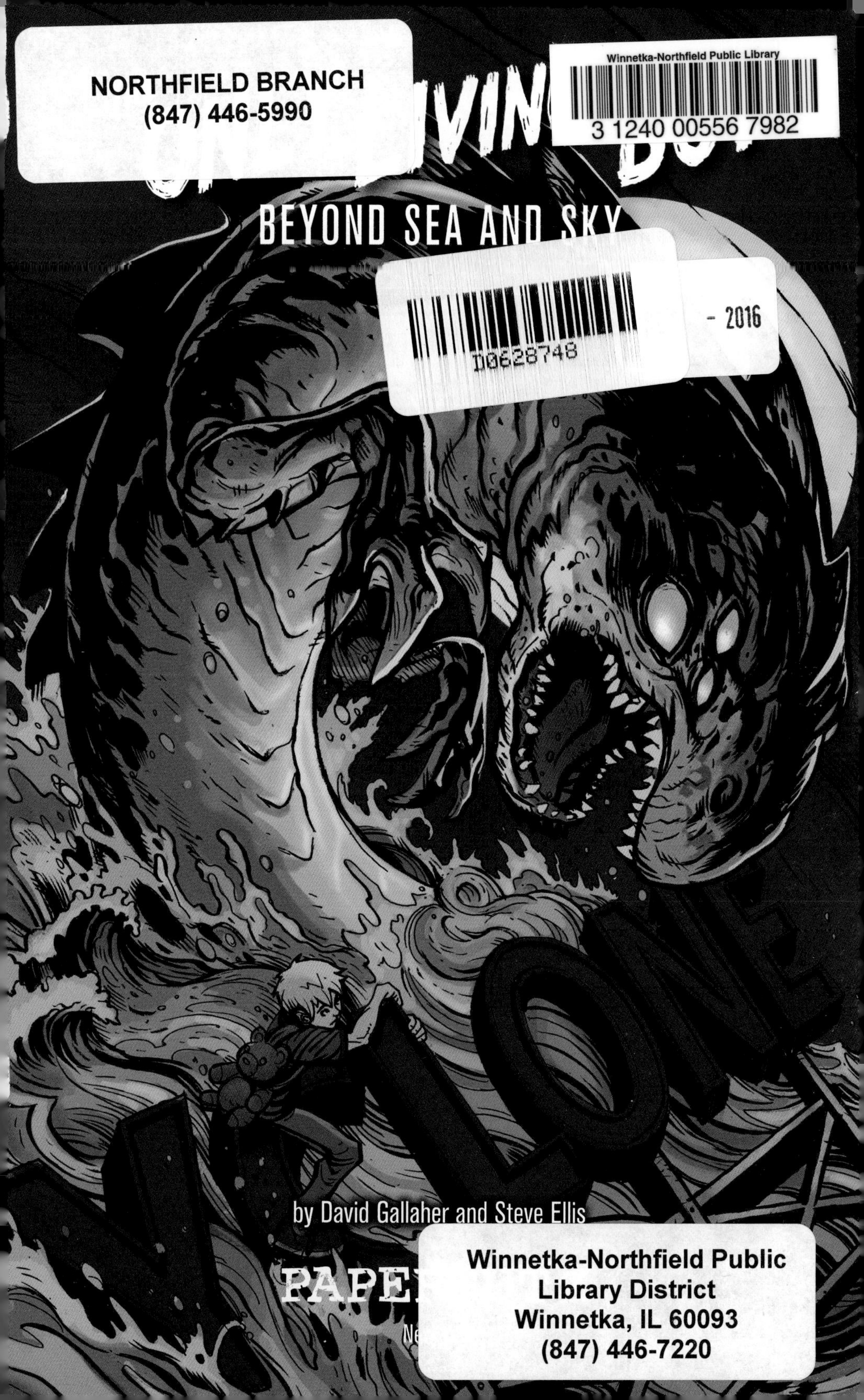
BEYOND SEA AND SKY
by David Gallaher and Steve Ellis

To my parents, who taught me how to slay dragons and fight fair.
– David

To my wife, Yamila, who has provided endless love, support, and inspiration.
– Steve

THE ONLY LIVING BOY #2 "Beyond Sea and Sky"

Chapter 3
Writer/ Co-Creator: David Gallaher
Artist/ Co-Creator: Steve Ellis
Color Flatting: Ten Van Winkle
Lettering: April Brown, Scott O. Brown
Consulting Editor: Tom Brennan
Art Corrections: Allison Strejlau

Chapter 4:
Writer/ Co-Creator: David Gallaher
Artist/ Co-Creator: Steve Ellis
Color Flatting: Holley McKend, Ten Van Winkle
Lettering: Christy Sawyer
Assistants: Emily Walton, Luke D. Blackwood
Consulting Editor: Janelle Asselin
Art Corrections: Allison Strejlau

Originally serialized at: www.the-only-living-boy.com

Papercutz books may be purchased for business or promotional use. For information on bulk purchases please contact Macmillan Corporate and Premium Sales Department at (800) 221-795 x5442.

Production – Dawn Guzzo
Cover Logo – Adam Grano
Production Coordinator/Assistant Managing Editor – Jeff Whitman
Associate Editor – Bethany Bryan
Special Thanks – Carol M. Burrell
Jim Salicrup
Editor-in-Chief

PB ISBN: 978-1-62991-473-2
HC ISBN: 978-1-62991-474-9

Printed in China July 2016 by Imago
2/F, Blk, 402, Cai Dian Industrial Zone
Huanggang North Road
Futian District, Shenzhen
China

Distributed by Macmillan
First Papercutz Printing

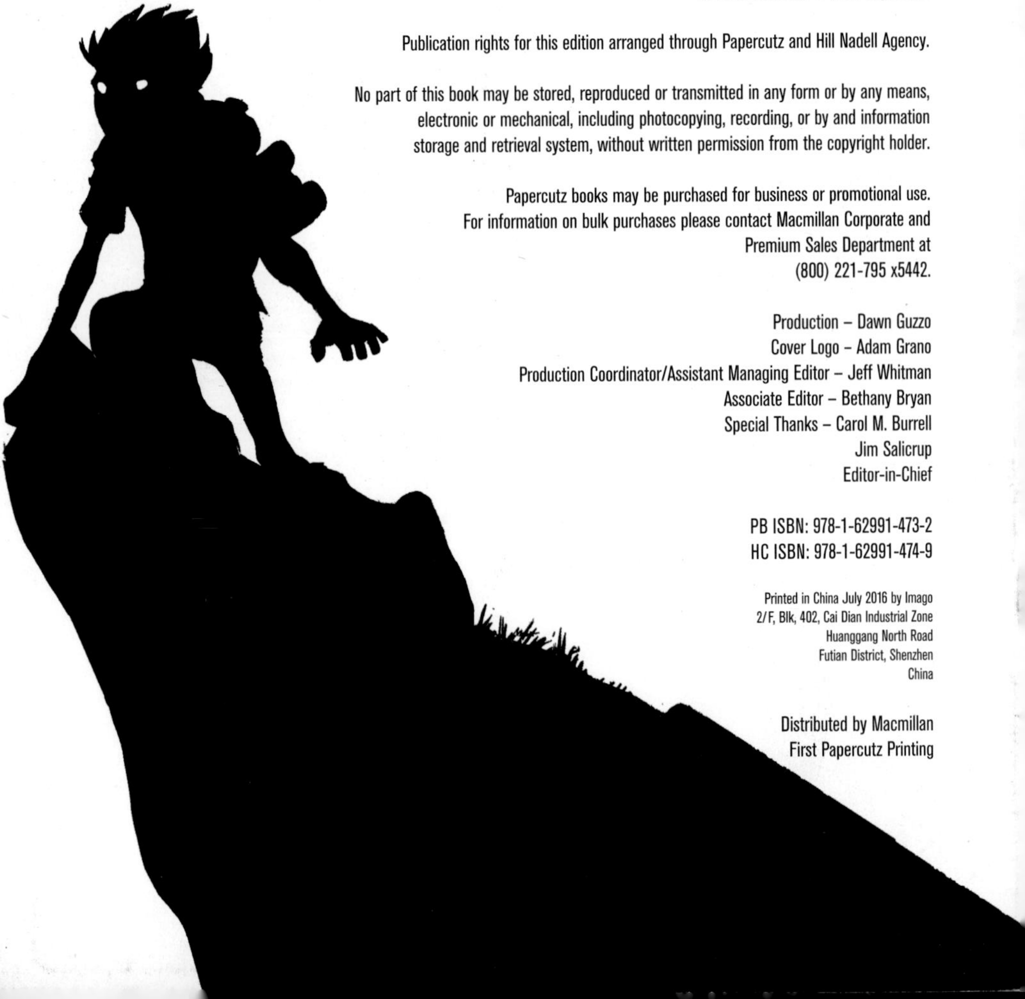

CHAPTER THREE

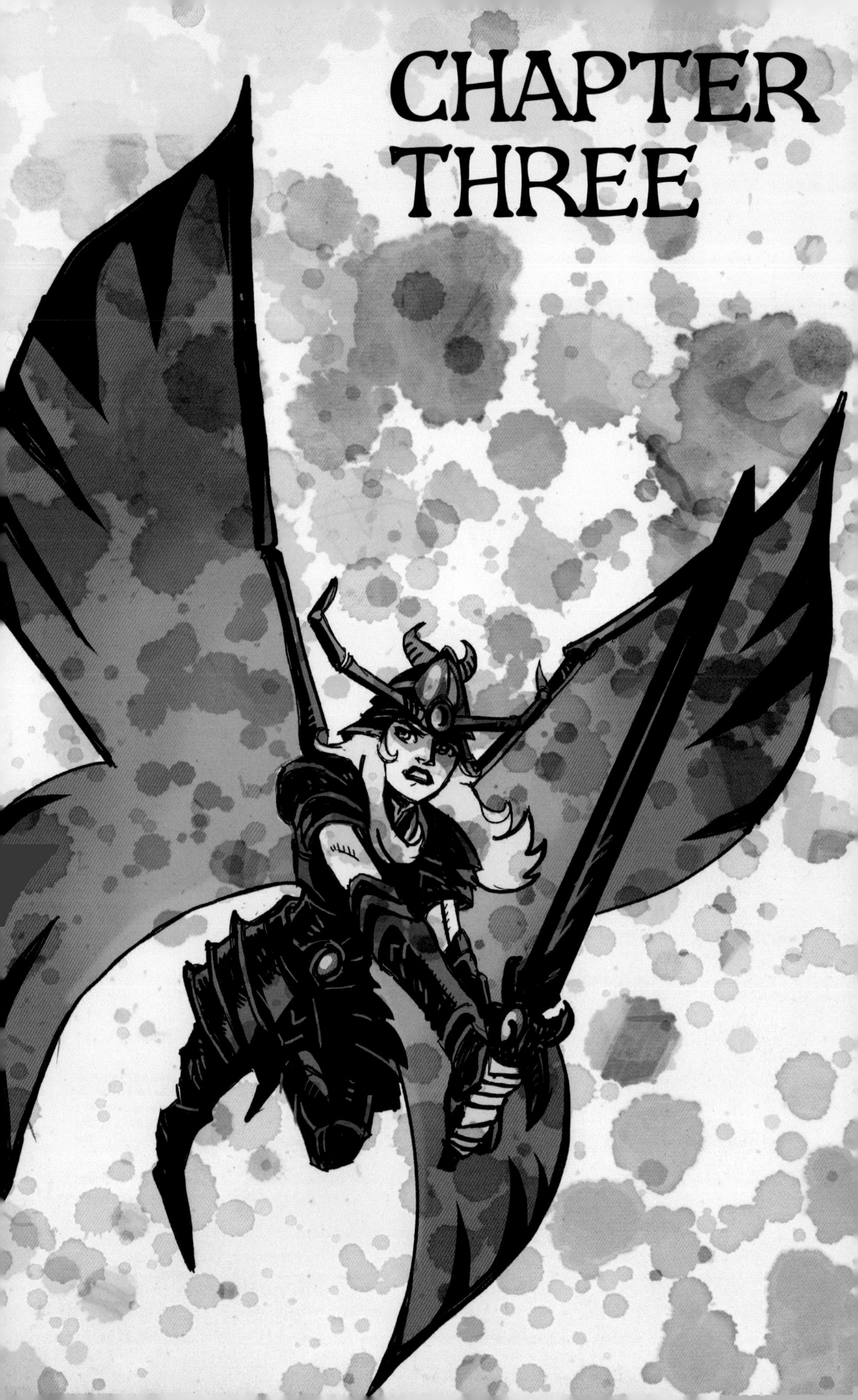

Previously in...

THE ONLY LIVING BOY

Twelve-year-old Erik Farrell ran away from home only to
wake up without his memory on a strange patchwork planet.
Surrounded by dangerous creatures, Erik fought alongside
Morgan, a Mermidonian warrior, but was captured by the evil
Doctor Once. While in his cell, Erik met other prisoners,
including Thea, a beautiful Sectaurian princess. Erik led a
daring escape but was separated from his new companions.
He stumbled into the underground land of the mapmaking
Groundlings and discovered startling secrets to the land
they call Chimerika. The Groundlings were hopeful Erik
could help them with their map, but when the city fell under
attack they blamed Erik for leading Doctor Once's minions to
their secret lair, and jailed him. Just when all seemed lost a
mysterious stranger arrived with startling news....

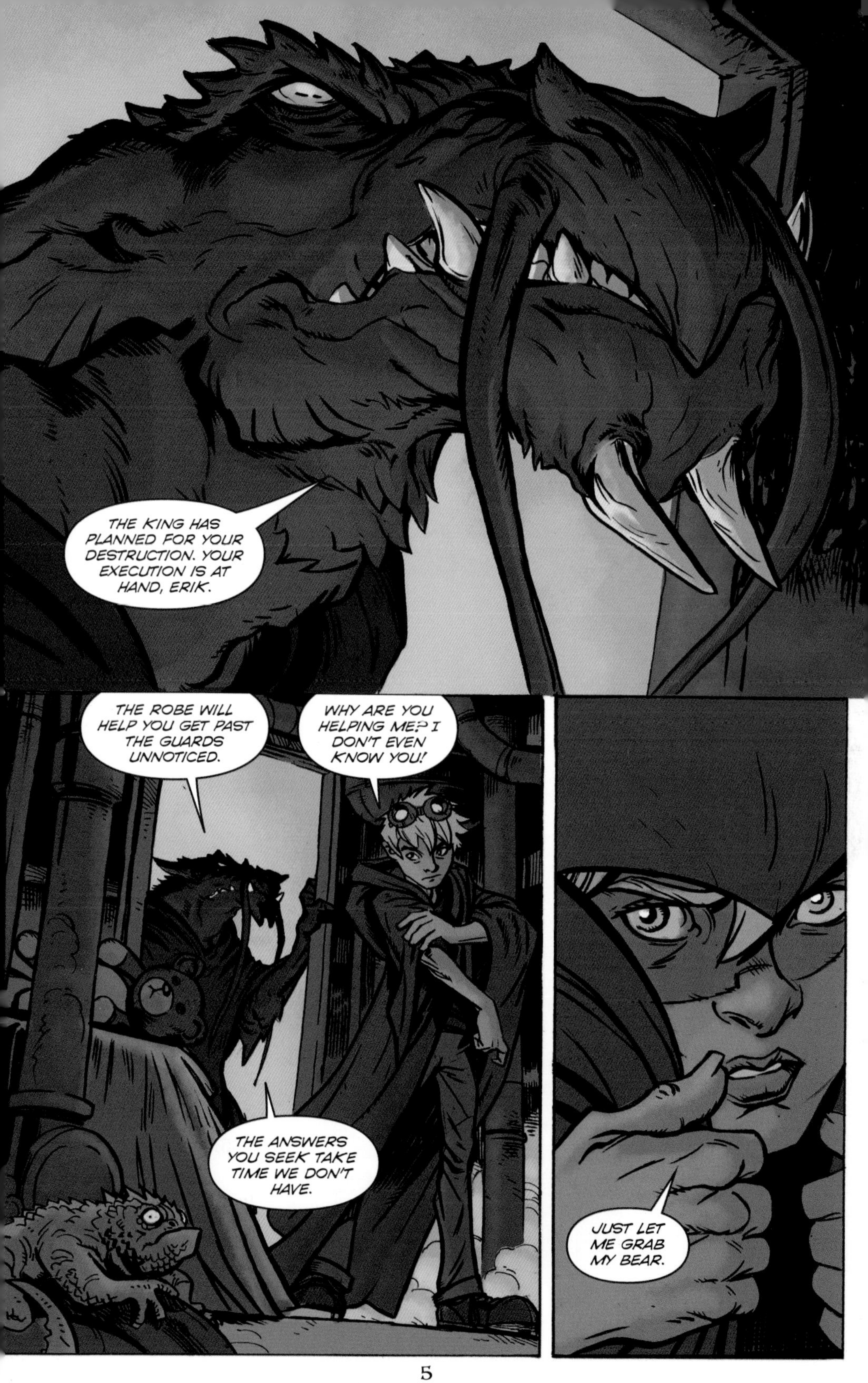
THE KING HAS PLANNED FOR YOUR DESTRUCTION. YOUR EXECUTION IS AT HAND, ERIK.
THE ROBE WILL HELP YOU GET PAST THE GUARDS UNNOTICED.
WHY ARE YOU HELPING ME? I DON'T EVEN KNOW YOU!
THE ANSWERS YOU SEEK TAKE TIME WE DON'T HAVE.
JUST LET ME GRAB MY BEAR.

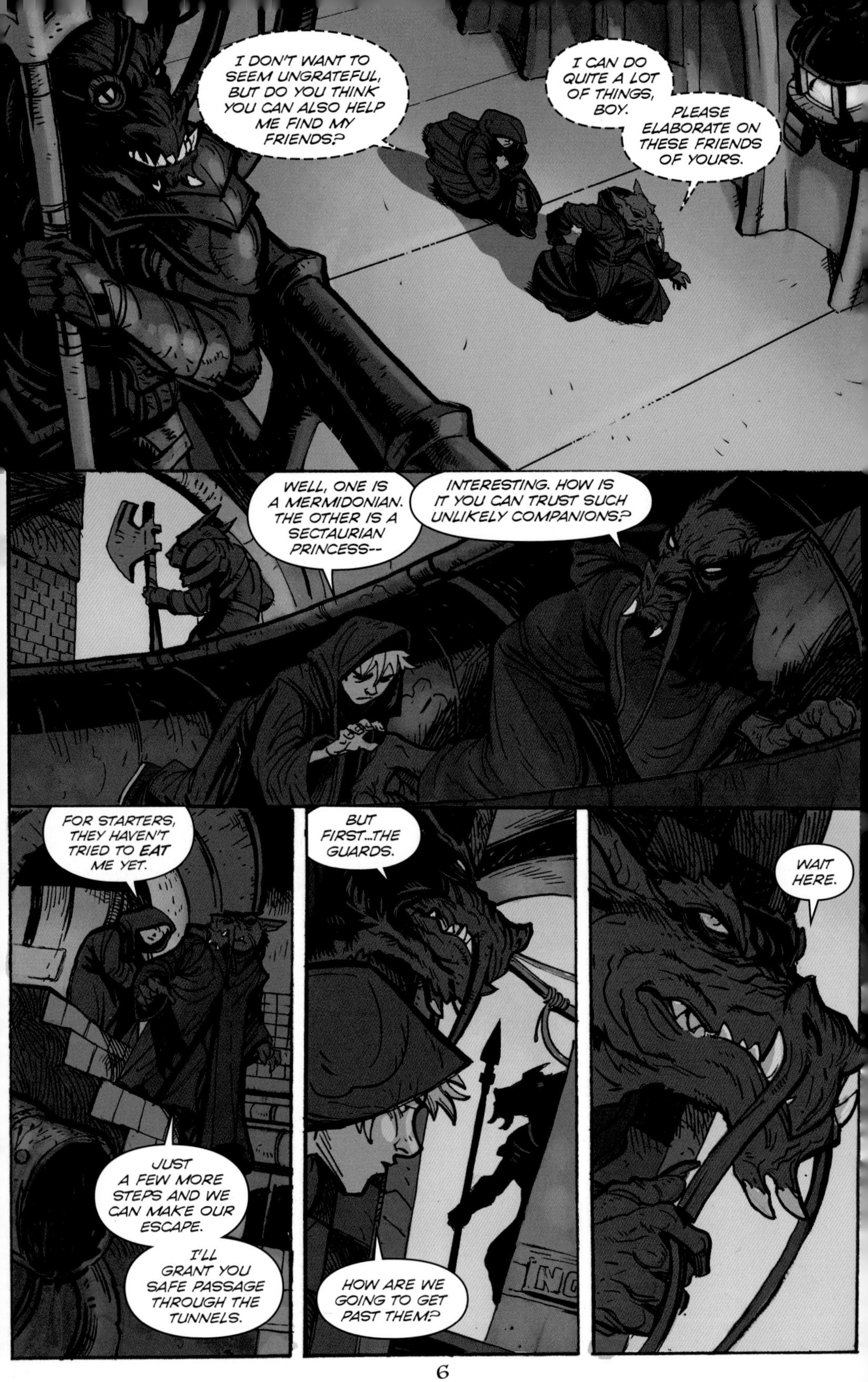
I DON'T WANT TO SEEM UNGRATEFUL, BUT DO YOU THINK YOU CAN ALSO HELP ME FIND MY FRIENDS?
I CAN DO QUITE A LOT OF THINGS, BOY.
PLEASE ELABORATE ON THESE FRIENDS OF YOURS.
WELL, ONE IS A MERMIDONIAN. THE OTHER IS A SECTAURIAN PRINCESS--
INTERESTING. HOW IS IT YOU CAN TRUST SUCH UNLIKELY COMPANIONS?
FOR STARTERS, THEY HAVEN'T TRIED TO EAT ME YET.
JUST A FEW MORE STEPS AND WE CAN MAKE OUR ESCAPE.
I'LL GRANT YOU SAFE PASSAGE THROUGH THE TUNNELS.
BUT FIRST...THE GUARDS.
HOW ARE WE GOING TO GET PAST THEM?
WAIT HERE.

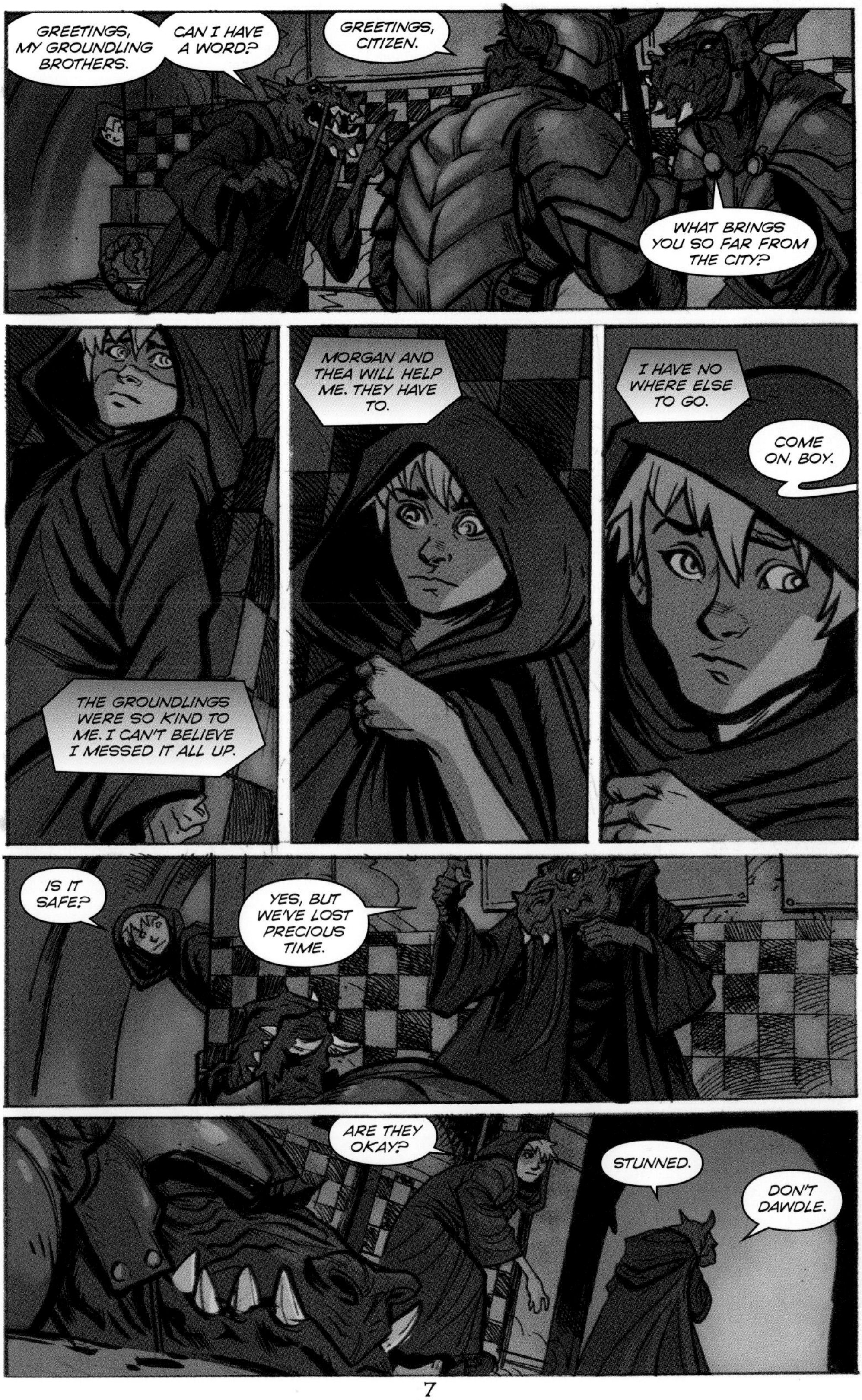
GREETINGS, MY GROUNDLING BROTHERS.
CAN I HAVE A WORD?
GREETINGS, CITIZEN.
WHAT BRINGS YOU SO FAR FROM THE CITY?
THE GROUNDLINGS WERE SO KIND TO ME. I CAN'T BELIEVE I MESSED IT ALL UP.
MORGAN AND THEA WILL HELP ME. THEY HAVE TO.
I HAVE NO WHERE ELSE TO GO.
COME ON, BOY.
IS IT SAFE?
YES, BUT WE'VE LOST PRECIOUS TIME.
ARE THEY OKAY?
STUNNED.
DON'T DAWDLE.

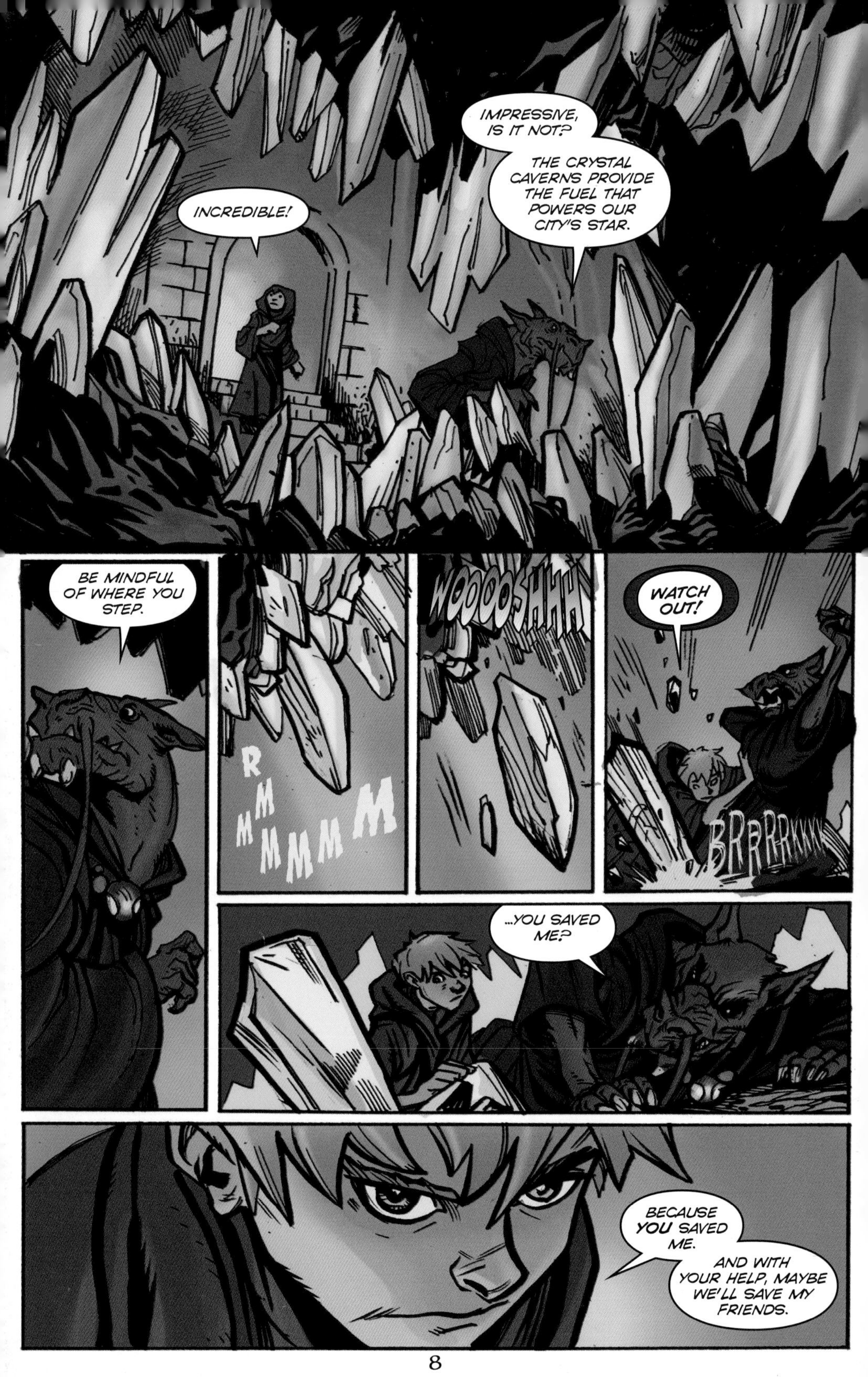
IMPRESSIVE, IS IT NOT?
THE CRYSTAL CAVERNS PROVIDE THE FUEL THAT POWERS OUR CITY'S STAR.
INCREDIBLE!
BE MINDFUL OF WHERE YOU STEP.
RMMMMMMM
WOOOOSHHH
WATCH OUT!
BRRRRKKK
...YOU SAVED ME?
BECAUSE YOU SAVED ME.
AND WITH YOUR HELP, MAYBE WE'LL SAVE MY FRIENDS.

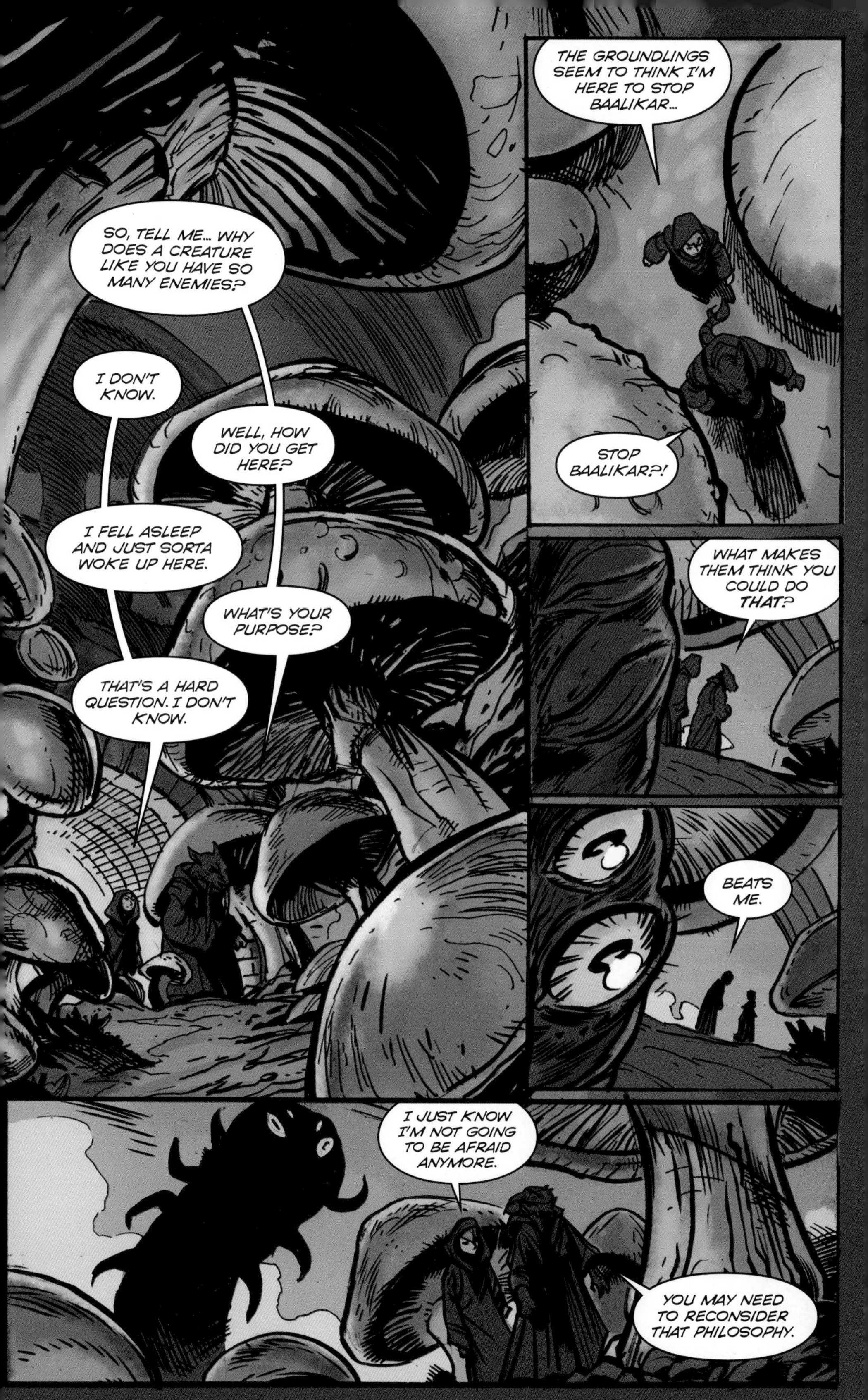
SO, TELL ME... WHY DOES A CREATURE LIKE YOU HAVE SO MANY ENEMIES?
I DON'T KNOW.
WELL, HOW DID YOU GET HERE?
I FELL ASLEEP AND JUST SORTA WOKE UP HERE.
WHAT'S YOUR PURPOSE?
THAT'S A HARD QUESTION. I DON'T KNOW.
THE GROUNDLINGS SEEM TO THINK I'M HERE TO STOP BAALIKAR...
STOP BAALIKAR?!
WHAT MAKES THEM THINK YOU COULD DO THAT?
BEATS ME.
I JUST KNOW I'M NOT GOING TO BE AFRAID ANYMORE.
YOU MAY NEED TO RECONSIDER THAT PHILOSOPHY.

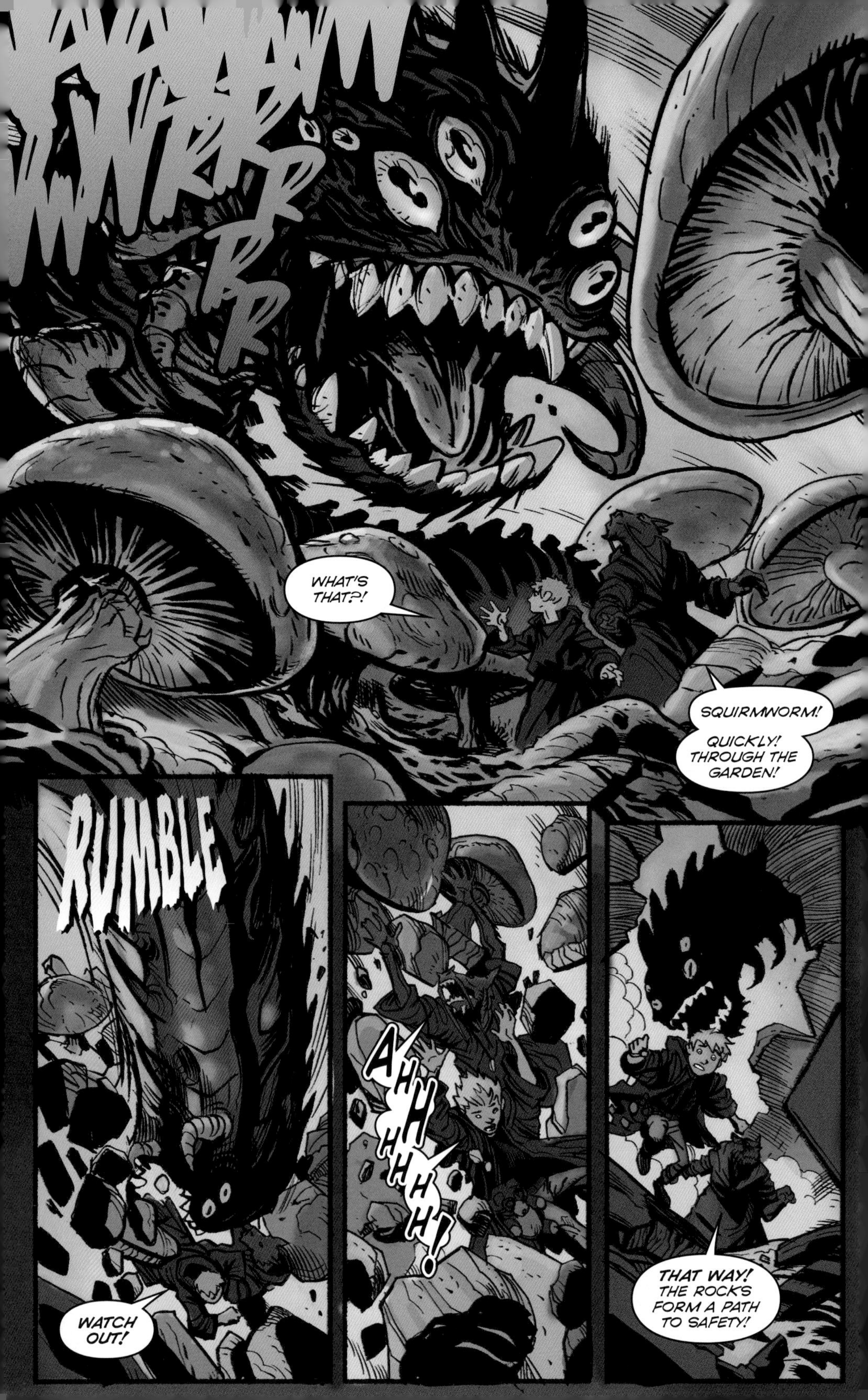
WHAT'S THAT?!
SQUIRMWORM!
QUICKLY! THROUGH THE GARDEN!
RUMBLE
WATCH OUT!
AHHHHHHH!
THAT WAY! THE ROCK'S FORM A PATH TO SAFETY!

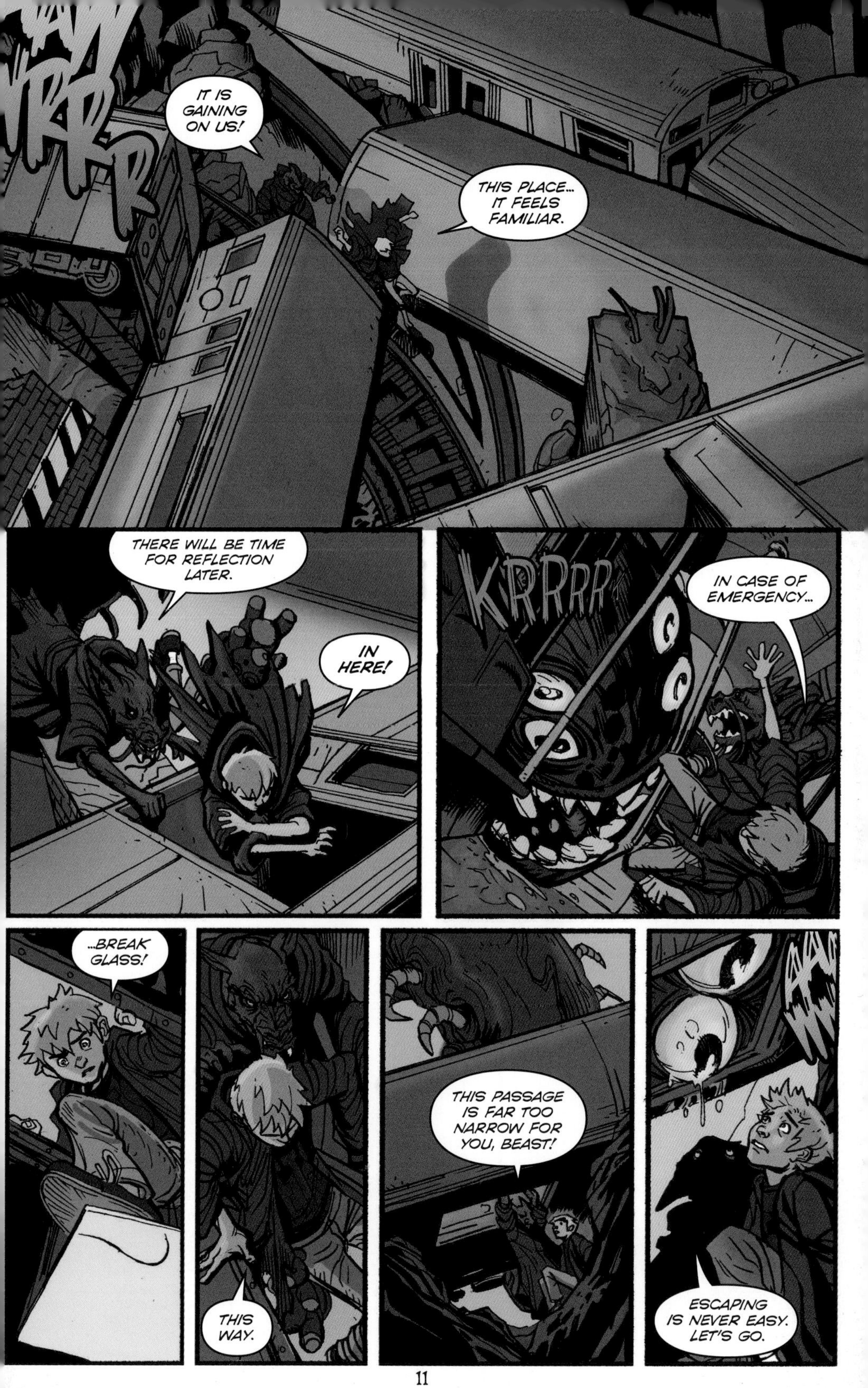
IT IS GAINING ON US!
THIS PLACE... IT FEELS FAMILIAR.
THERE WILL BE TIME FOR REFLECTION LATER.
IN HERE!
KRRRR
IN CASE OF EMERGENCY...
...BREAK GLASS!
THIS WAY.
THIS PASSAGE IS FAR TOO NARROW FOR YOU, BEAST!
ESCAPING IS NEVER EASY. LET'S GO.

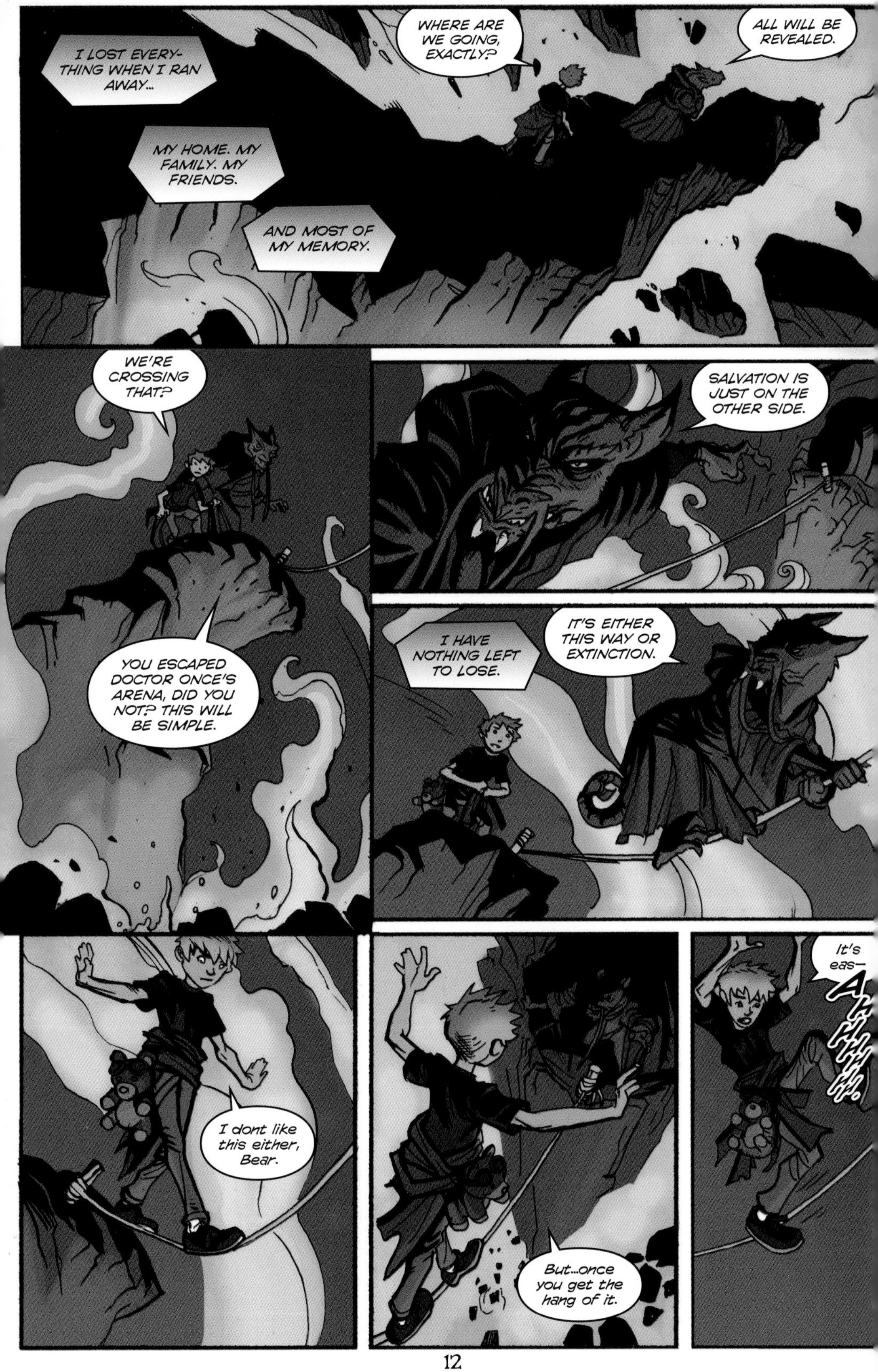
I LOST EVERY-THING WHEN I RAN AWAY...
WHERE ARE WE GOING, EXACTLY?
ALL WILL BE REVEALED.
MY HOME. MY FAMILY. MY FRIENDS.
AND MOST OF MY MEMORY.
WE'RE CROSSING THAT?
YOU ESCAPED DOCTOR ONCE'S ARENA, DID YOU NOT? THIS WILL BE SIMPLE.
SALVATION IS JUST ON THE OTHER SIDE.
I HAVE NOTHING LEFT TO LOSE.
IT'S EITHER THIS WAY OR EXTINCTION.
I dont like this either, Bear.
But...once you get the hang of it.
It's eas—
AHHHHH.

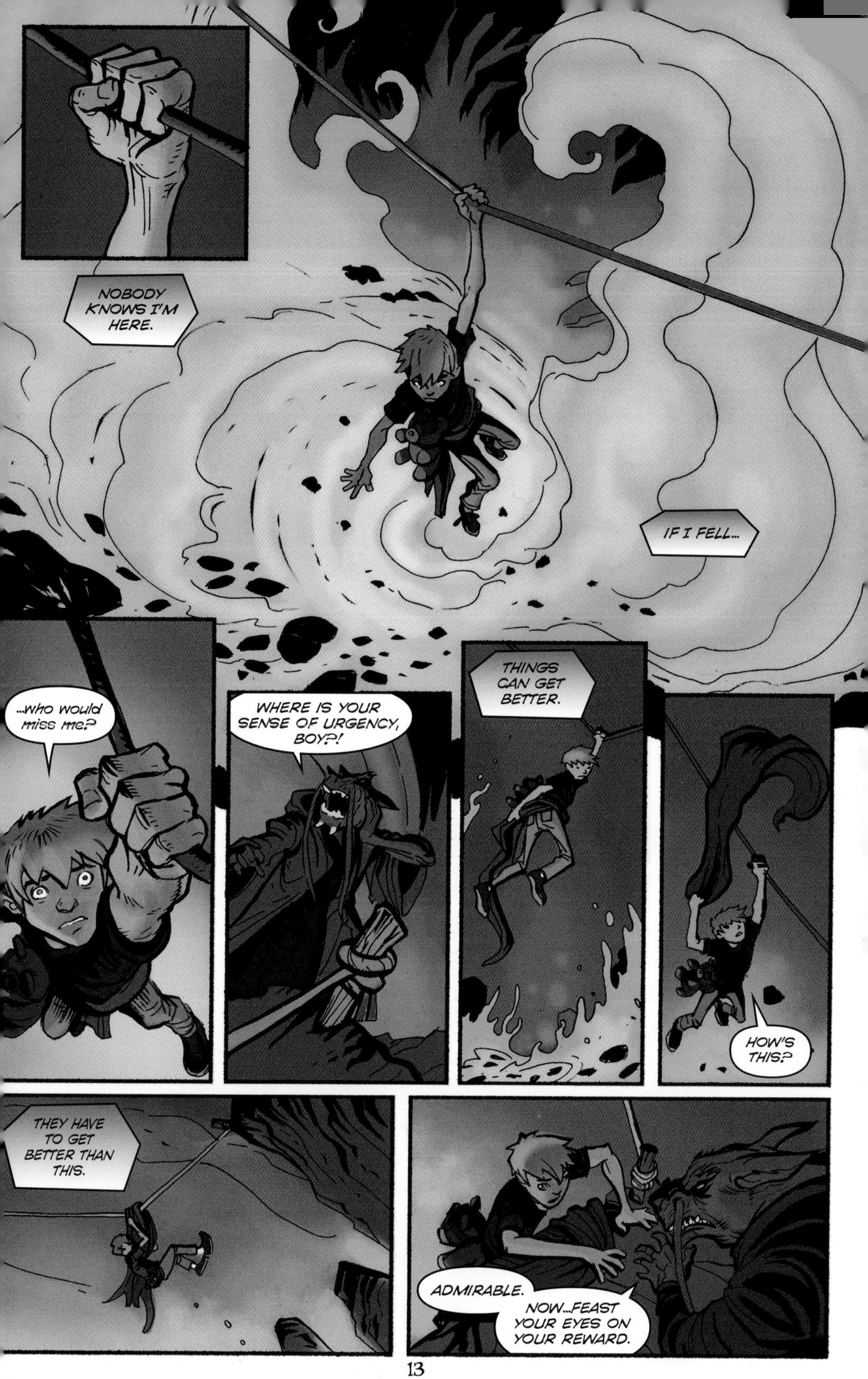
NOBODY KNOWS I'M HERE.
IF I FELL...
...who would miss me?
WHERE IS YOUR SENSE OF URGENCY, BOY?!
THINGS CAN GET BETTER.
HOW'S THIS?
THEY HAVE TO GET BETTER THAN THIS.
ADMIRABLE.
NOW...FEAST YOUR EYES ON YOUR REWARD.

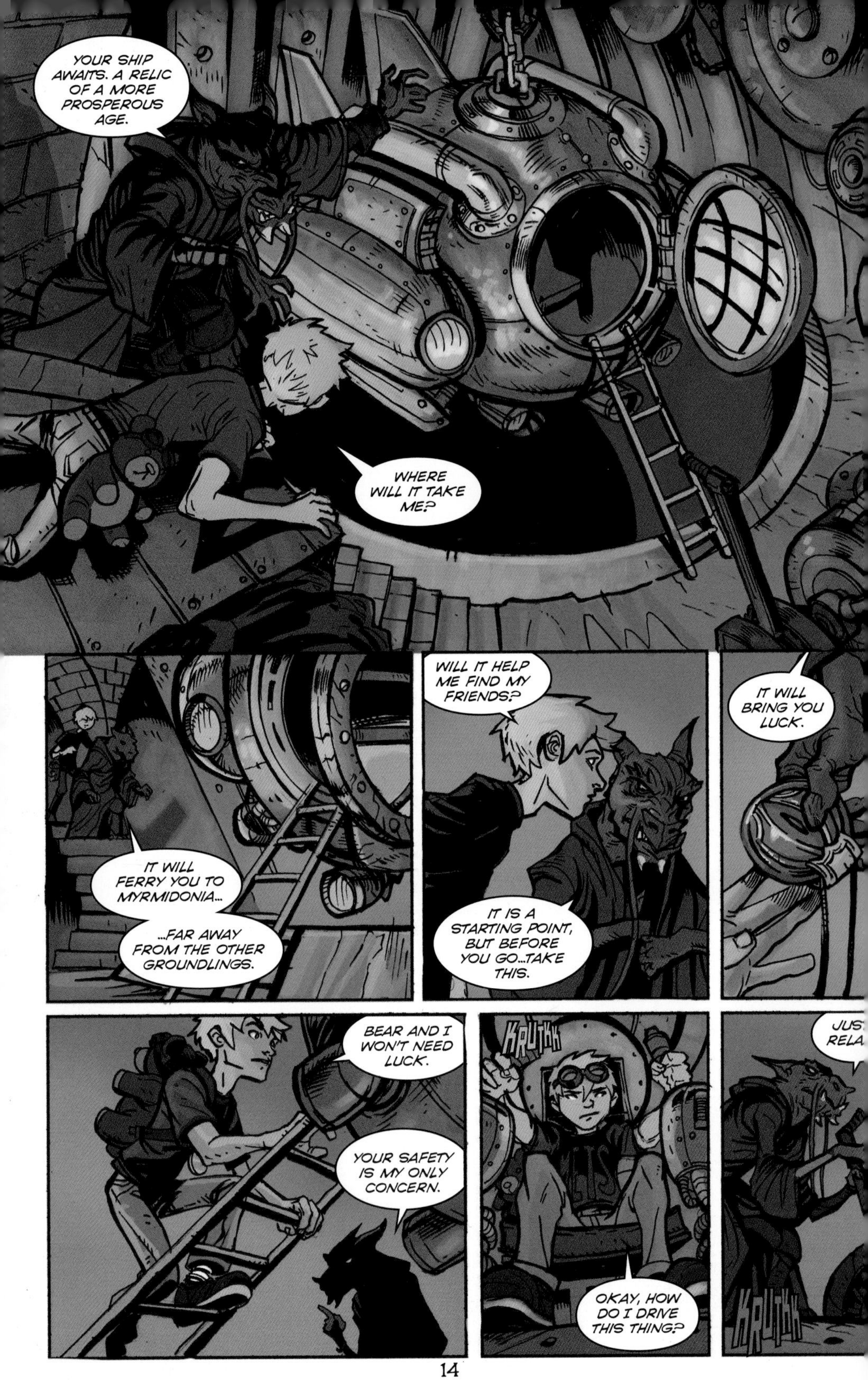
YOUR SHIP AWAITS. A RELIC OF A MORE PROSPEROUS AGE.
WHERE WILL IT TAKE ME?
IT WILL FERRY YOU TO MYRMIDONIA...
...FAR AWAY FROM THE OTHER GROUNDLINGS.
WILL IT HELP ME FIND MY FRIENDS?
IT IS A STARTING POINT, BUT BEFORE YOU GO...TAKE THIS.
IT WILL BRING YOU LUCK.
BEAR AND I WON'T NEED LUCK.
YOUR SAFETY IS MY ONLY CONCERN.
KRUTKK
OKAY, HOW DO I DRIVE THIS THING?
JUS
RELA
KRUTKK

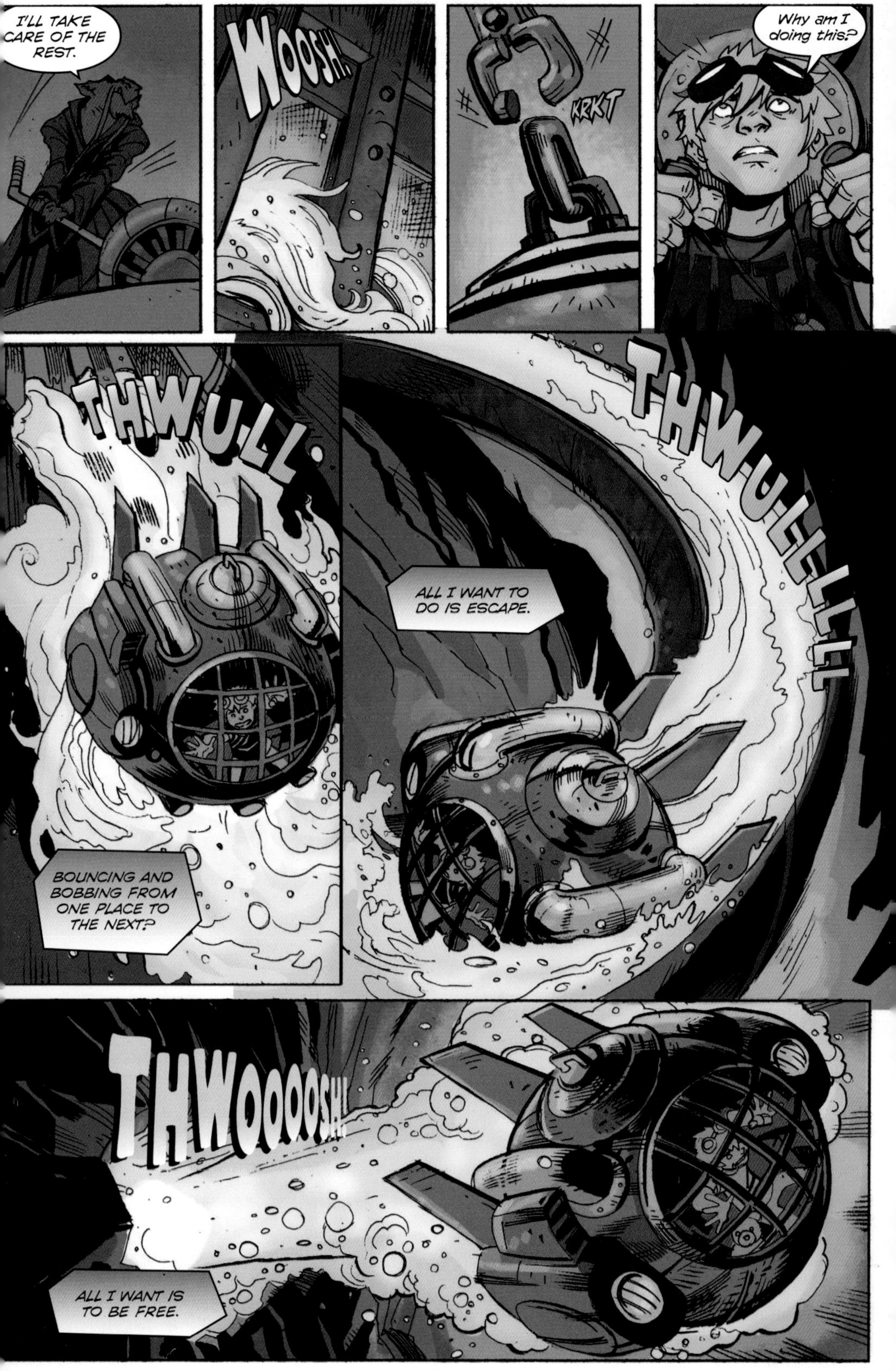

I'LL TAKE CARE OF THE REST.
WOOSH!
KRKT
Why am I doing this?
THWULL
ALL I WANT TO DO IS ESCAPE.
THWULLLLL
BOUNCING AND BOBBING FROM ONE PLACE TO THE NEXT?
THWOOOOSH!
ALL I WANT IS TO BE FREE.

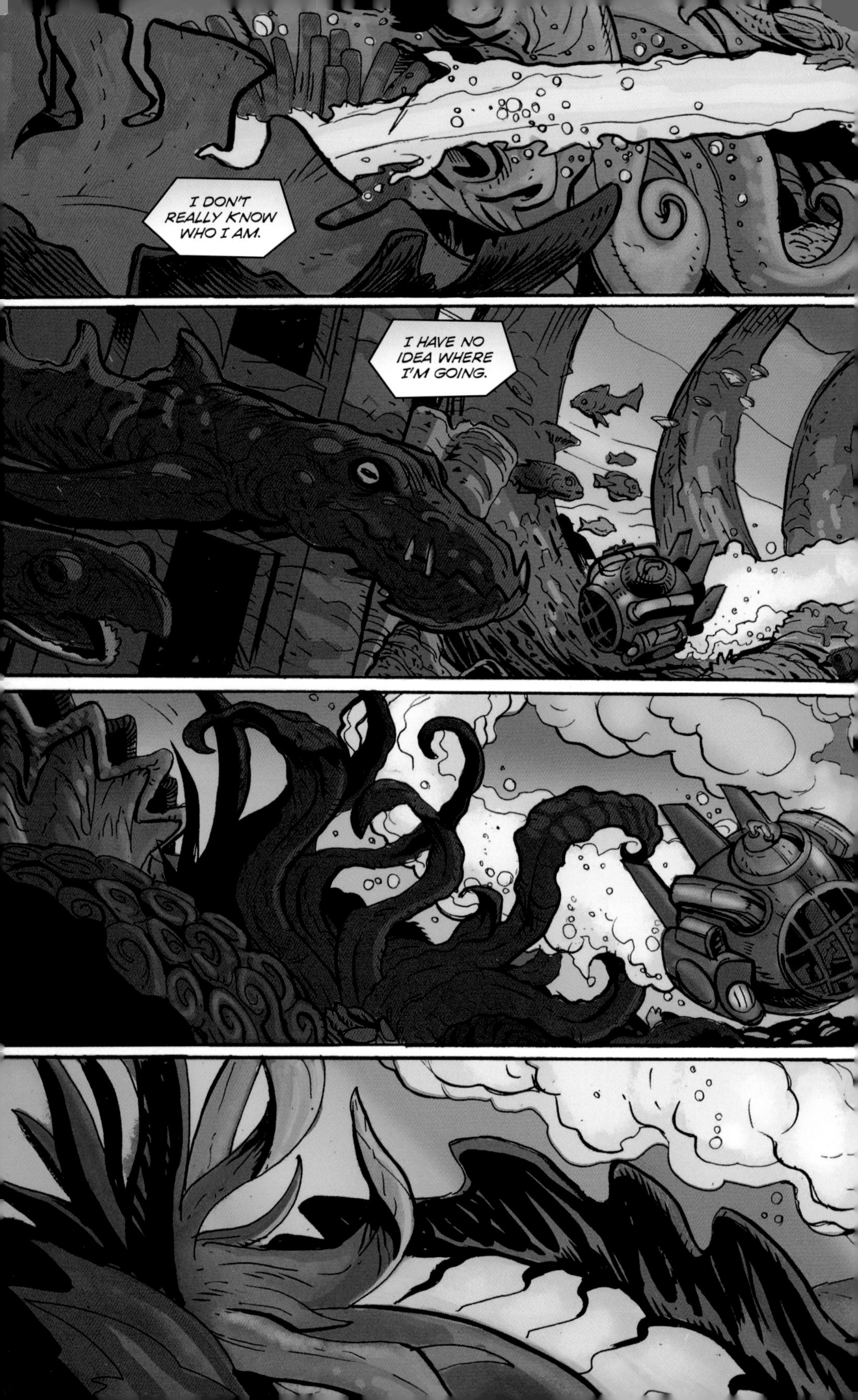
I DON'T REALLY KNOW WHO I AM.
I HAVE NO IDEA WHERE I'M GOING.

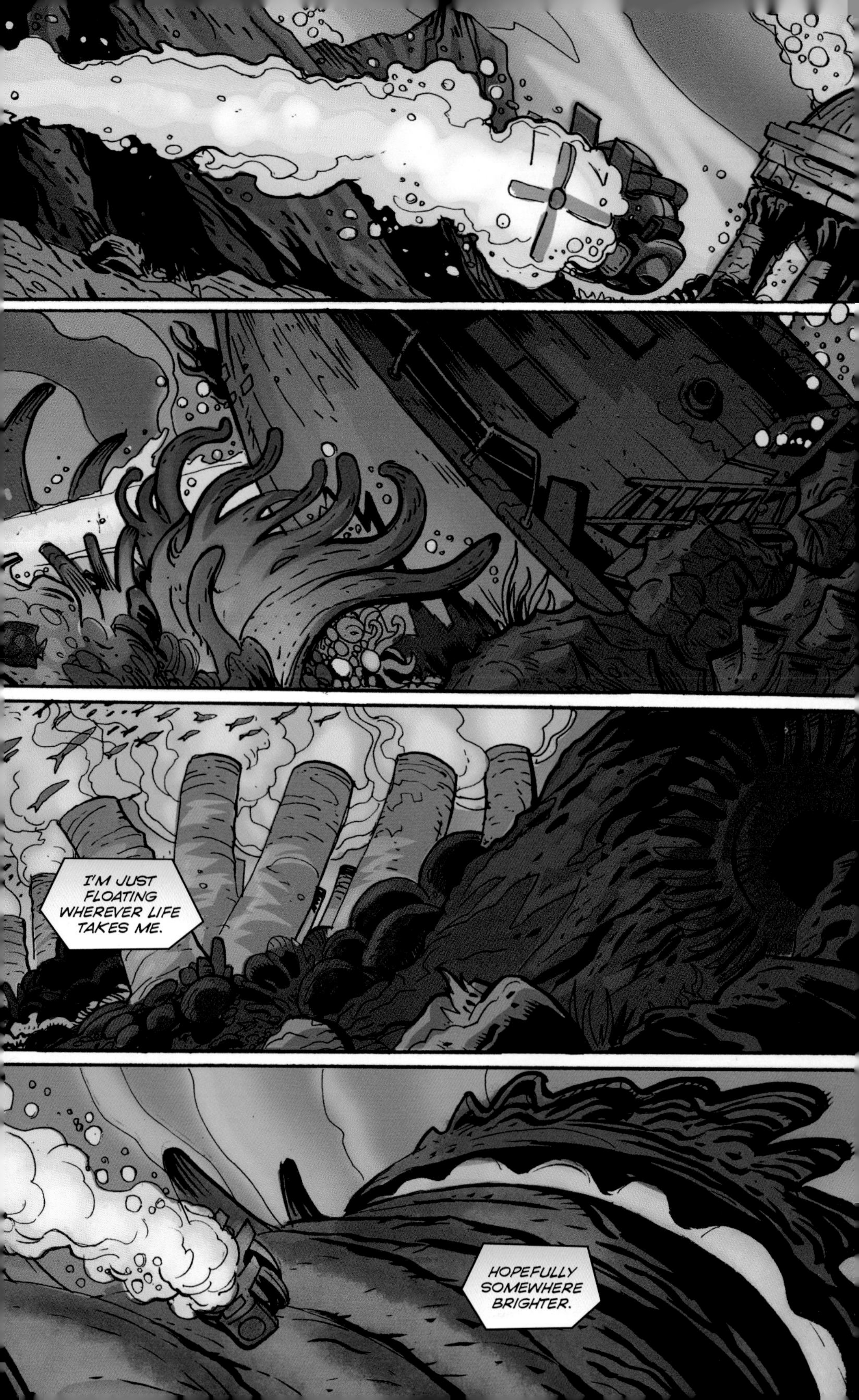
I'M JUST FLOATING WHEREVER LIFE TAKES ME.
HOPEFULLY SOMEWHERE BRIGHTER.

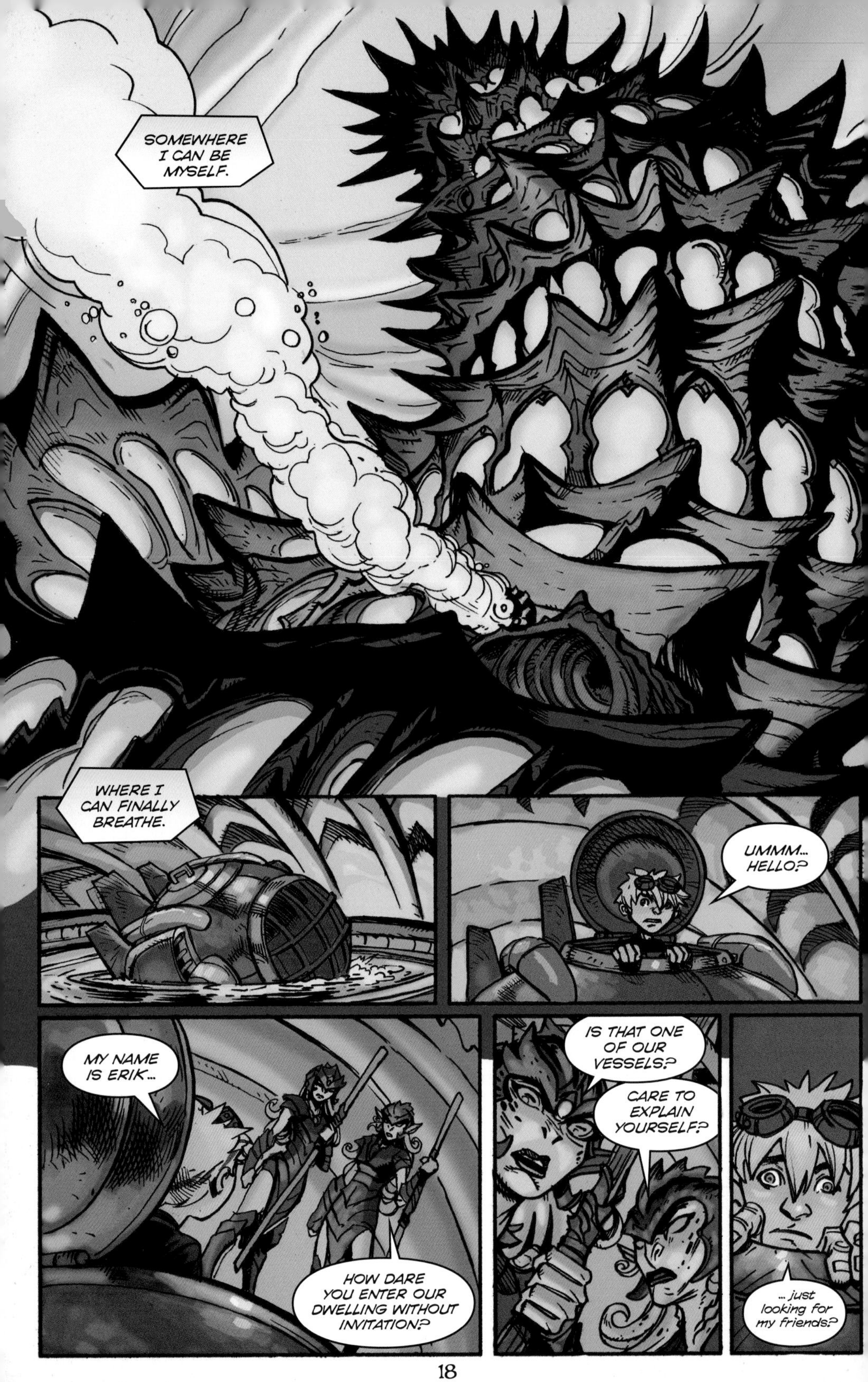
SOMEWHERE I CAN BE MYSELF.
WHERE I CAN FINALLY BREATHE.
UMMM... HELLO?
MY NAME IS ERIK...
HOW DARE YOU ENTER OUR DWELLING WITHOUT INVITATION?
IS THAT ONE OF OUR VESSELS?
CARE TO EXPLAIN YOURSELF?
... just looking for my friends?

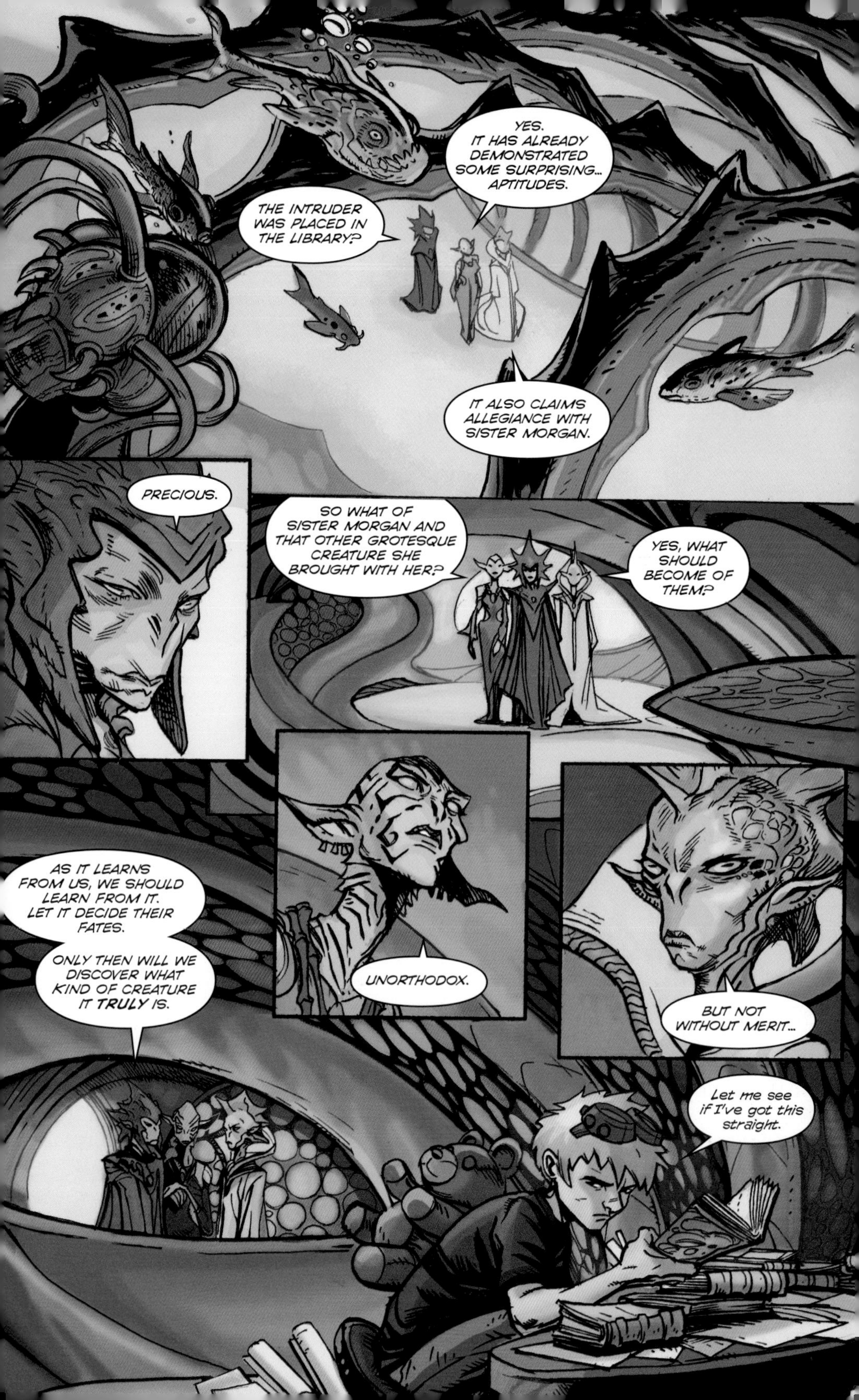
THE INTRUDER WAS PLACED IN THE LIBRARY?
YES. IT HAS ALREADY DEMONSTRATED SOME SURPRISING... APTITUDES.
IT ALSO CLAIMS ALLEGIANCE WITH SISTER MORGAN.
PRECIOUS.
SO WHAT OF SISTER MORGAN AND THAT OTHER GROTESQUE CREATURE SHE BROUGHT WITH HER?
YES, WHAT SHOULD BECOME OF THEM?
UNORTHODOX.
BUT NOT WITHOUT MERIT...
AS IT LEARNS FROM US, WE SHOULD LEARN FROM IT. LET IT DECIDE THEIR FATES.
ONLY THEN WILL WE DISCOVER WHAT KIND OF CREATURE IT TRULY IS.
Let me see if I've got this straight.

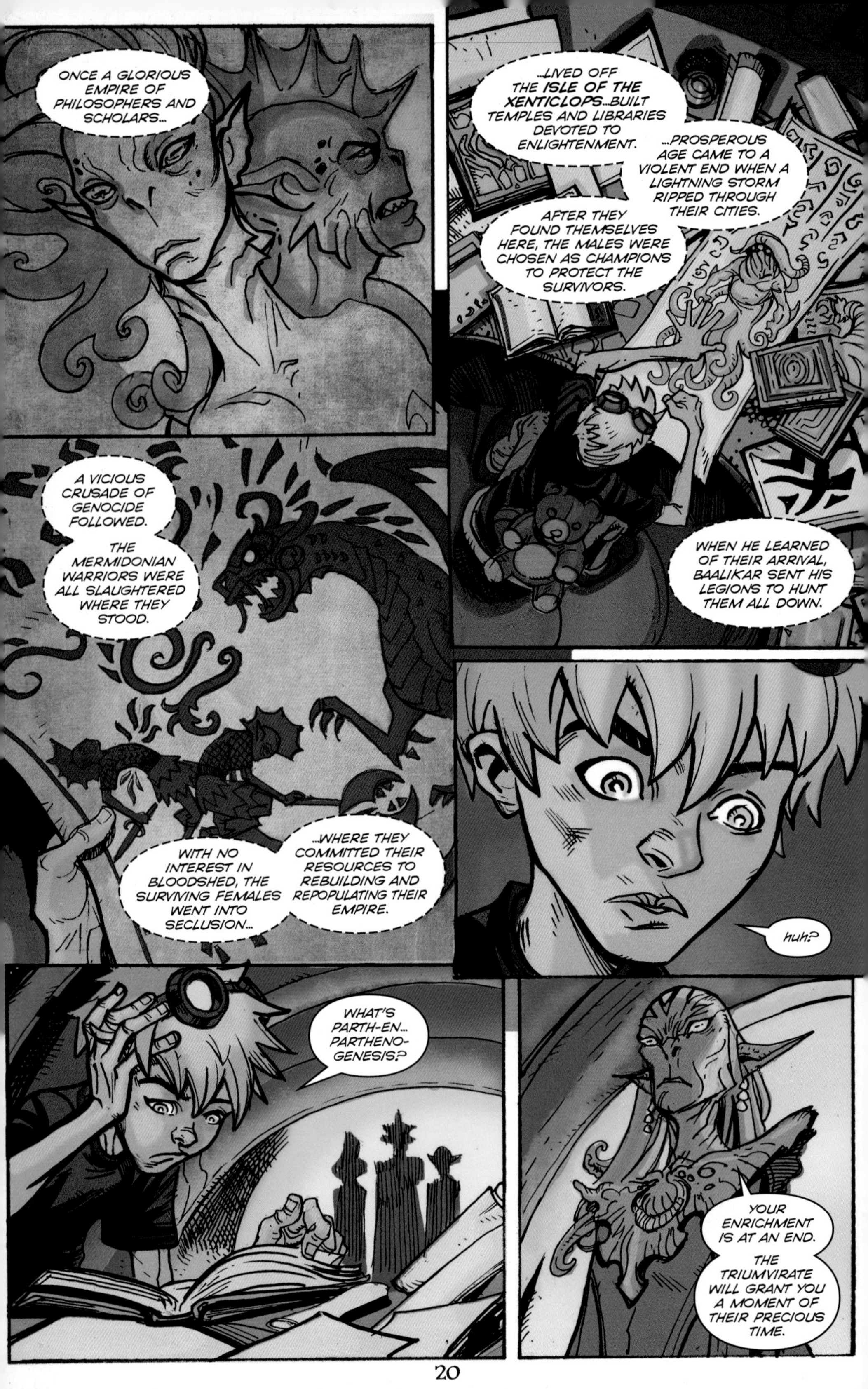
ONCE A GLORIOUS EMPIRE OF PHILOSOPHERS AND SCHOLARS...
...LIVED OFF THE ISLE OF THE XENTICLOPS...BUILT TEMPLES AND LIBRARIES DEVOTED TO ENLIGHTENMENT.
...PROSPEROUS AGE CAME TO A VIOLENT END WHEN A LIGHTNING STORM RIPPED THROUGH THEIR CITIES.
AFTER THEY FOUND THEMSELVES HERE, THE MALES WERE CHOSEN AS CHAMPIONS TO PROTECT THE SURVIVORS.
WHEN HE LEARNED OF THEIR ARRIVAL, BAALIKAR SENT HIS LEGIONS TO HUNT THEM ALL DOWN.
A VICIOUS CRUSADE OF GENOCIDE FOLLOWED.
THE MERMIDONIAN WARRIORS WERE ALL SLAUGHTERED WHERE THEY STOOD.
WITH NO INTEREST IN BLOODSHED, THE SURVIVING FEMALES WENT INTO SECLUSION...
...WHERE THEY COMMITTED THEIR RESOURCES TO REBUILDING AND REPOPULATING THEIR EMPIRE.
huh?
WHAT'S PARTH-EN... PARTHENO-GENESIS?
YOUR ENRICHMENT IS AT AN END.
THE TRIUMVIRATE WILL GRANT YOU A MOMENT OF THEIR PRECIOUS TIME.

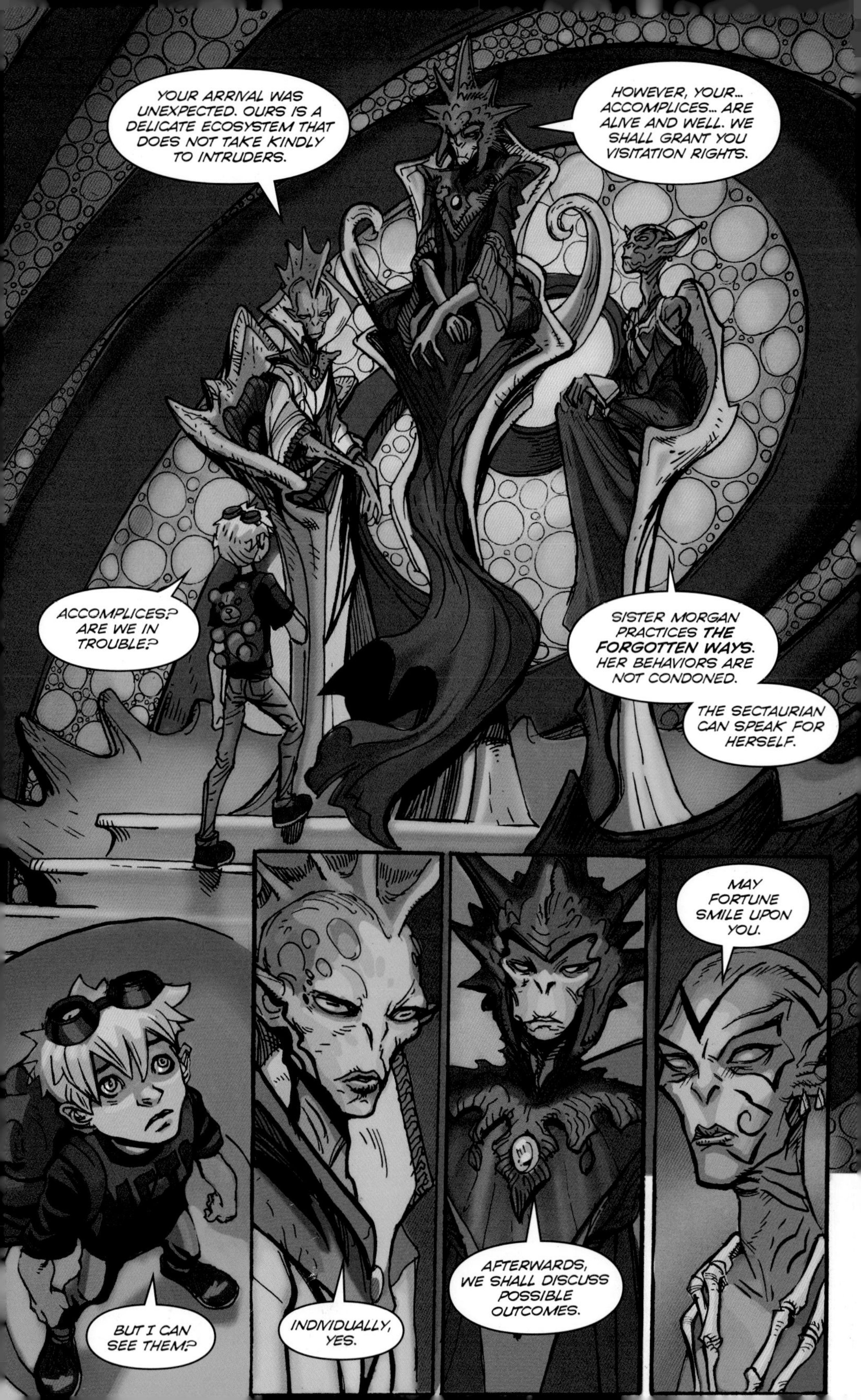
YOUR ARRIVAL WAS UNEXPECTED. OURS IS A DELICATE ECOSYSTEM THAT DOES NOT TAKE KINDLY TO INTRUDERS.
HOWEVER, YOUR... ACCOMPLICES... ARE ALIVE AND WELL. WE SHALL GRANT YOU VISITATION RIGHTS.
ACCOMPLICES? ARE WE IN TROUBLE?
SISTER MORGAN PRACTICES **THE FORGOTTEN WAYS**. HER BEHAVIORS ARE NOT CONDONED.
THE SECTAURIAN CAN SPEAK FOR HERSELF.
BUT I CAN SEE THEM?
INDIVIDUALLY, YES.
AFTERWARDS, WE SHALL DISCUSS POSSIBLE OUTCOMES.
MAY FORTUNE SMILE UPON YOU.

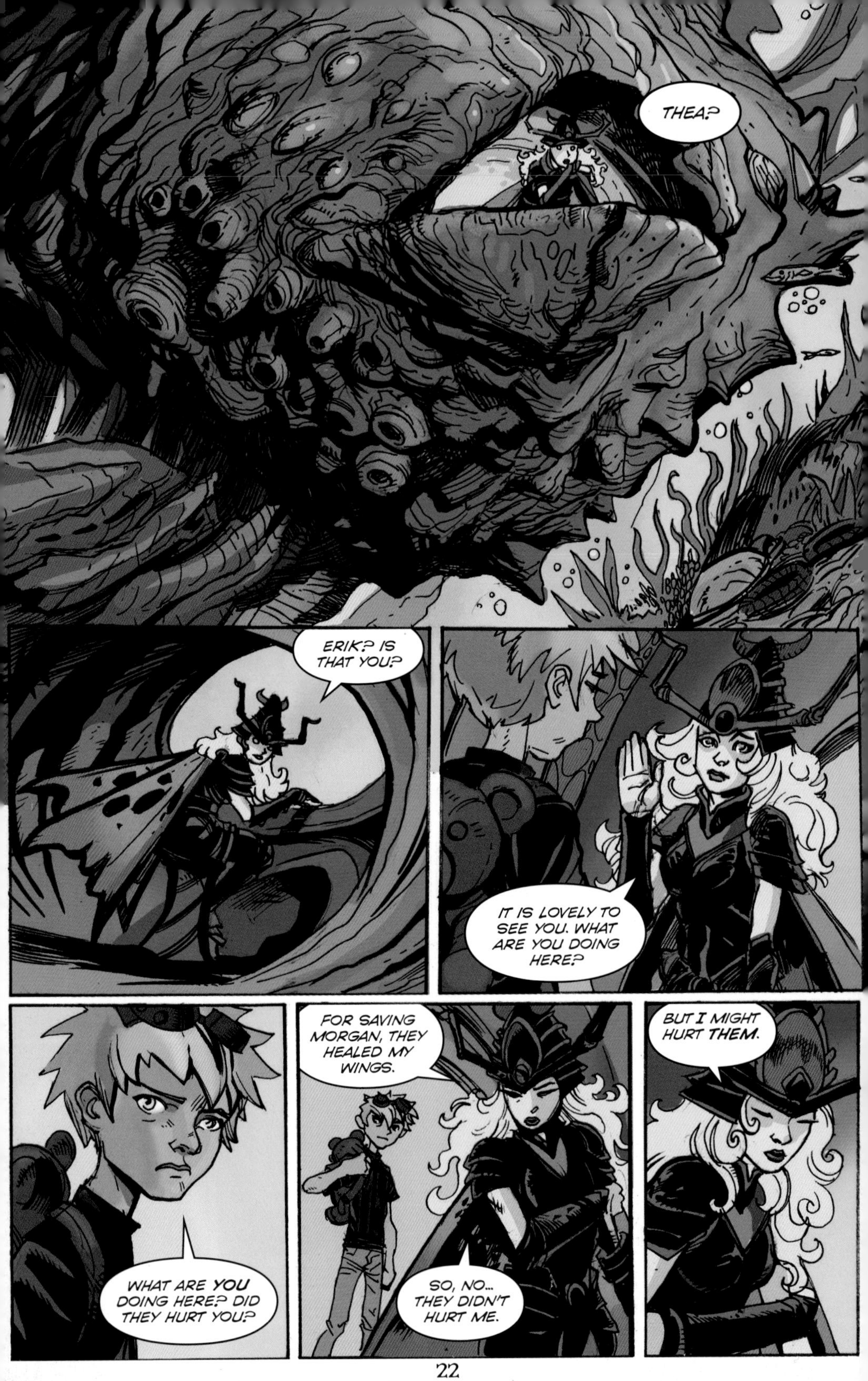
THEA?
ERIK? IS THAT YOU?
IT IS LOVELY TO SEE YOU. WHAT ARE YOU DOING HERE?
WHAT ARE YOU DOING HERE? DID THEY HURT YOU?
FOR SAVING MORGAN, THEY HEALED MY WINGS.
SO, NO... THEY DIDN'T HURT ME.
BUT I MIGHT HURT THEM.

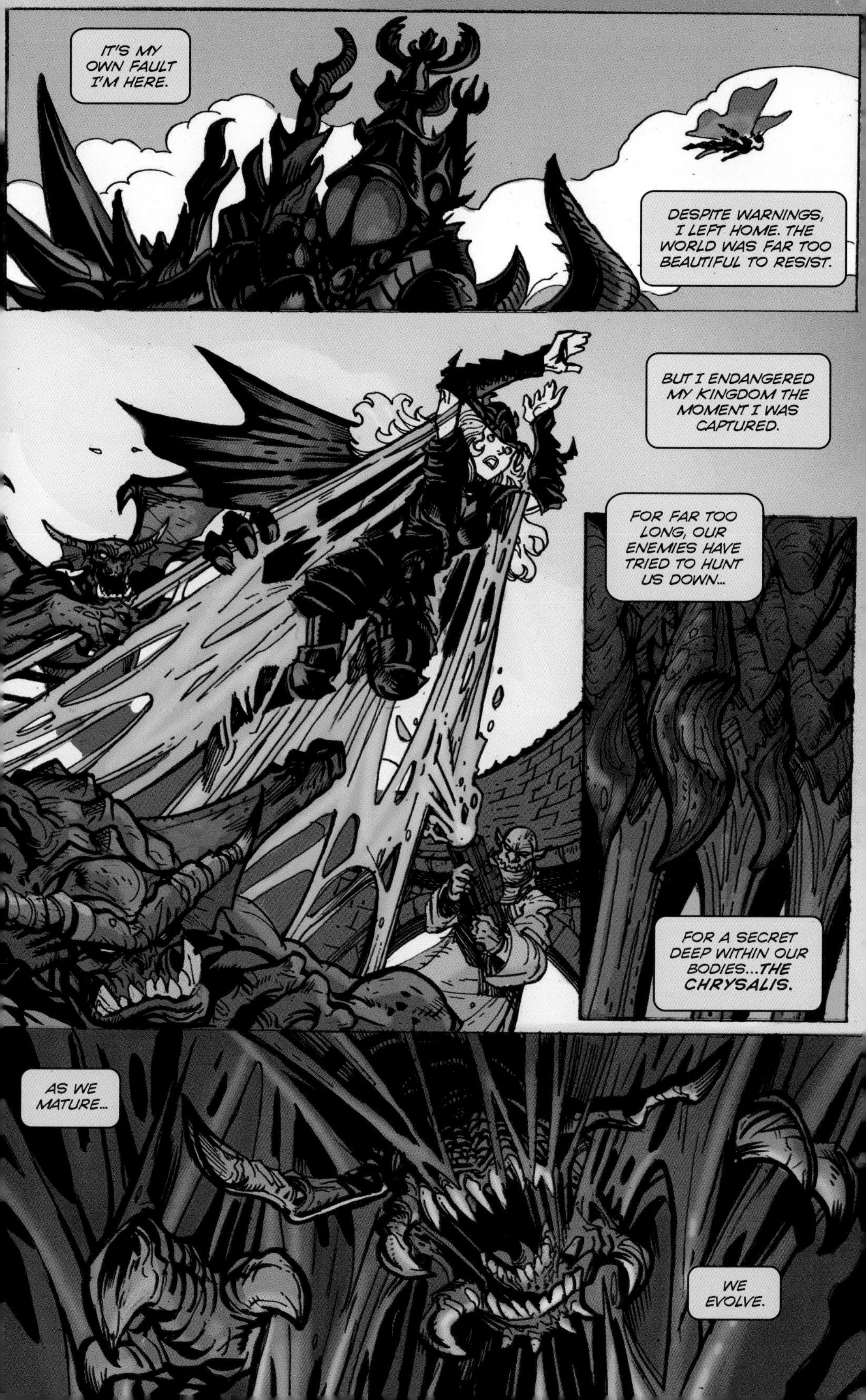
IT'S MY OWN FAULT I'M HERE.
DESPITE WARNINGS, I LEFT HOME. THE WORLD WAS FAR TOO BEAUTIFUL TO RESIST.
BUT I ENDANGERED MY KINGDOM THE MOMENT I WAS CAPTURED.
FOR FAR TOO LONG, OUR ENEMIES HAVE TRIED TO HUNT US DOWN...
FOR A SECRET DEEP WITHIN OUR BODIES...THE CHRYSALIS.
AS WE MATURE...
WE EVOLVE.

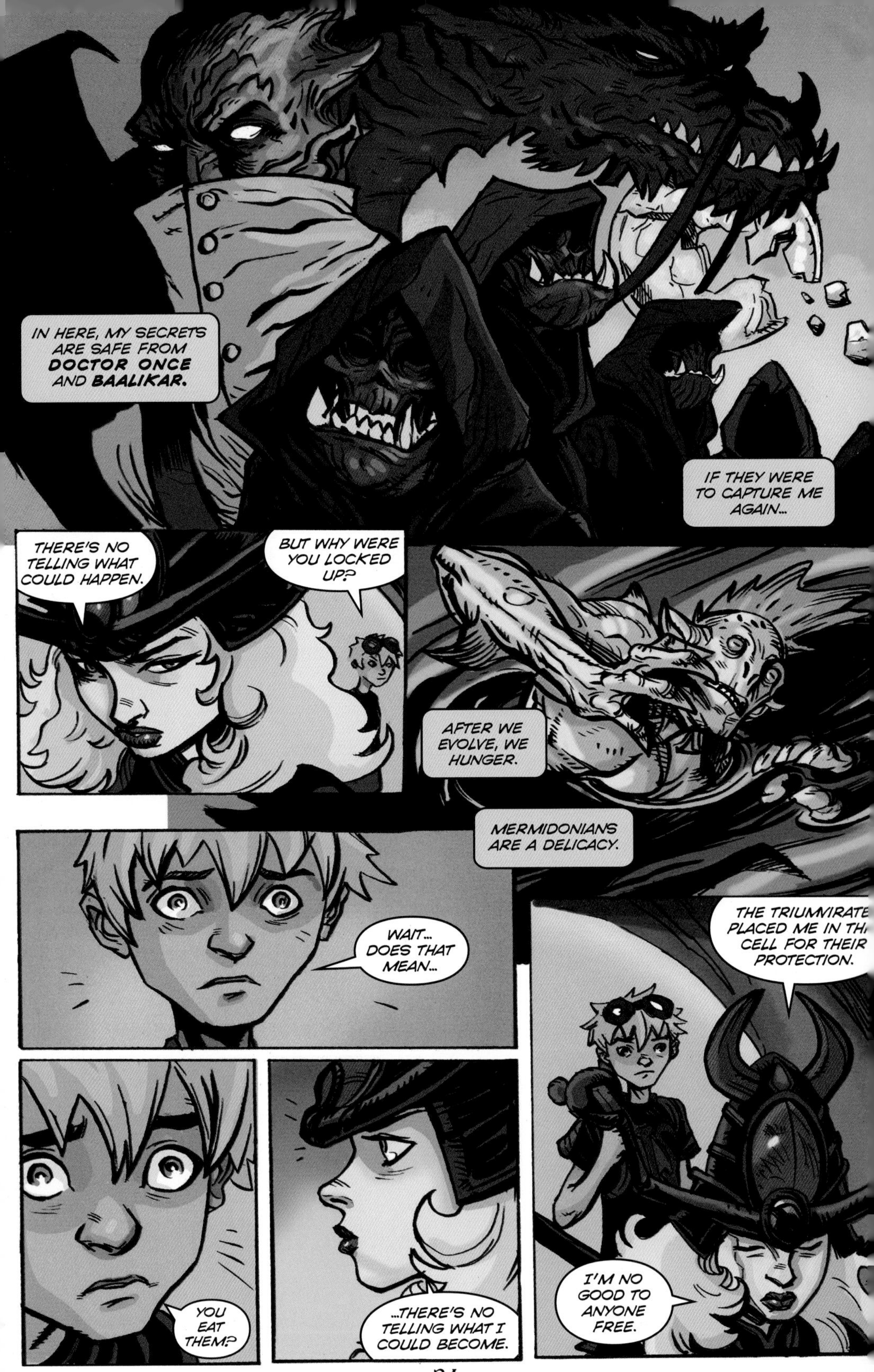
IN HERE, MY SECRETS ARE SAFE FROM **DOCTOR ONCE** AND **BAALIKAR.**
IF THEY WERE TO CAPTURE ME AGAIN...
THERE'S NO TELLING WHAT COULD HAPPEN.
BUT WHY WERE YOU LOCKED UP?
AFTER WE EVOLVE, WE HUNGER.
MERMIDONIANS ARE A DELICACY.
WAIT... DOES THAT MEAN...
THE TRIUMVIRATE PLACED ME IN TH
CELL FOR THEIR PROTECTION.
YOU EAT THEM?
...THERE'S NO TELLING WHAT I COULD BECOME.
I'M NO GOOD TO ANYONE FREE.

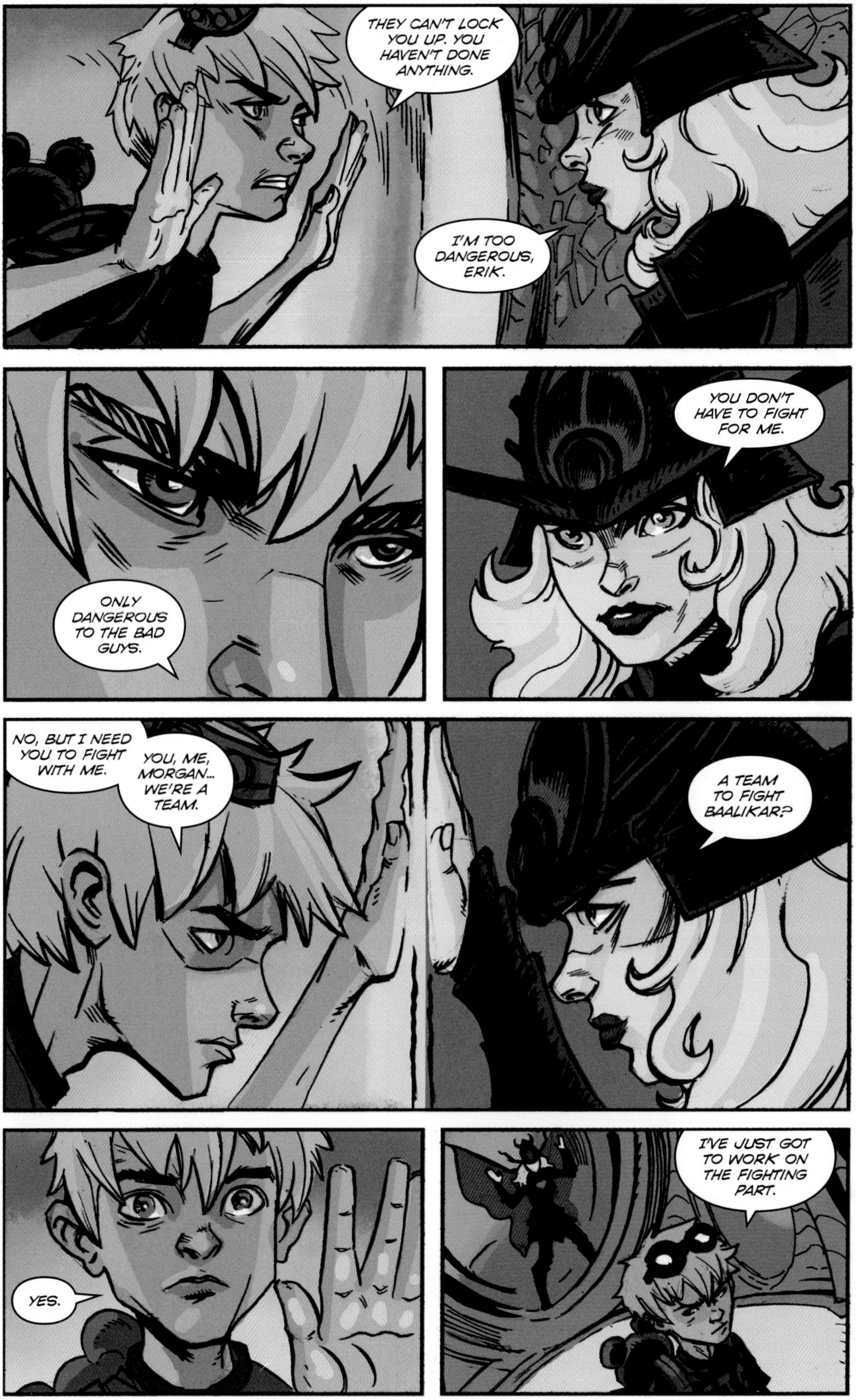
THEY CAN'T LOCK YOU UP. YOU HAVEN'T DONE ANYTHING.
I'M TOO DANGEROUS, ERIK.
ONLY DANGEROUS TO THE BAD GUYS.
YOU DON'T HAVE TO FIGHT FOR ME.
NO, BUT I NEED YOU TO FIGHT WITH ME.
YOU, ME, MORGAN... WE'RE A TEAM.
A TEAM TO FIGHT BAALIKAR?
YES.
I'VE JUST GOT TO WORK ON THE FIGHTING PART.

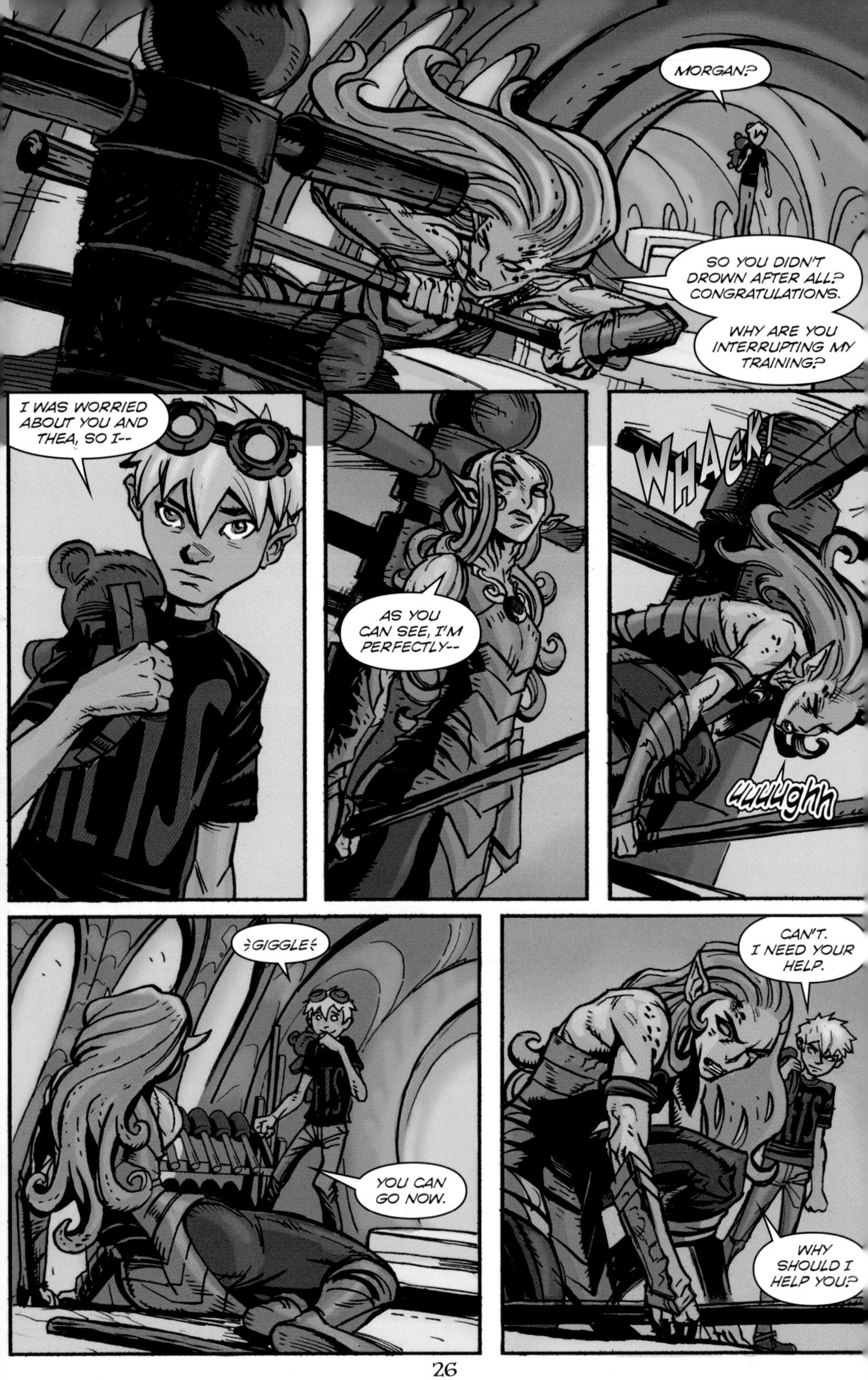
MORGAN?
SO YOU DIDN'T DROWN AFTER ALL? CONGRATULATIONS.
WHY ARE YOU INTERRUPTING MY TRAINING?
I WAS WORRIED ABOUT YOU AND THEA, SO I--
AS YOU CAN SEE, I'M PERFECTLY--
WHACK!
uuuughn
GIGGLE
YOU CAN GO NOW.
CAN'T. I NEED YOUR HELP.
WHY SHOULD I HELP YOU?

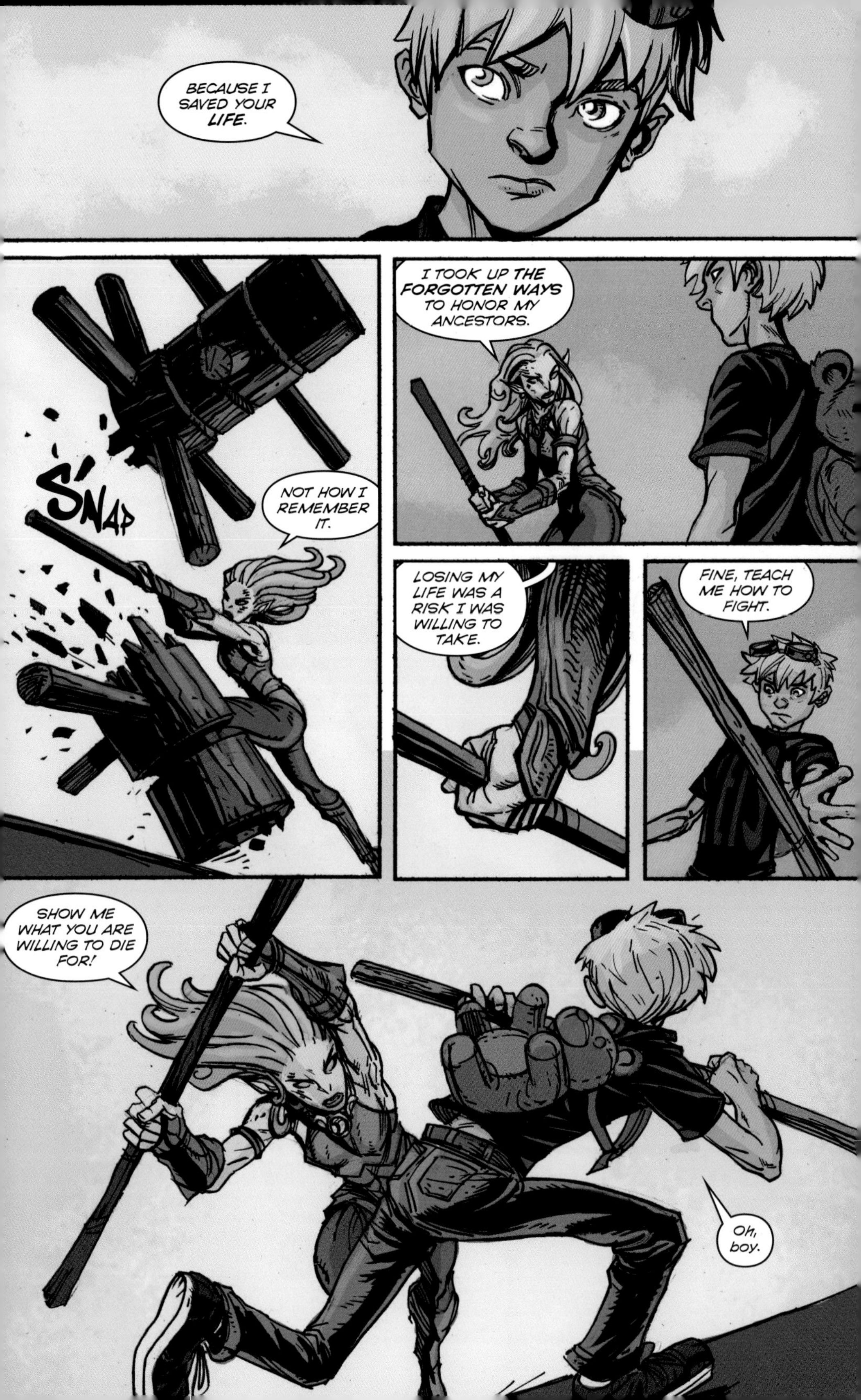
BECAUSE I SAVED YOUR LIFE.
SNAP
NOT HOW I REMEMBER IT.
I TOOK UP THE FORGOTTEN WAYS TO HONOR MY ANCESTORS.
LOSING MY LIFE WAS A RISK I WAS WILLING TO TAKE.
FINE, TEACH ME HOW TO FIGHT.
SHOW ME WHAT YOU ARE WILLING TO DIE FOR!
Oh, boy.

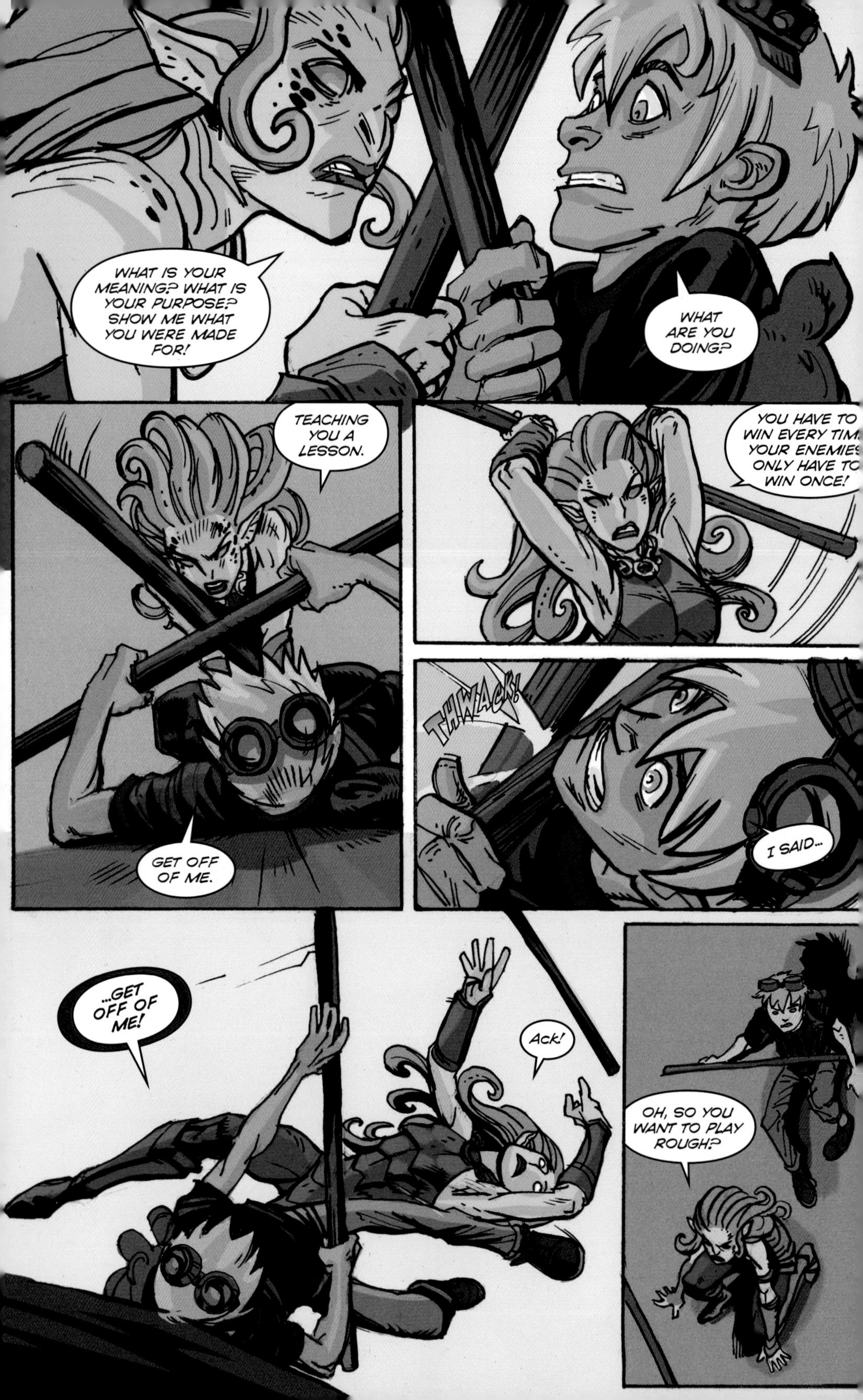
WHAT IS YOUR MEANING? WHAT IS YOUR PURPOSE? SHOW ME WHAT YOU WERE MADE FOR!
WHAT ARE YOU DOING?
TEACHING YOU A LESSON.
GET OFF OF ME.
YOU HAVE TO WIN EVERY TIM YOUR ENEMIES ONLY HAVE TO WIN ONCE!
THWACK!
I SAID...
...GET OFF OF ME!
Ack!
OH, SO YOU WANT TO PLAY ROUGH?

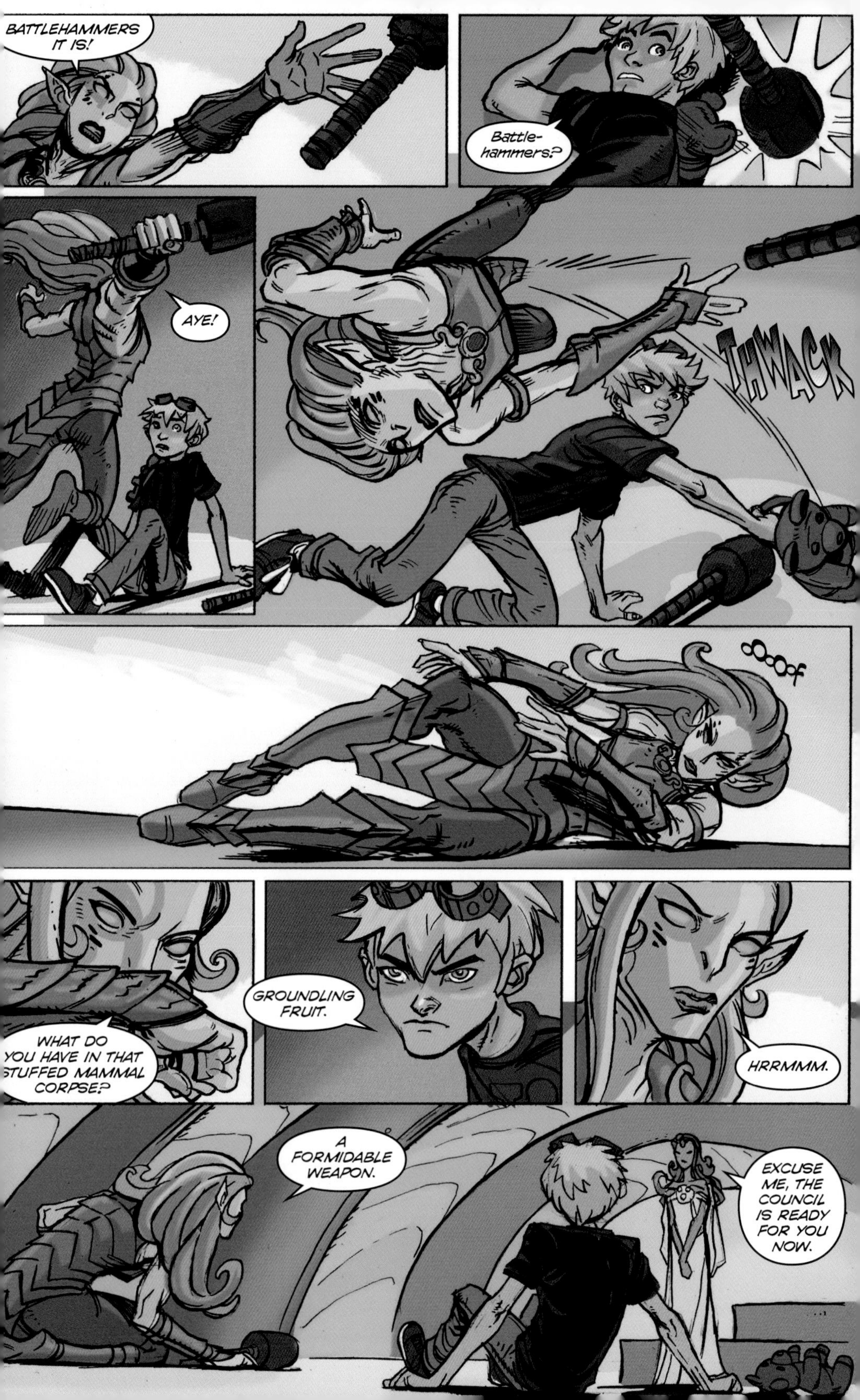
BATTLEHAMMERS IT IS!
Battle-hammers?
AYE!
THWACK
OooOf
WHAT DO YOU HAVE IN THAT STUFFED MAMMAL CORPSE?
GROUNDLING FRUIT.
HRRMMM.
A FORMIDABLE WEAPON.
EXCUSE ME, THE COUNCIL IS READY FOR YOU NOW.

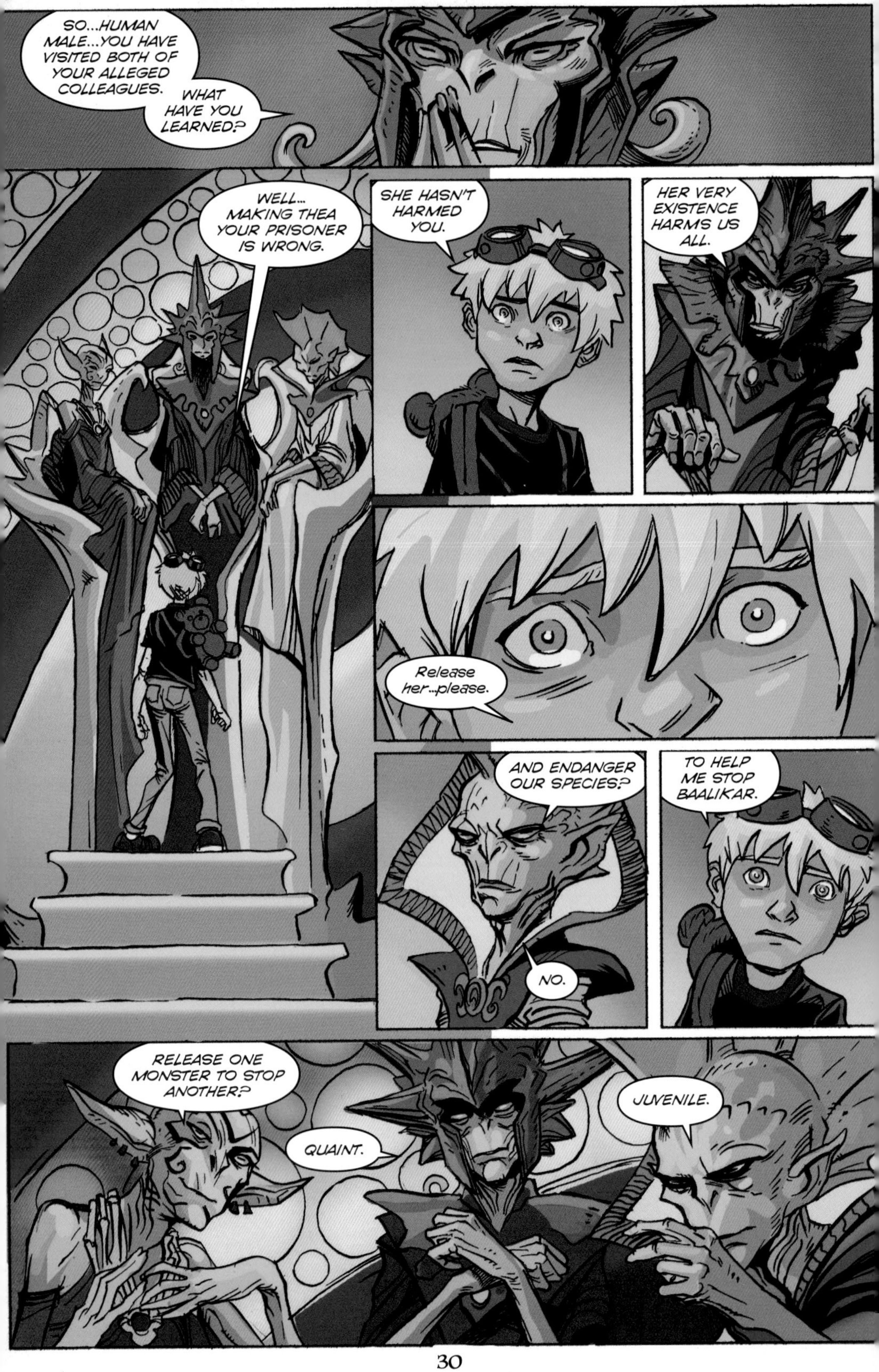
SO...HUMAN MALE...YOU HAVE VISITED BOTH OF YOUR ALLEGED COLLEAGUES.
WHAT HAVE YOU LEARNED?
WELL... MAKING THEA YOUR PRISONER IS WRONG.
SHE HASN'T HARMED YOU.
HER VERY EXISTENCE HARMS US ALL.
Release her...please.
AND ENDANGER OUR SPECIES?
NO.
TO HELP ME STOP BAALIKAR.
RELEASE ONE MONSTER TO STOP ANOTHER?
QUAINT.
JUVENILE.

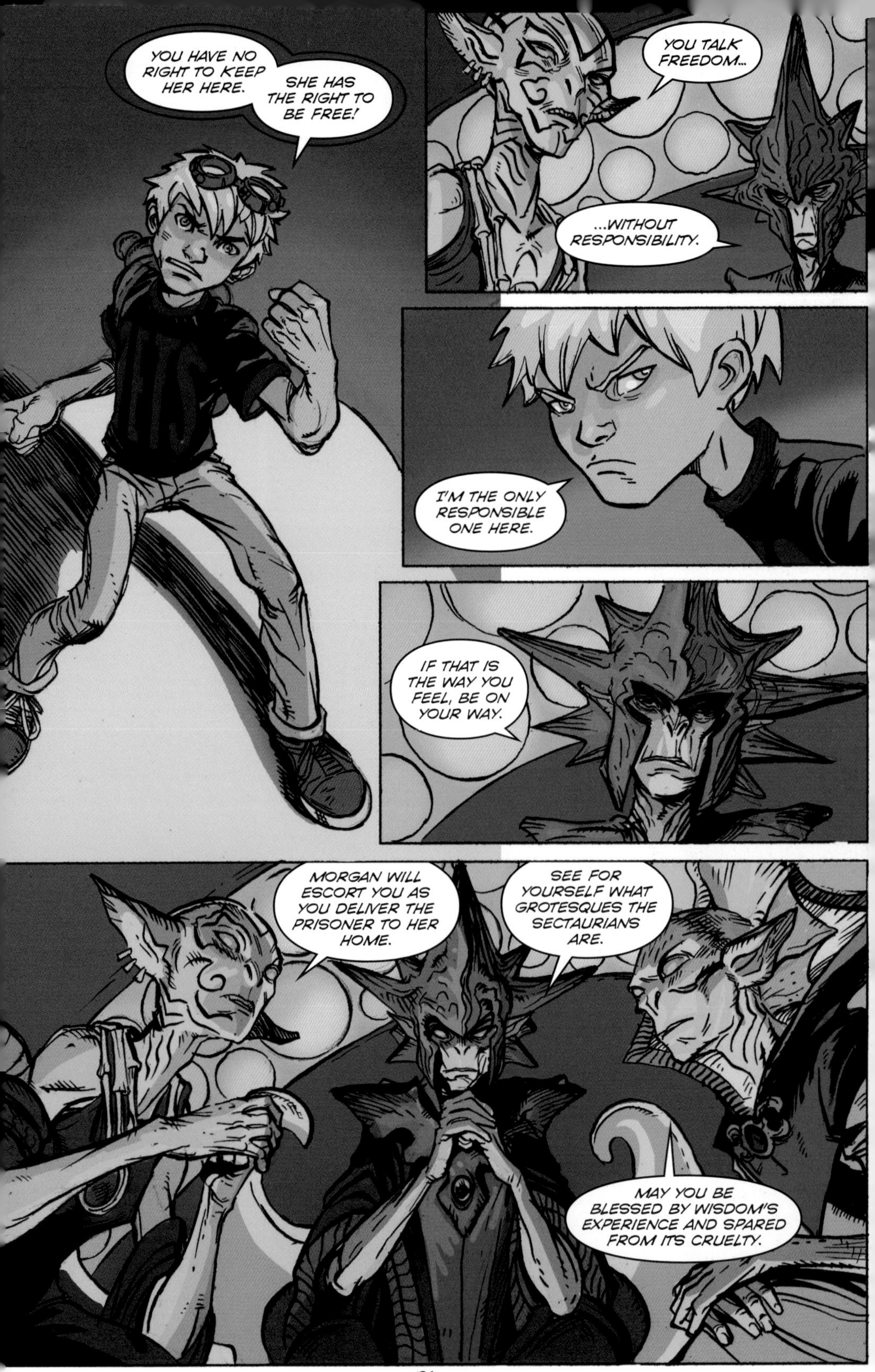
YOU HAVE NO RIGHT TO KEEP HER HERE.
SHE HAS THE RIGHT TO BE FREE!
YOU TALK FREEDOM...
...WITHOUT RESPONSIBILITY.
I'M THE ONLY RESPONSIBLE ONE HERE.
IF THAT IS THE WAY YOU FEEL, BE ON YOUR WAY.
MORGAN WILL ESCORT YOU AS YOU DELIVER THE PRISONER TO HER HOME.
SEE FOR YOURSELF WHAT GROTESQUES THE SECTAURIANS ARE.
MAY YOU BE BLESSED BY WISDOM'S EXPERIENCE AND SPARED FROM ITS CRUELTY.

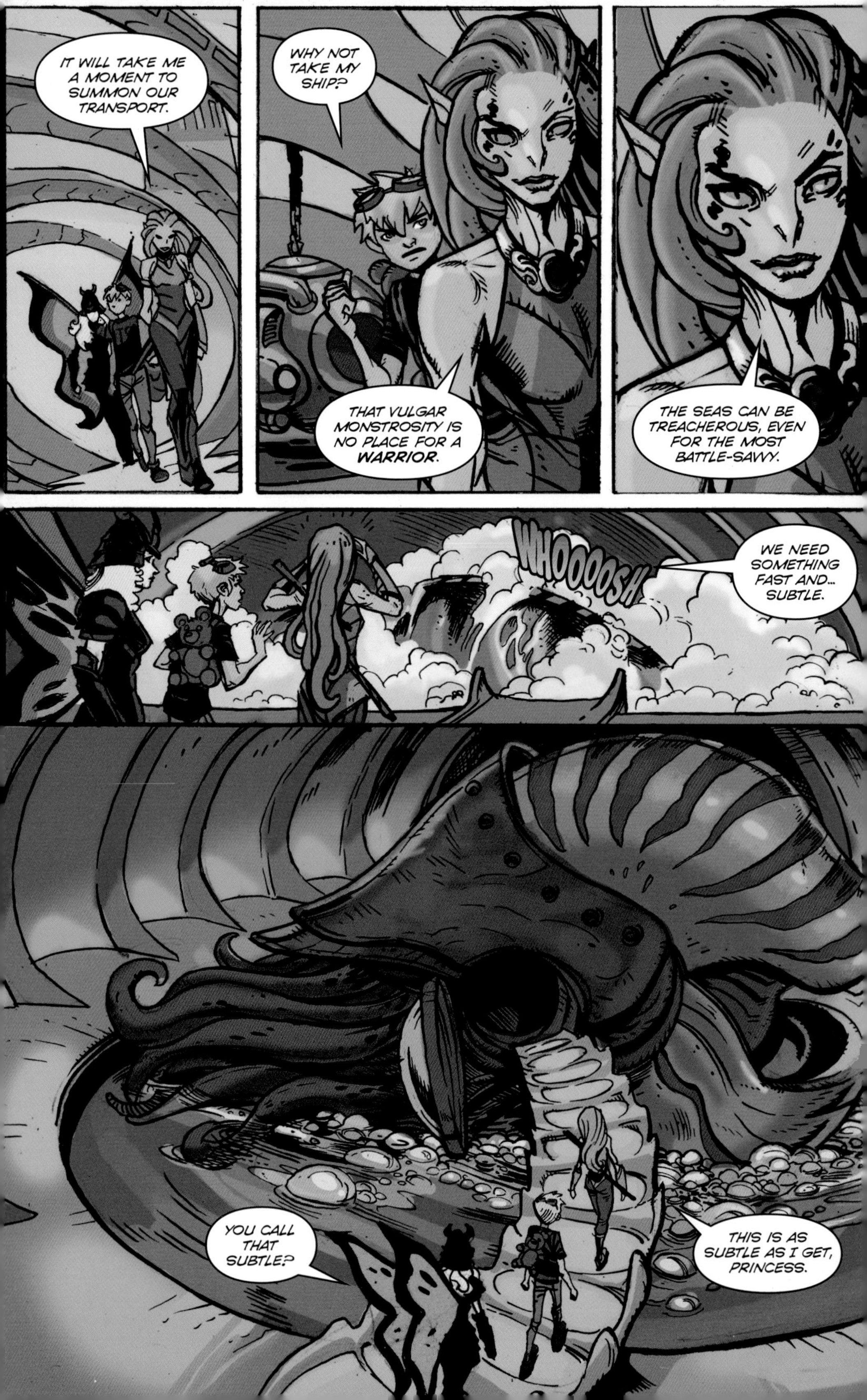
IT WILL TAKE ME A MOMENT TO SUMMON OUR TRANSPORT.
WHY NOT TAKE MY SHIP?
THAT VULGAR MONSTROSITY IS NO PLACE FOR A WARRIOR.
THE SEAS CAN BE TREACHEROUS, EVEN FOR THE MOST BATTLE-SAVVY.
WHOOOOSH
WE NEED SOMETHING FAST AND... SUBTLE.
YOU CALL THAT SUBTLE?
THIS IS AS SUBTLE AS I GET, PRINCESS.

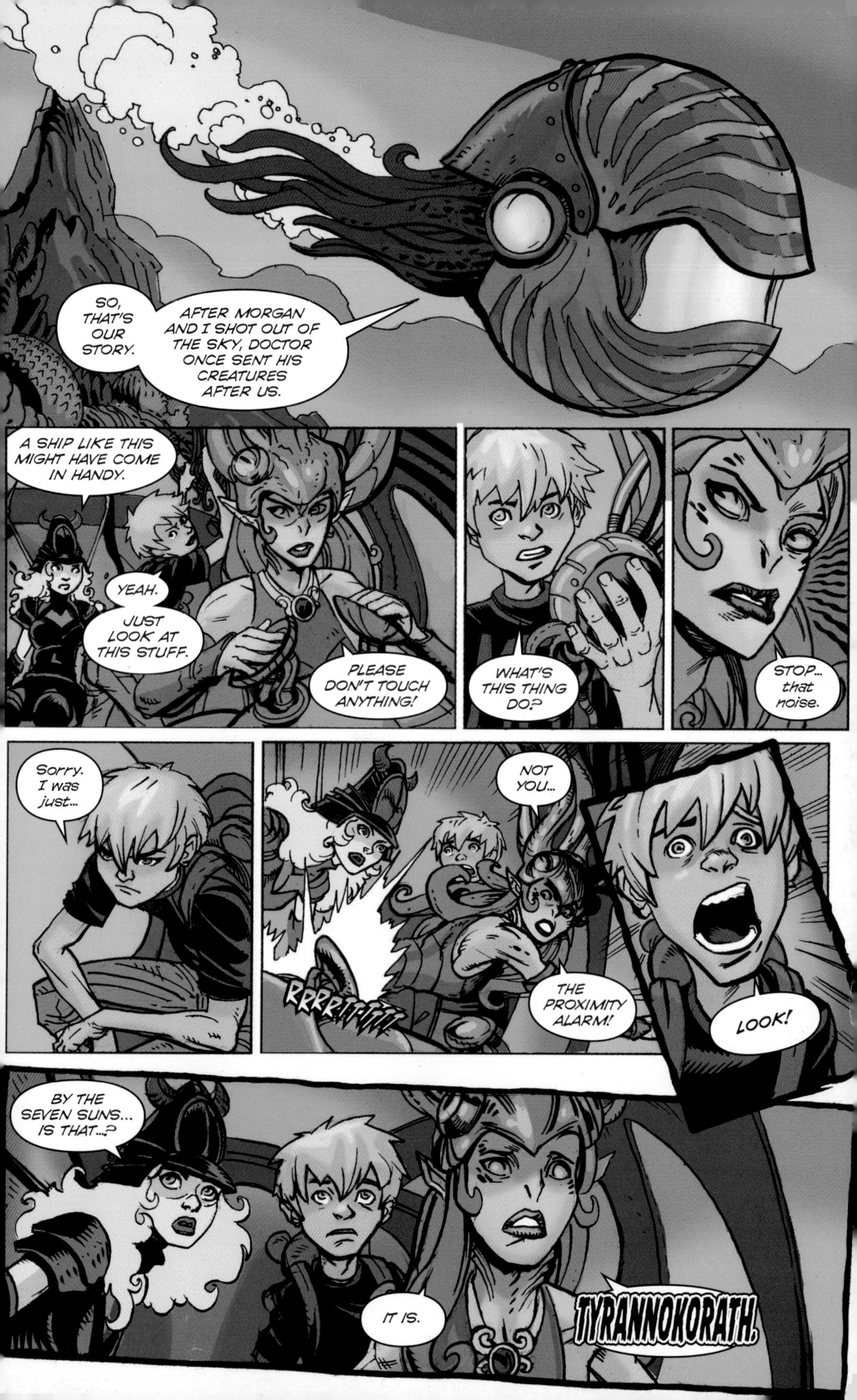
SO, THAT'S OUR STORY.
AFTER MORGAN AND I SHOT OUT OF THE SKY, DOCTOR ONCE SENT HIS CREATURES AFTER US.
A SHIP LIKE THIS MIGHT HAVE COME IN HANDY.
YEAH.
JUST LOOK AT THIS STUFF.
PLEASE DON'T TOUCH ANYTHING!
WHAT'S THIS THING DO?
STOP... that noise.
Sorry. I was just...
NOT YOU...
RRRRIIIIIII
THE PROXIMITY ALARM!
LOOK!
BY THE SEVEN SUNS... IS THAT...?
IT IS.
TYRANNOKORATH.

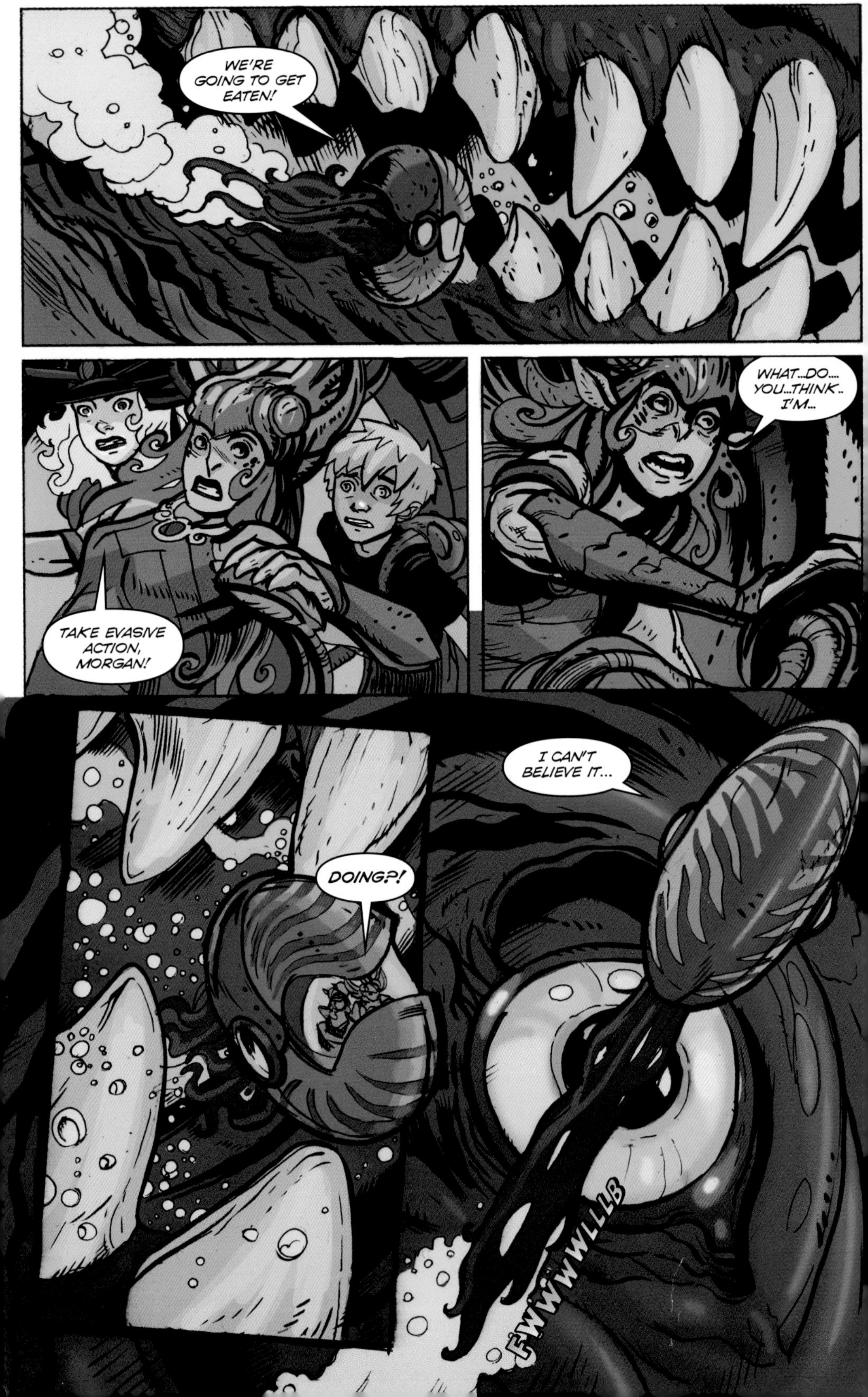
WE'RE GOING TO GET EATEN!
TAKE EVASIVE ACTION, MORGAN!
WHAT...DO.... YOU...THINK.. I'M...
I CAN'T BELIEVE IT...
DOING?!
FWWWWLLLB

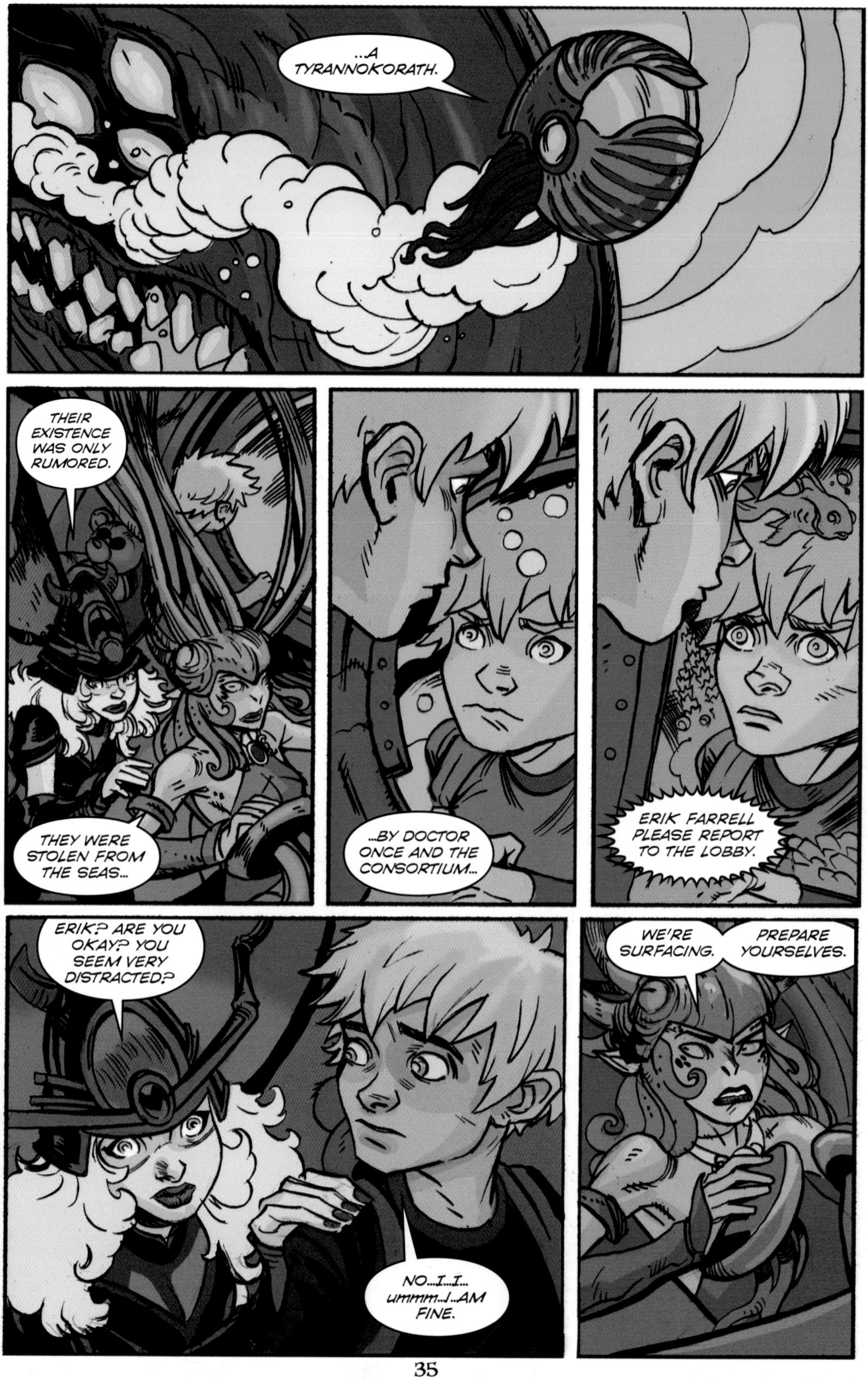
...A TYRANNOKORATH.
THEIR EXISTENCE WAS ONLY RUMORED.
THEY WERE STOLEN FROM THE SEAS...
...BY DOCTOR ONCE AND THE CONSORTIUM...
ERIK FARRELL PLEASE REPORT TO THE LOBBY.
ERIK? ARE YOU OKAY? YOU SEEM VERY DISTRACTED?
NO...I...I... ummm...I...AM FINE.
WE'RE SURFACING.
PREPARE YOURSELVES.

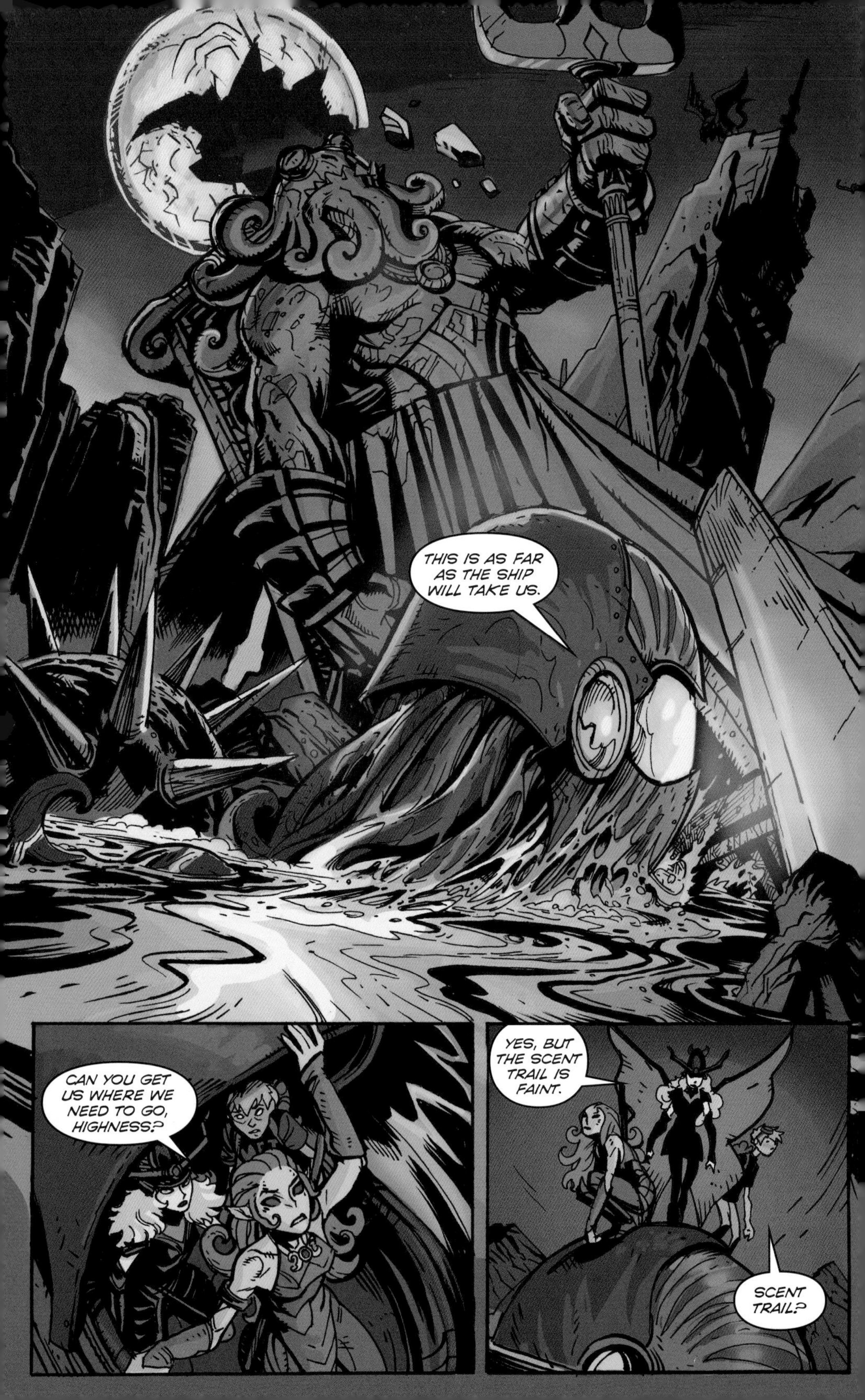
THIS IS AS FAR AS THE SHIP WILL TAKE US.
CAN YOU GET US WHERE WE NEED TO GO, HIGHNESS?
YES, BUT THE SCENT TRAIL IS FAINT.
SCENT TRAIL?

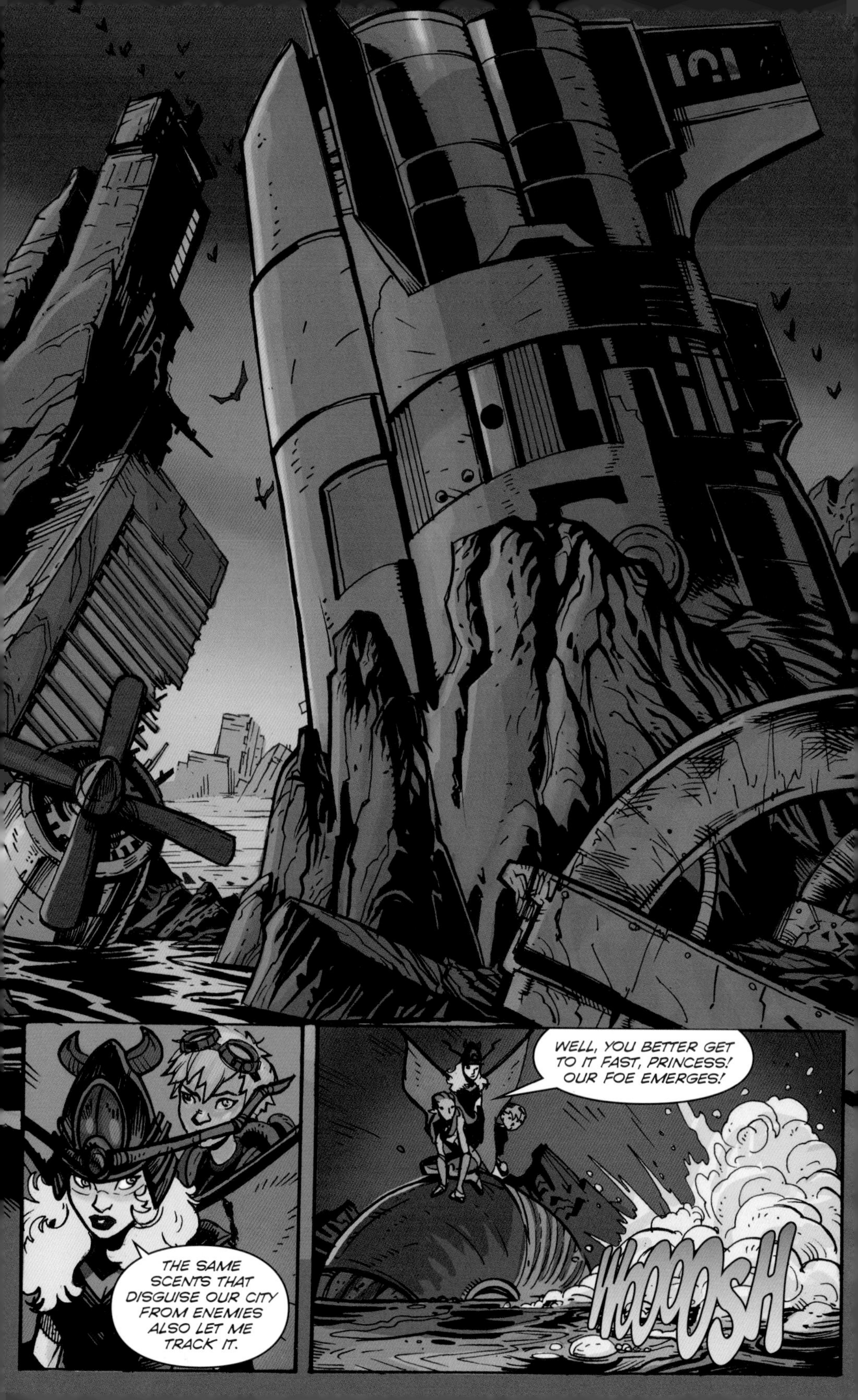
THE SAME SCENTS THAT DISGUISE OUR CITY FROM ENEMIES ALSO LET ME TRACK IT.
WELL, YOU BETTER GET TO IT FAST, PRINCESS! OUR FOE EMERGES!
WHOOOSH

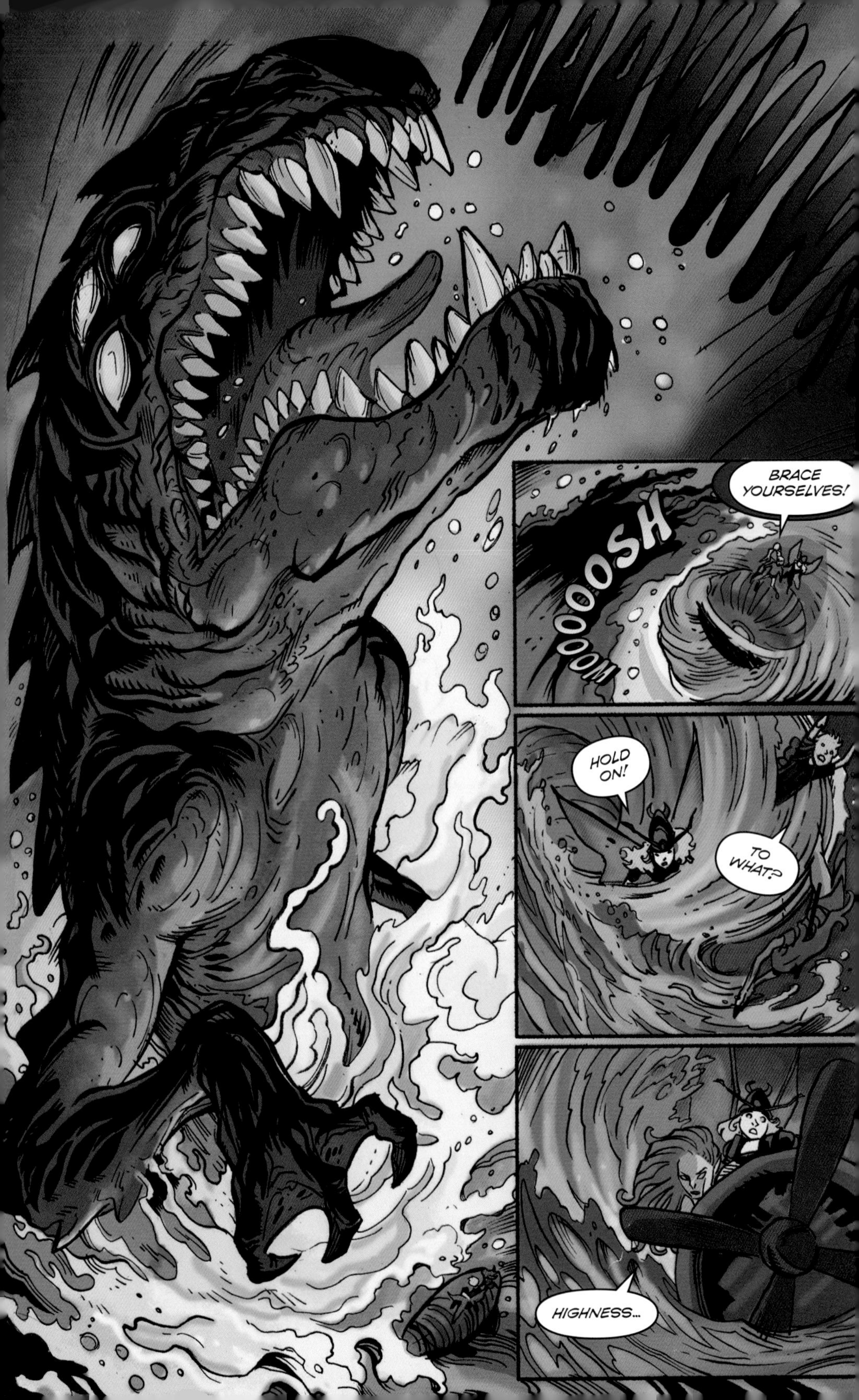
RRAAAHHWWW
BRACE YOURSELVES!
WOOOOOOSH
HOLD ON!
TO WHAT?
HIGHNESS...

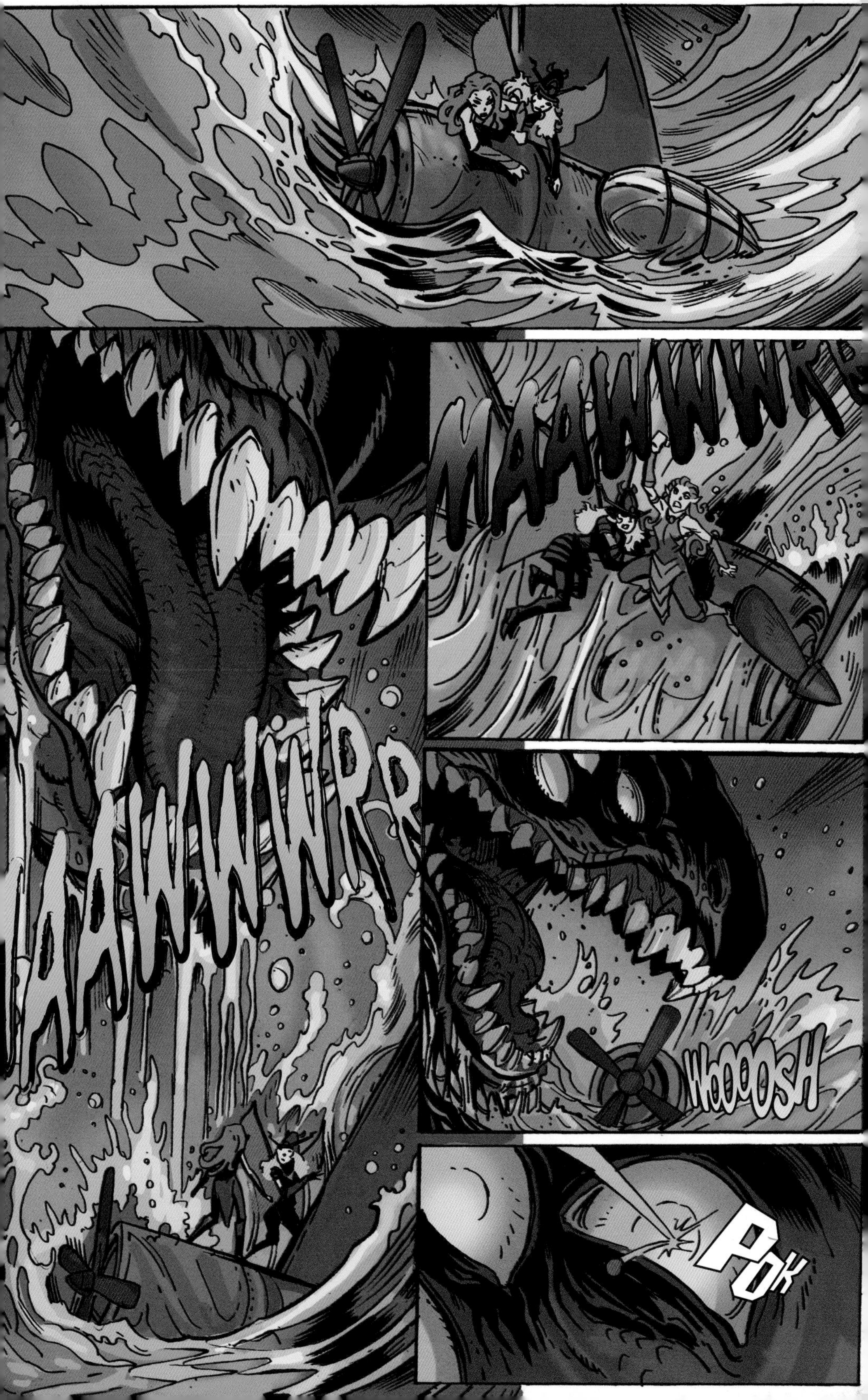

AAWWWRR
MAAWWWR
WOOOOSH
POK

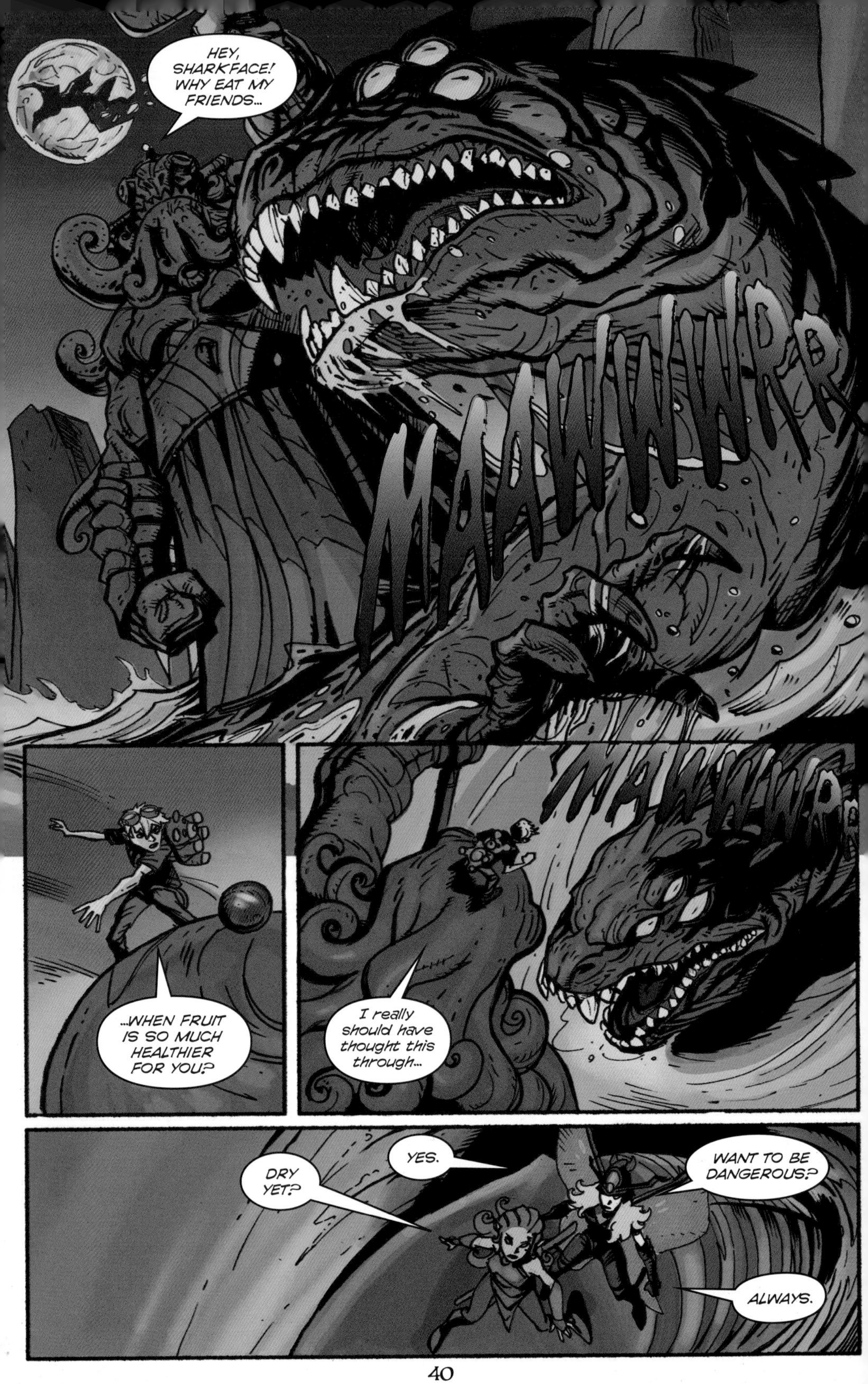

HEY, SHARKFACE! WHY EAT MY FRIENDS...
MAAWWWRR
...WHEN FRUIT IS SO MUCH HEALTHIER FOR YOU?
MAWWWR
I really should have thought this through...
DRY YET?
YES.
WANT TO BE DANGEROUS?
ALWAYS.

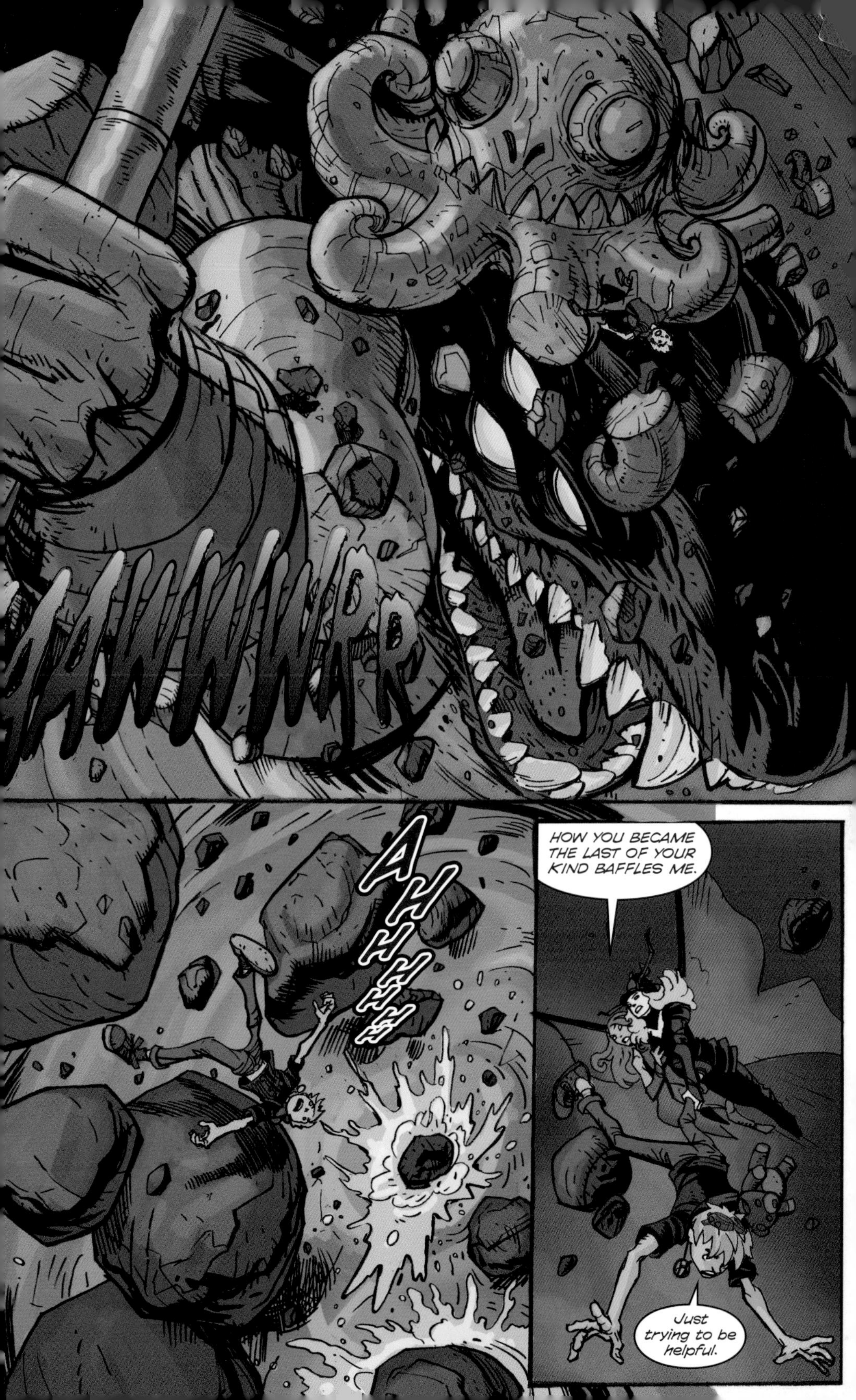
RAWWWWRR
AHHHHHH
HOW YOU BECAME THE LAST OF YOUR KIND BAFFLES ME.
Just trying to be helpful.

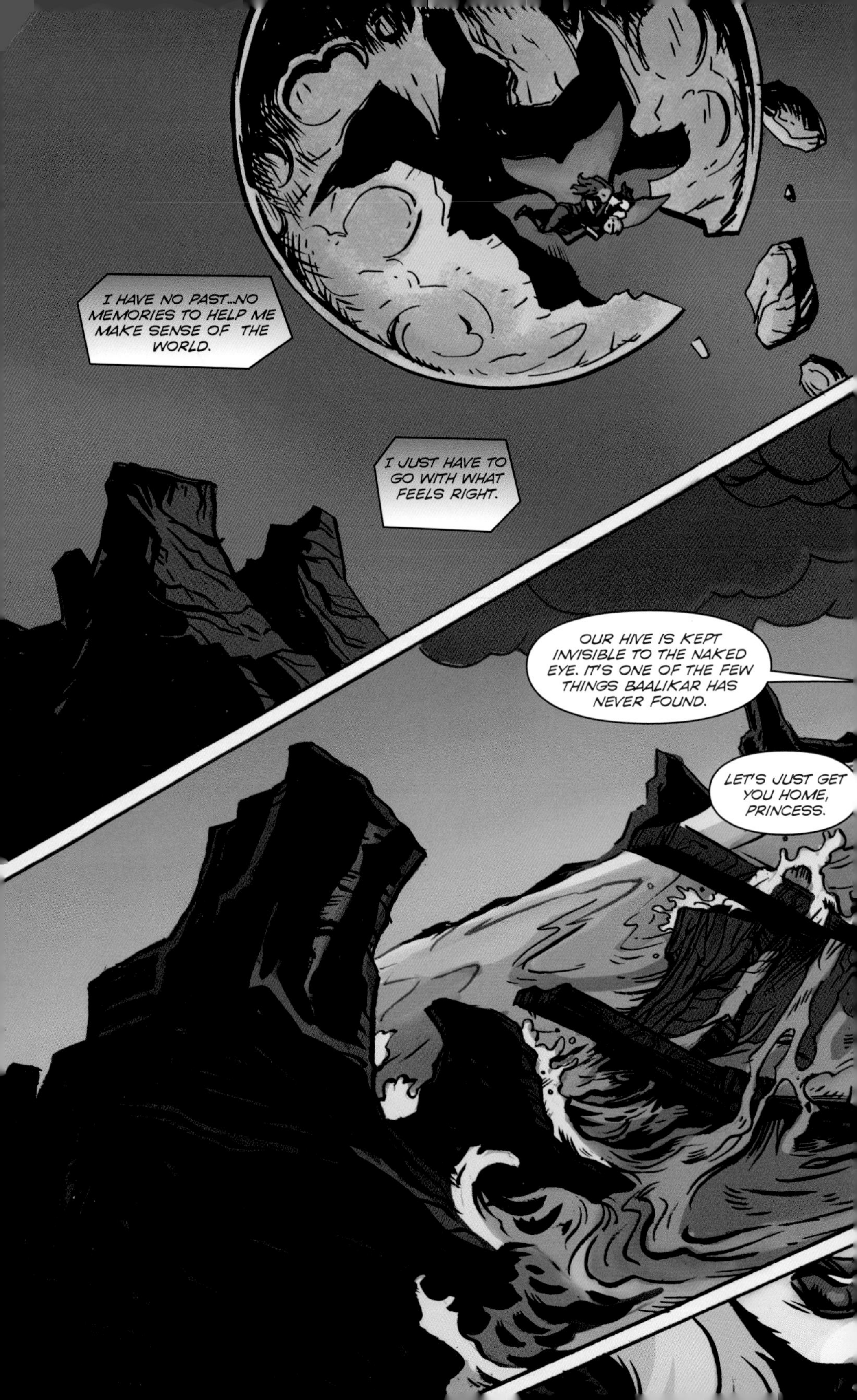
I HAVE NO PAST...NO MEMORIES TO HELP ME MAKE SENSE OF THE WORLD.
I JUST HAVE TO GO WITH WHAT FEELS RIGHT.
OUR HIVE IS KEPT INVISIBLE TO THE NAKED EYE. IT'S ONE OF THE FEW THINGS BAALIKAR HAS NEVER FOUND.
LET'S JUST GET YOU HOME, PRINCESS.

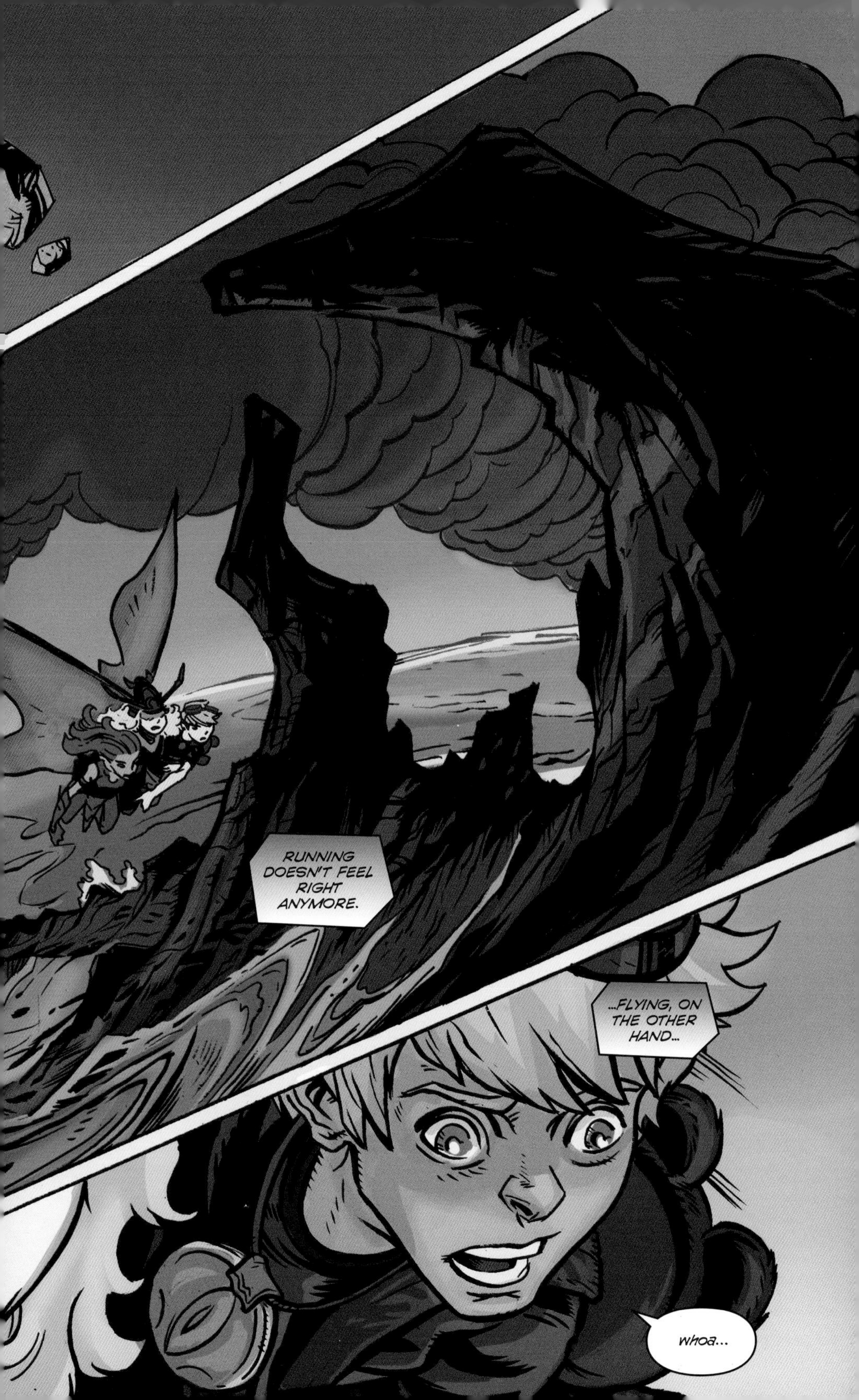
RUNNING DOESN'T FEEL RIGHT ANYMORE.
...FLYING, ON THE OTHER HAND...
whoa...

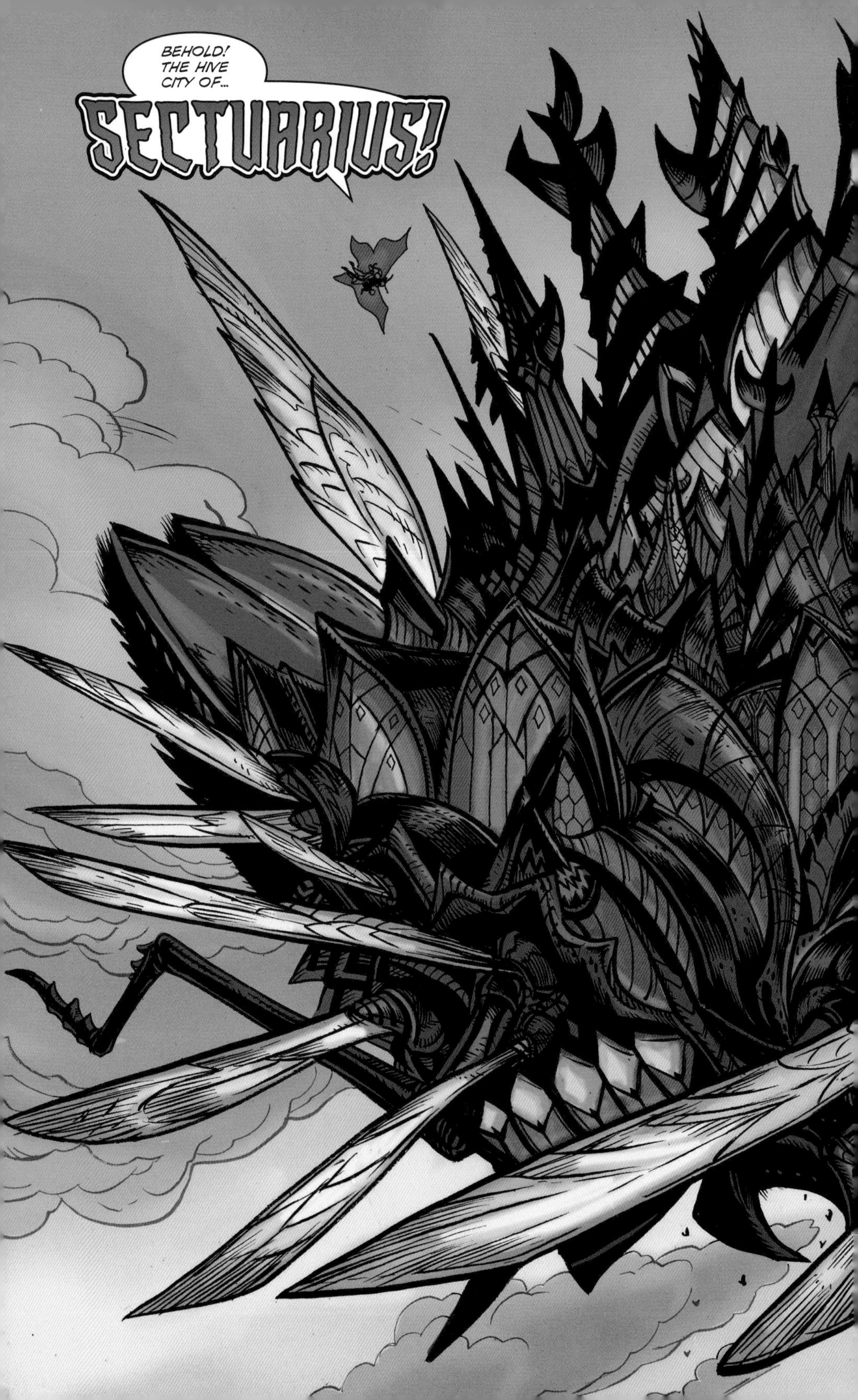
BEHOLD! THE HIVE CITY OF... SECTUARIUS!

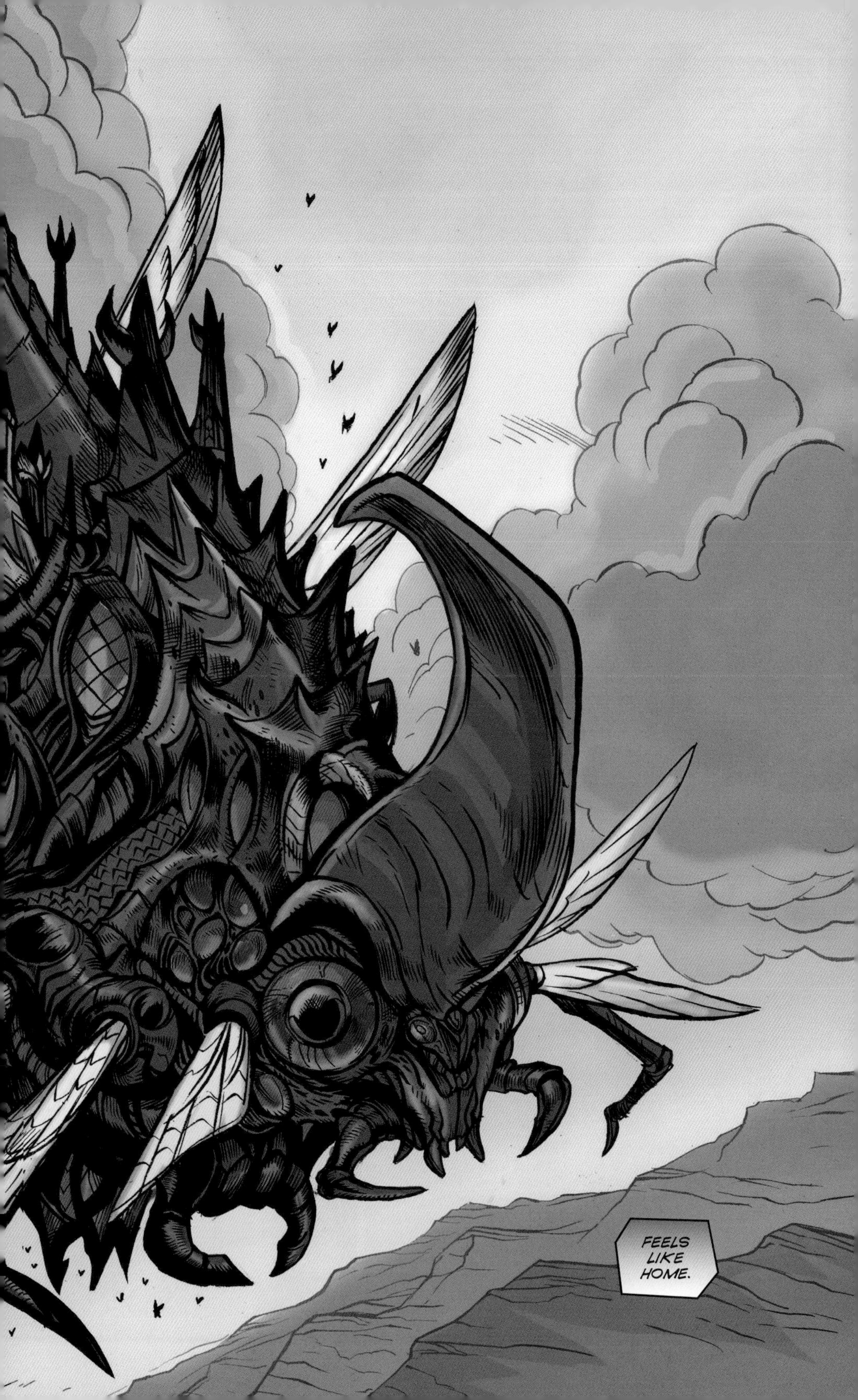
FEELS LIKE HOME.

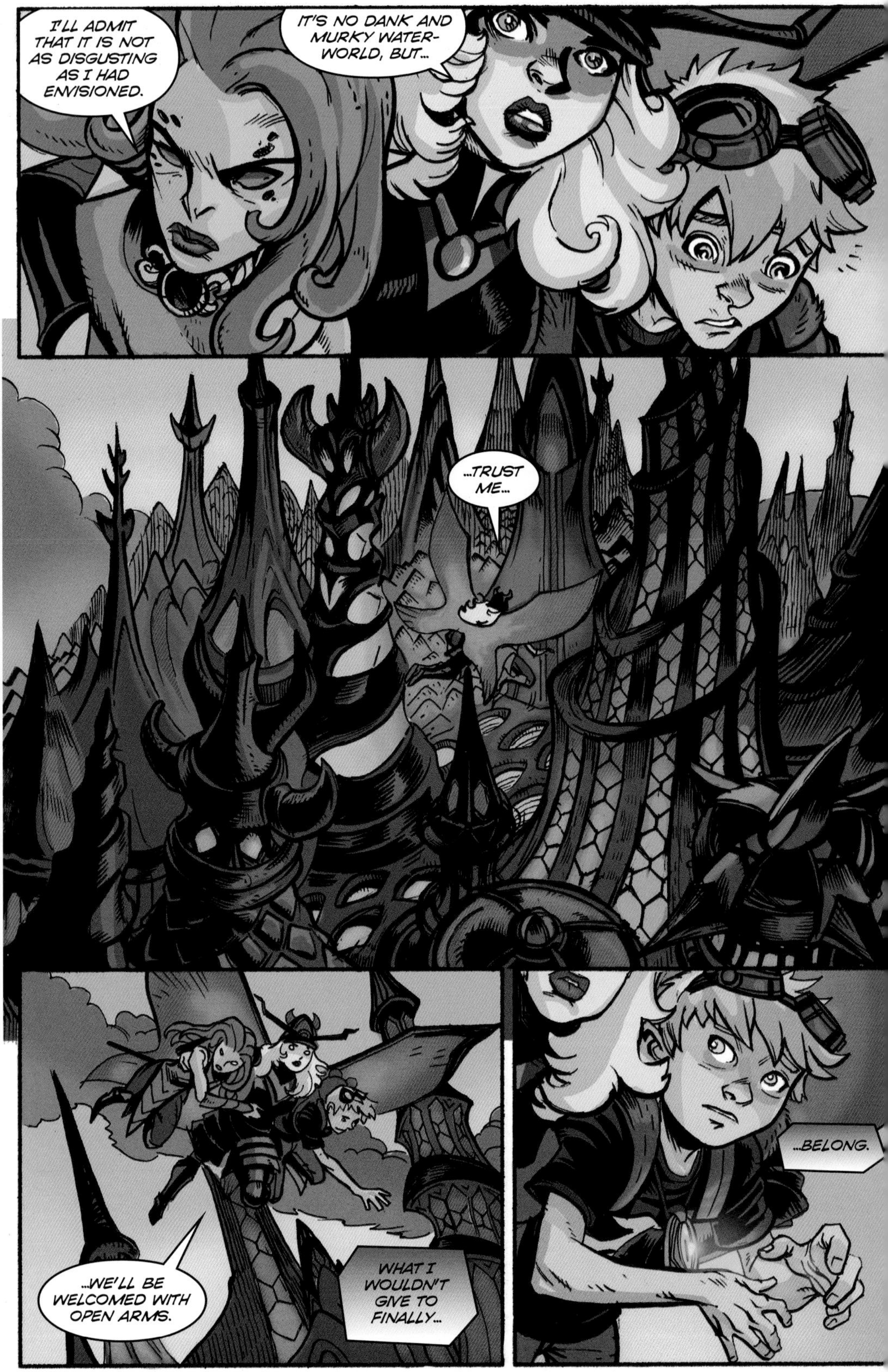
I'LL ADMIT THAT IT IS NOT AS DISGUSTING AS I HAD ENVISIONED.
IT'S NO DANK AND MURKY WATER-WORLD, BUT...
...TRUST ME...
...WE'LL BE WELCOMED WITH OPEN ARMS.
WHAT I WOULDN'T GIVE TO FINALLY...
...BELONG.

CHAPTER FOUR

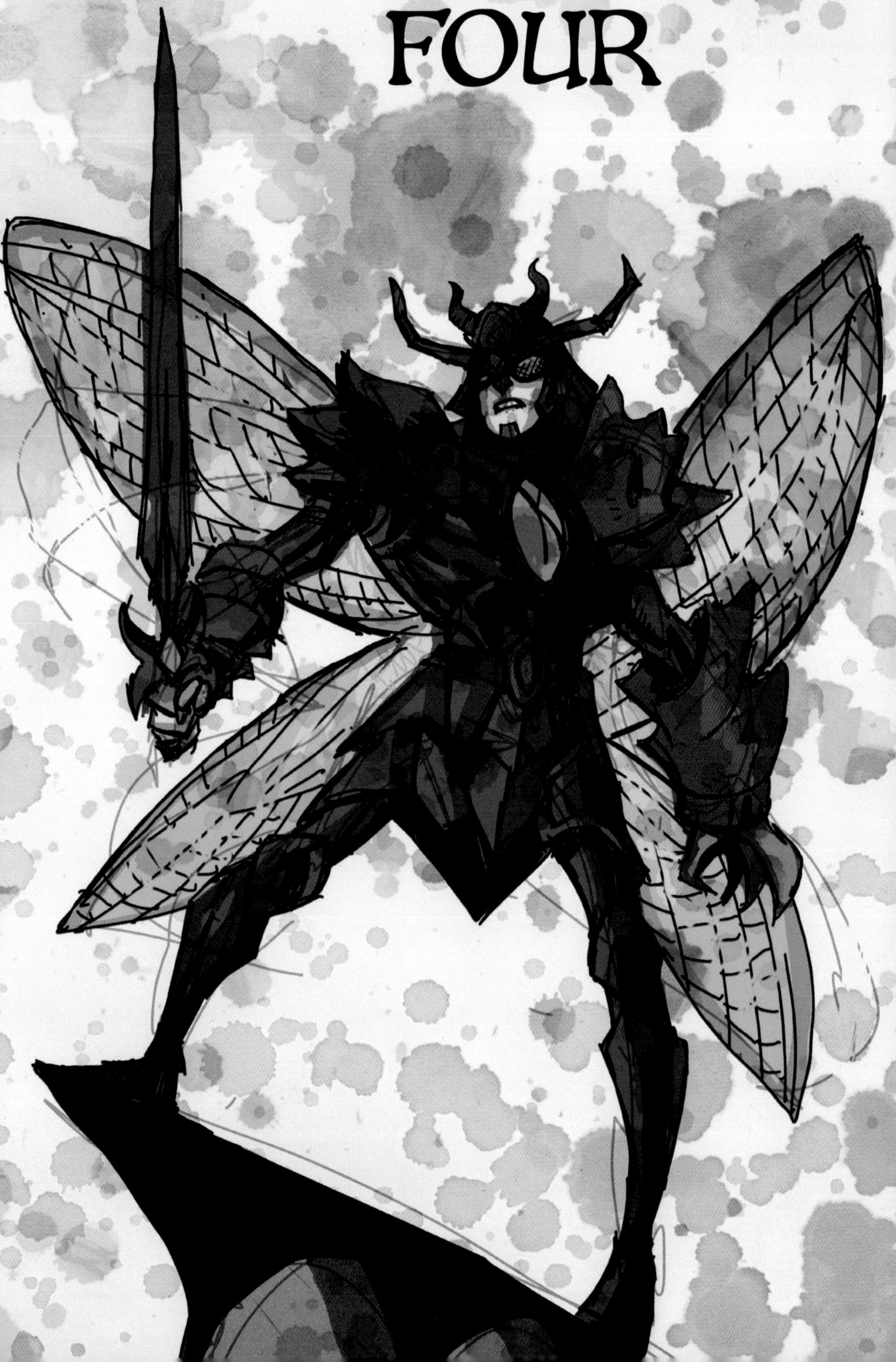

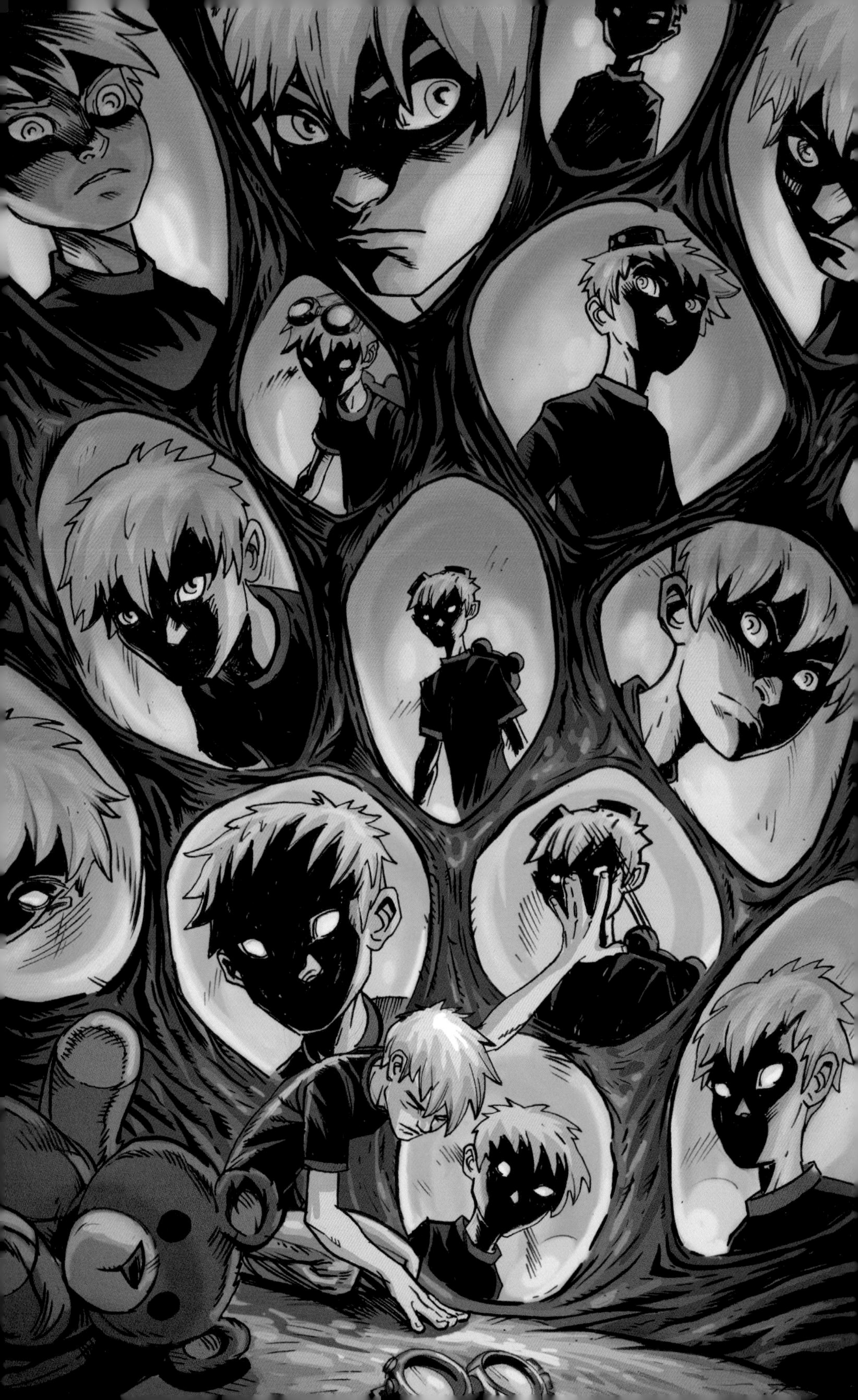

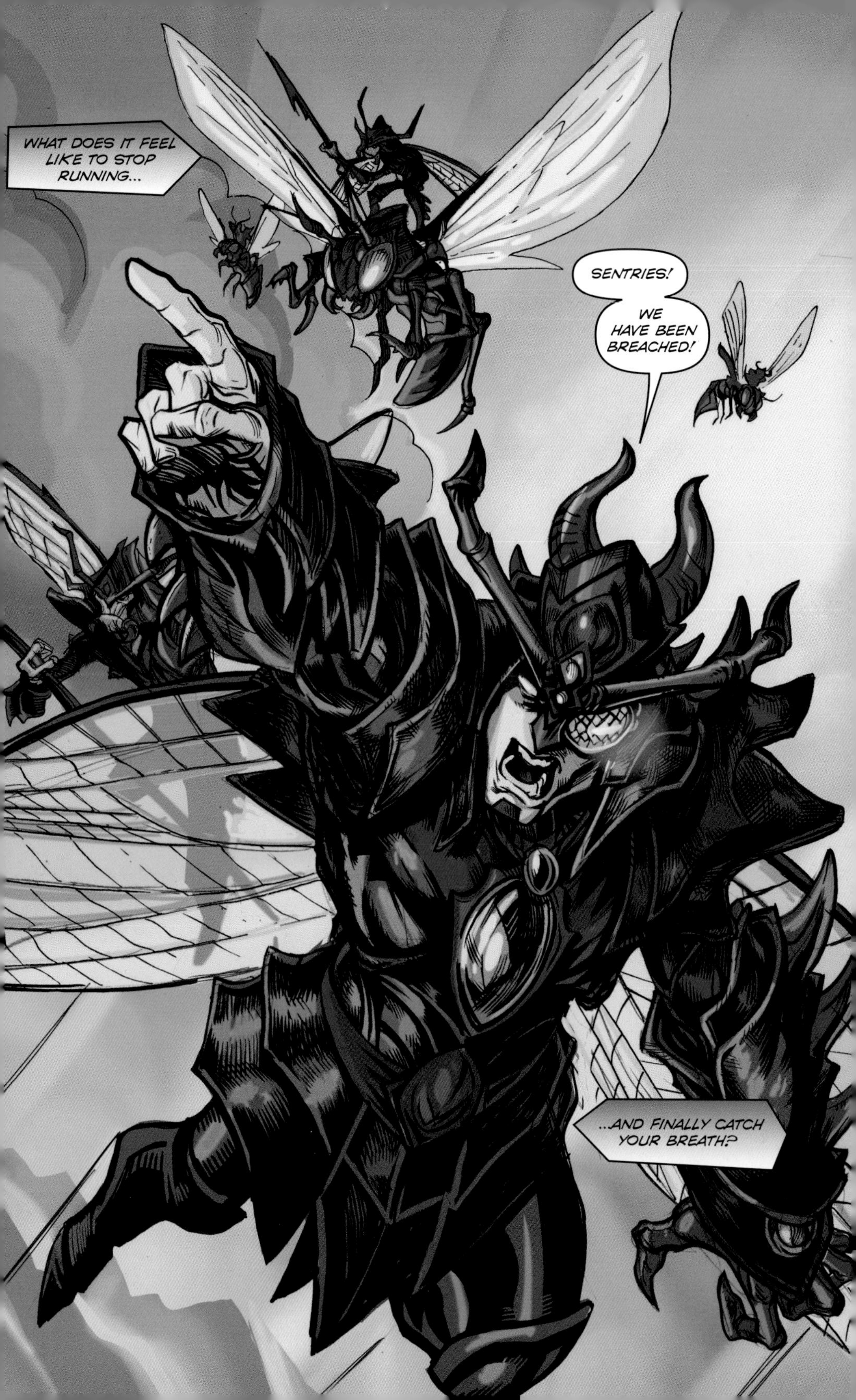
WHAT DOES IT FEEL LIKE TO STOP RUNNING...
SENTRIES!
WE HAVE BEEN BREACHED!
...AND FINALLY CATCH YOUR BREATH?

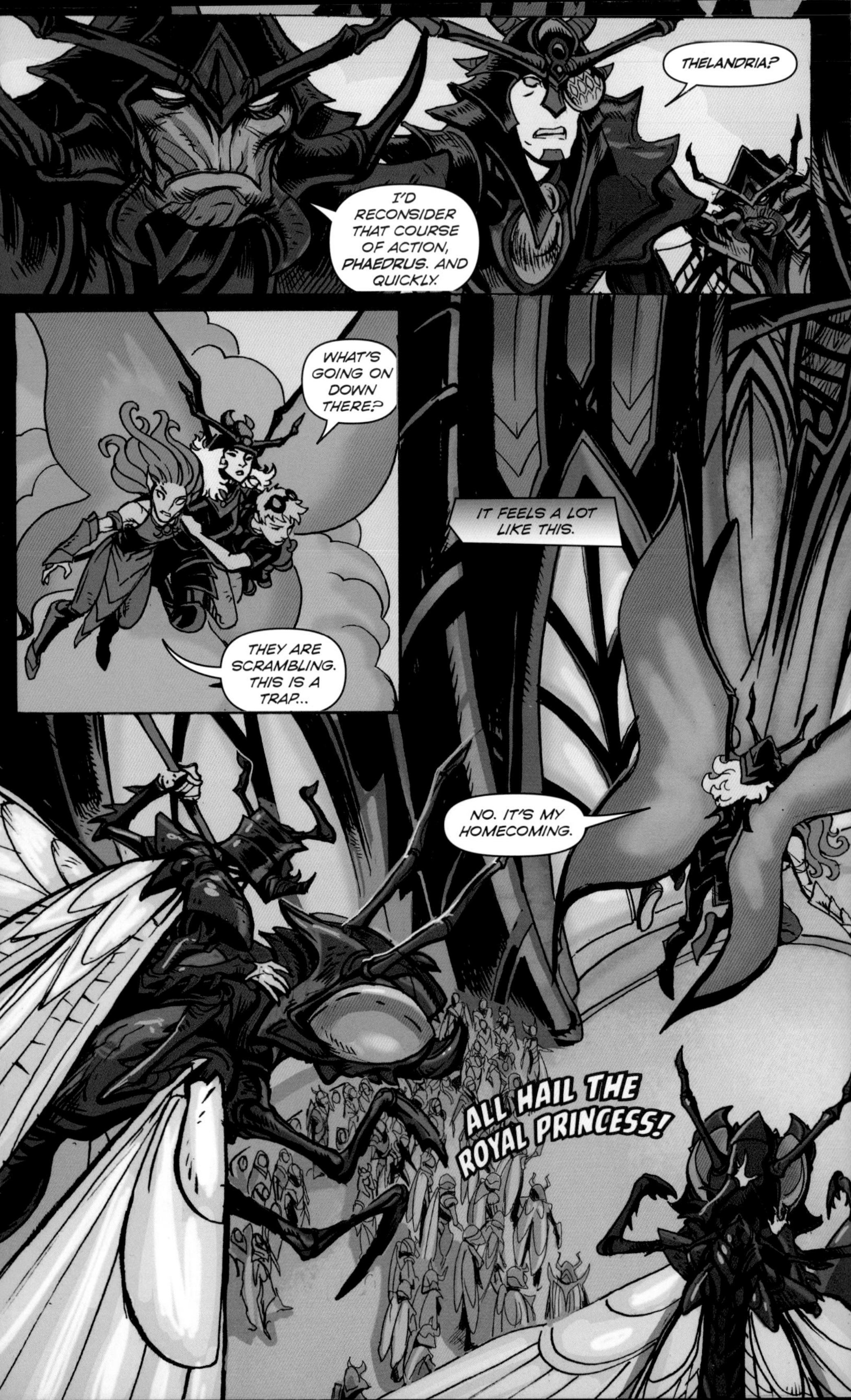
THELANDRIA?
I'D RECONSIDER THAT COURSE OF ACTION, PHAEDRUS. AND QUICKLY.
WHAT'S GOING ON DOWN THERE?
THEY ARE SCRAMBLING. THIS IS A TRAP...
IT FEELS A LOT LIKE THIS.
NO. IT'S MY HOMECOMING.
ALL HAIL THE ROYAL PRINCESS!

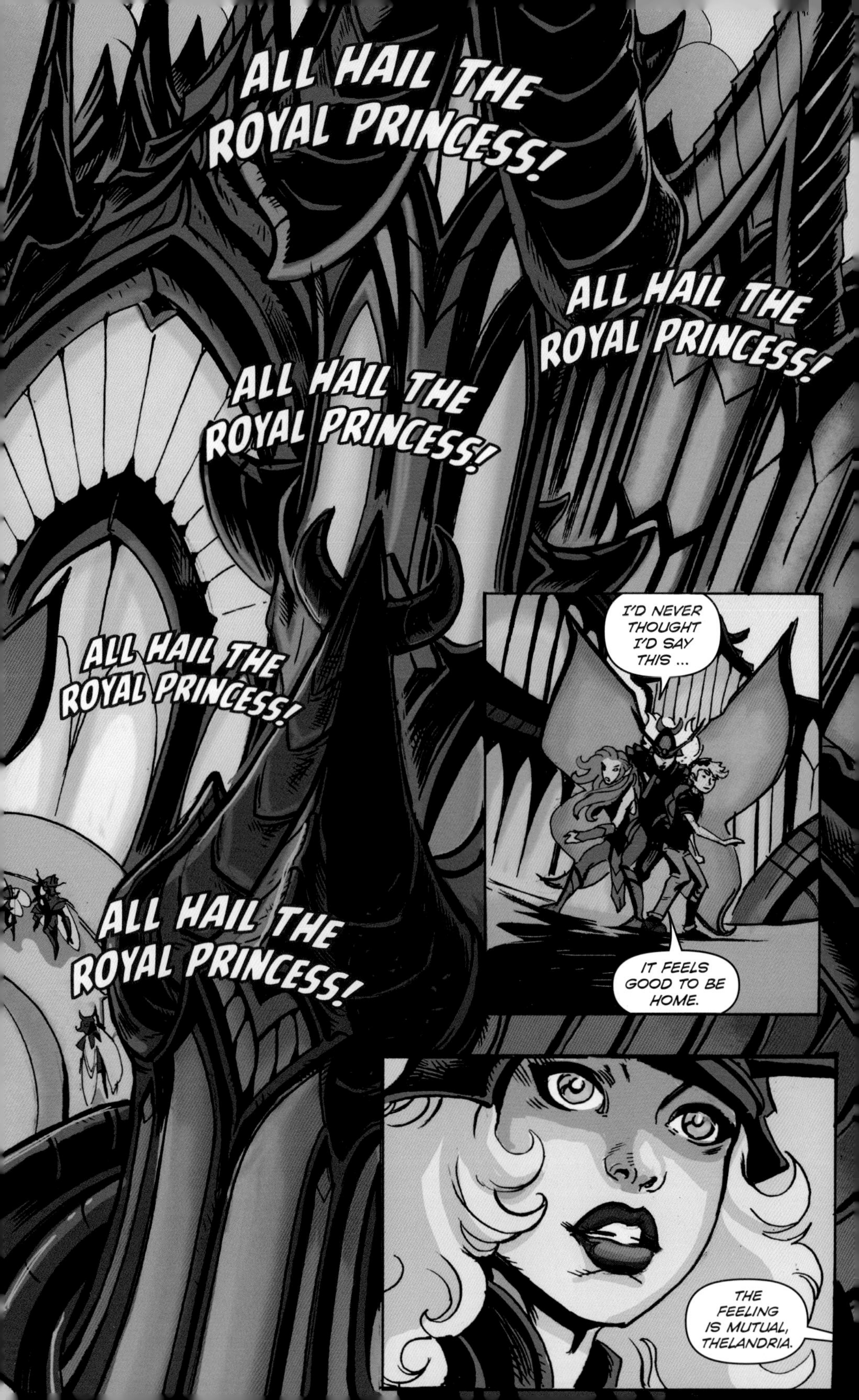
ALL HAIL THE ROYAL PRINCESS!
ALL HAIL THE ROYAL PRINCESS!
ALL HAIL THE ROYAL PRINCESS!
ALL HAIL THE ROYAL PRINCESS!
ALL HAIL THE ROYAL PRINCESS!
I'D NEVER THOUGHT I'D SAY THIS ...
IT FEELS GOOD TO BE HOME.
THE FEELING IS MUTUAL, THELANDRIA.

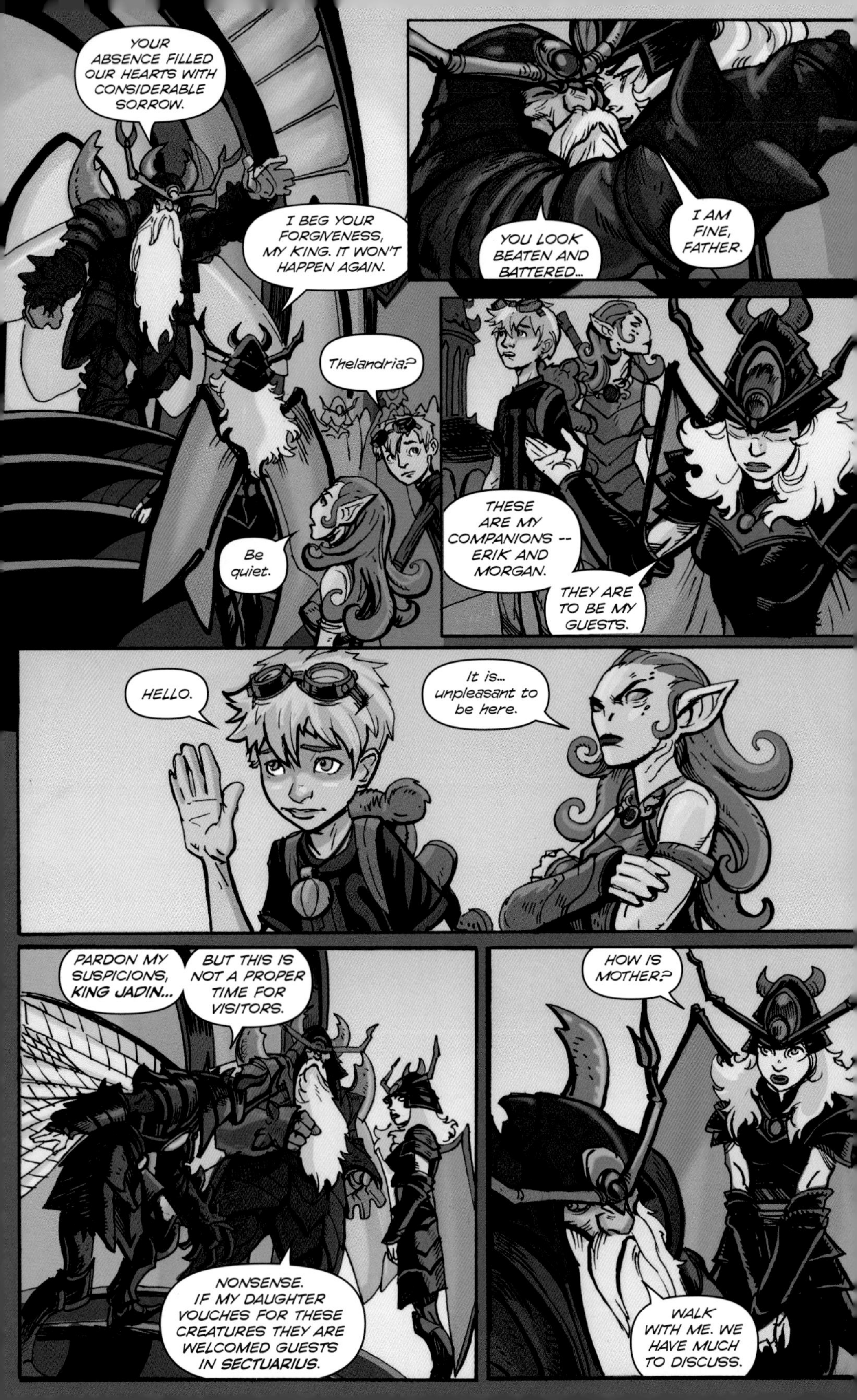
YOUR ABSENCE FILLED OUR HEARTS WITH CONSIDERABLE SORROW.
I BEG YOUR FORGIVENESS, MY KING. IT WON'T HAPPEN AGAIN.
Thelandria?
Be quiet.
YOU LOOK BEATEN AND BATTERED...
I AM FINE, FATHER.
THESE ARE MY COMPANIONS -- ERIK AND MORGAN.
THEY ARE TO BE MY GUESTS.
HELLO.
It is... unpleasant to be here.
PARDON MY SUSPICIONS, KING JADIN...
BUT THIS IS NOT A PROPER TIME FOR VISITORS.
NONSENSE. IF MY DAUGHTER VOUCHES FOR THESE CREATURES THEY ARE WELCOMED GUESTS IN SECTUARIUS.
HOW IS MOTHER?
WALK WITH ME. WE HAVE MUCH TO DISCUSS.

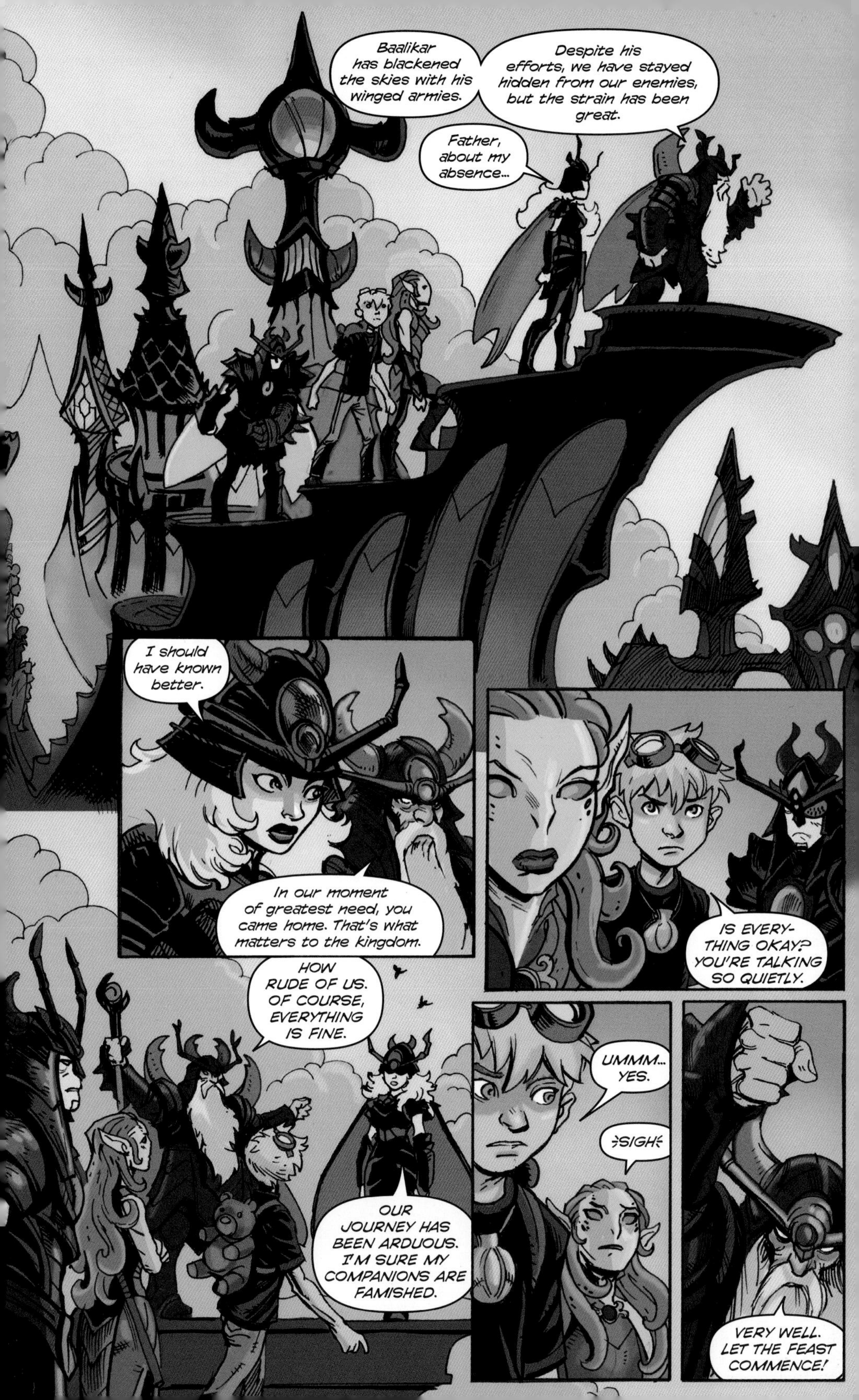
Baalikar has blackened the skies with his winged armies.
Despite his efforts, we have stayed hidden from our enemies, but the strain has been great.
Father, about my absence...
I should have known better.
In our moment of greatest need, you came home. That's what matters to the kingdom.
IS EVERY-THING OKAY? YOU'RE TALKING SO QUIETLY.
HOW RUDE OF US. OF COURSE, EVERYTHING IS FINE.
UMMM... YES.
SIGH
OUR JOURNEY HAS BEEN ARDUOUS. I'M SURE MY COMPANIONS ARE FAMISHED.
VERY WELL. LET THE FEAST COMMENCE!

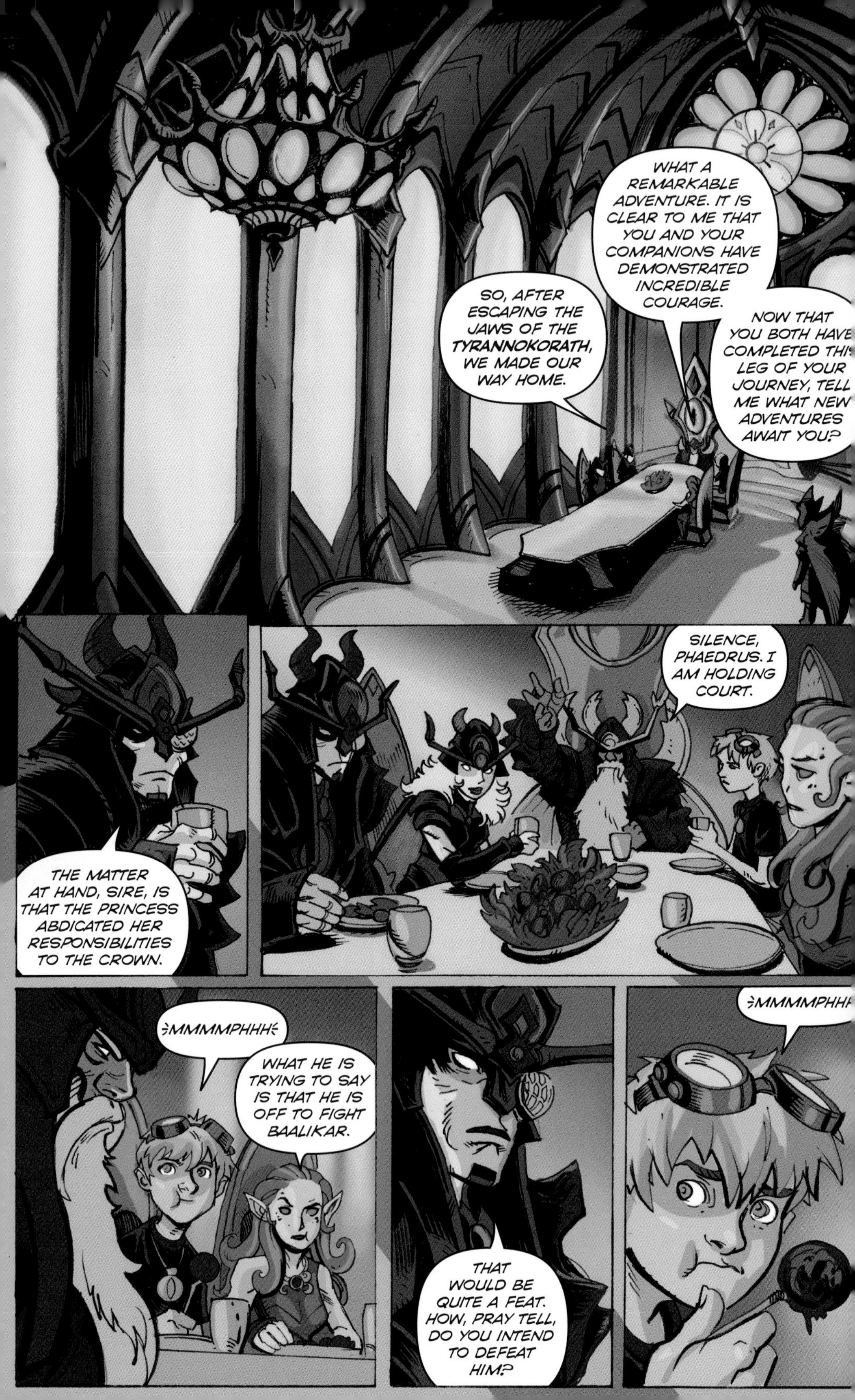
SO, AFTER ESCAPING THE JAWS OF THE TYRANNOKORATH, WE MADE OUR WAY HOME.
WHAT A REMARKABLE ADVENTURE. IT IS CLEAR TO ME THAT YOU AND YOUR COMPANIONS HAVE DEMONSTRATED INCREDIBLE COURAGE.
NOW THAT YOU BOTH HAVE COMPLETED THIS LEG OF YOUR JOURNEY, TELL ME WHAT NEW ADVENTURES AWAIT YOU?
THE MATTER AT HAND, SIRE, IS THAT THE PRINCESS ABDICATED HER RESPONSIBILITIES TO THE CROWN.
SILENCE, PHAEDRUS. I AM HOLDING COURT.
MMMMPHHH
WHAT HE IS TRYING TO SAY IS THAT HE IS OFF TO FIGHT BAALIKAR.
THAT WOULD BE QUITE A FEAT. HOW, PRAY TELL, DO YOU INTEND TO DEFEAT HIM?
MMMMPHH

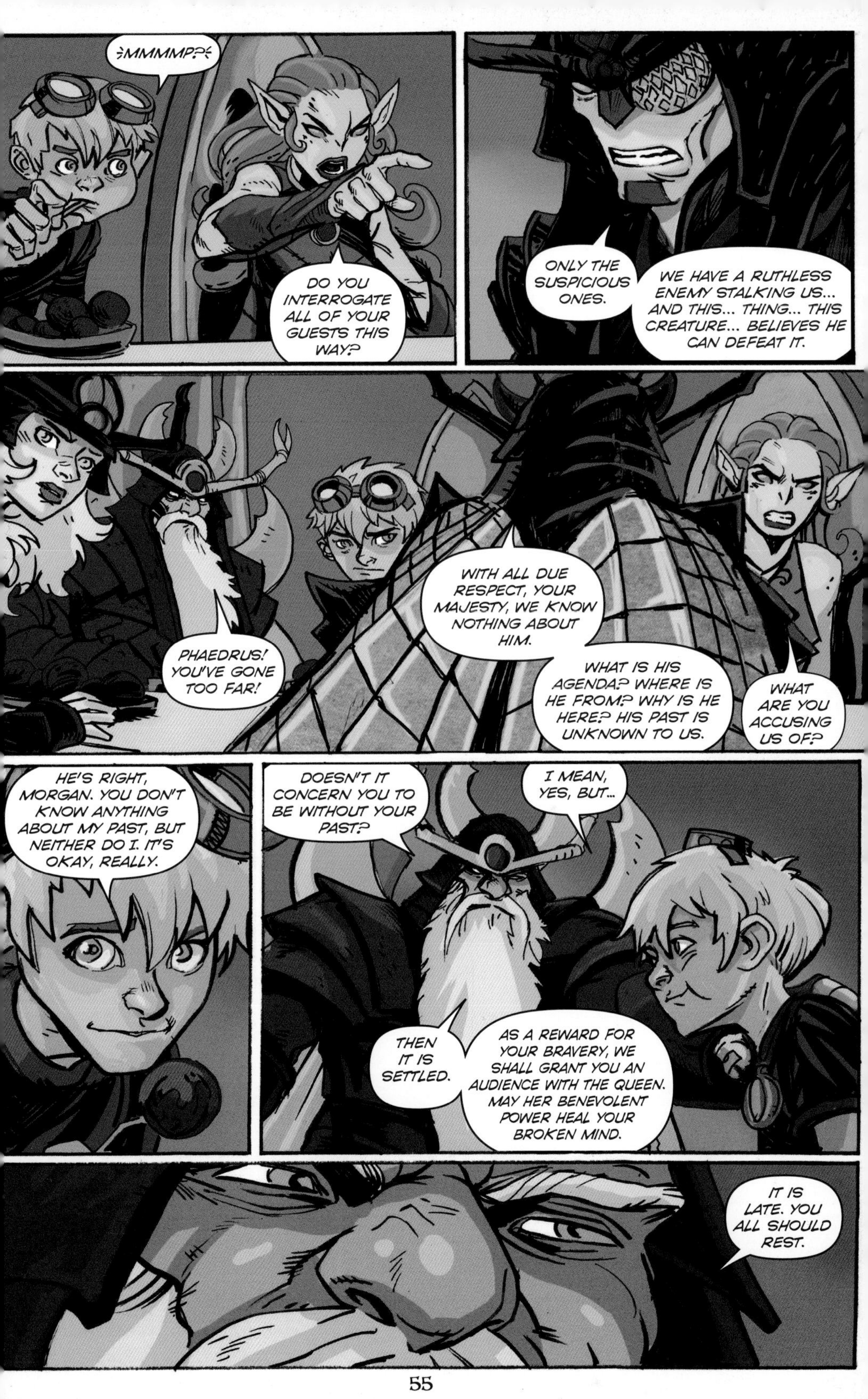

:MMMMP?:
DO YOU INTERROGATE ALL OF YOUR GUESTS THIS WAY?
ONLY THE SUSPICIOUS ONES.
WE HAVE A RUTHLESS ENEMY STALKING US... AND THIS... THING... THIS CREATURE... BELIEVES HE CAN DEFEAT IT.
PHAEDRUS! YOU'VE GONE TOO FAR!
WITH ALL DUE RESPECT, YOUR MAJESTY, WE KNOW NOTHING ABOUT HIM.
WHAT IS HIS AGENDA? WHERE IS HE FROM? WHY IS HE HERE? HIS PAST IS UNKNOWN TO US.
WHAT ARE YOU ACCUSING US OF?
HE'S RIGHT, MORGAN. YOU DON'T KNOW ANYTHING ABOUT MY PAST, BUT NEITHER DO I. IT'S OKAY, REALLY.
DOESN'T IT CONCERN YOU TO BE WITHOUT YOUR PAST?
I MEAN, YES, BUT...
THEN IT IS SETTLED.
AS A REWARD FOR YOUR BRAVERY, WE SHALL GRANT YOU AN AUDIENCE WITH THE QUEEN. MAY HER BENEVOLENT POWER HEAL YOUR BROKEN MIND.
IT IS LATE. YOU ALL SHOULD REST.

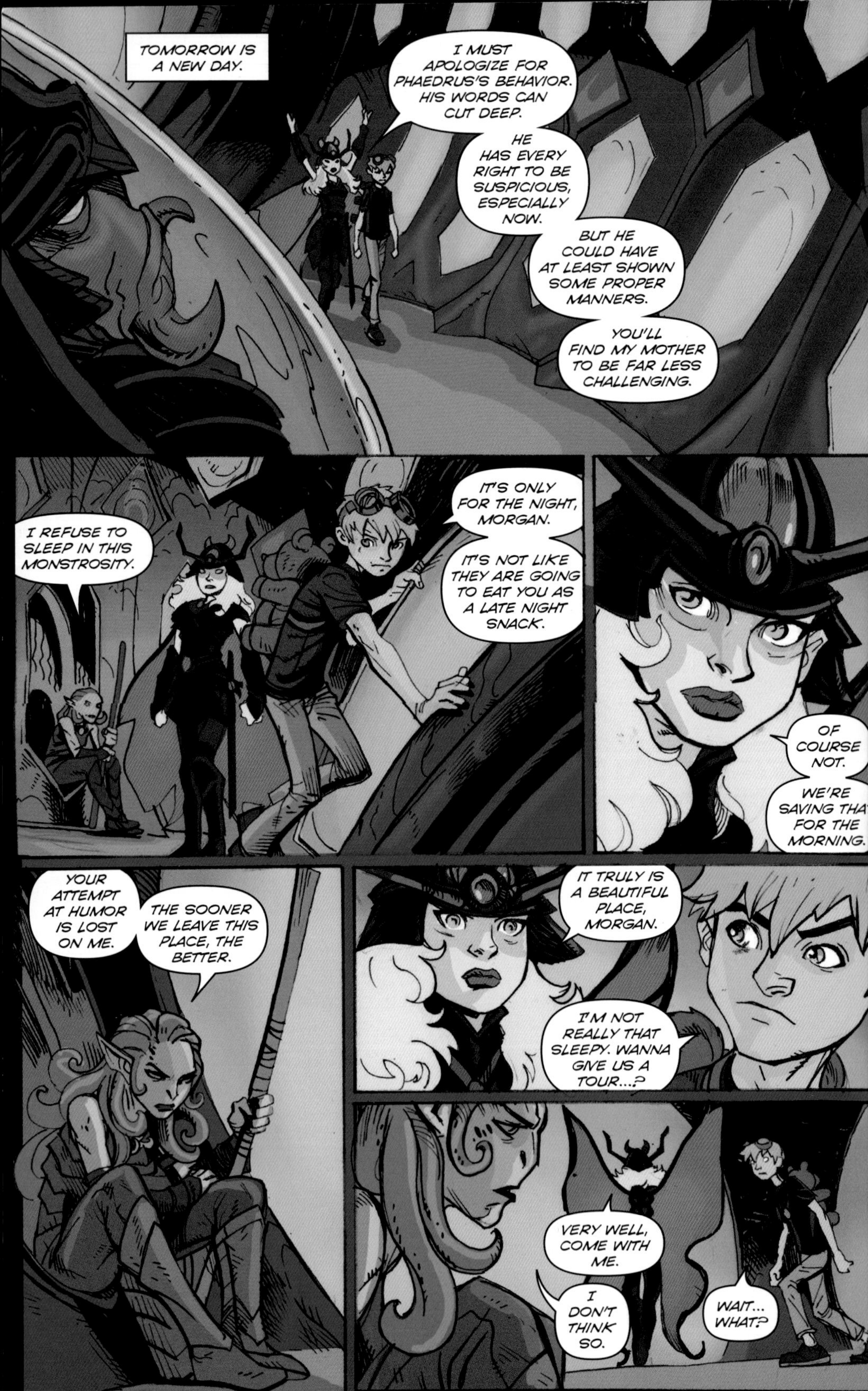
TOMORROW IS A NEW DAY.
I MUST APOLOGIZE FOR PHAEDRUS'S BEHAVIOR. HIS WORDS CAN CUT DEEP.
HE HAS EVERY RIGHT TO BE SUSPICIOUS, ESPECIALLY NOW.
BUT HE COULD HAVE AT LEAST SHOWN SOME PROPER MANNERS.
YOU'LL FIND MY MOTHER TO BE FAR LESS CHALLENGING.
I REFUSE TO SLEEP IN THIS MONSTROSITY.
IT'S ONLY FOR THE NIGHT, MORGAN.
IT'S NOT LIKE THEY ARE GOING TO EAT YOU AS A LATE NIGHT SNACK.
OF COURSE NOT.
WE'RE SAVING THAT FOR THE MORNING.
YOUR ATTEMPT AT HUMOR IS LOST ON ME.
THE SOONER WE LEAVE THIS PLACE, THE BETTER.
IT TRULY IS A BEAUTIFUL PLACE, MORGAN.
I'M NOT REALLY THAT SLEEPY. WANNA GIVE US A TOUR...?
VERY WELL, COME WITH ME.
I DON'T THINK SO.
WAIT... WHAT?

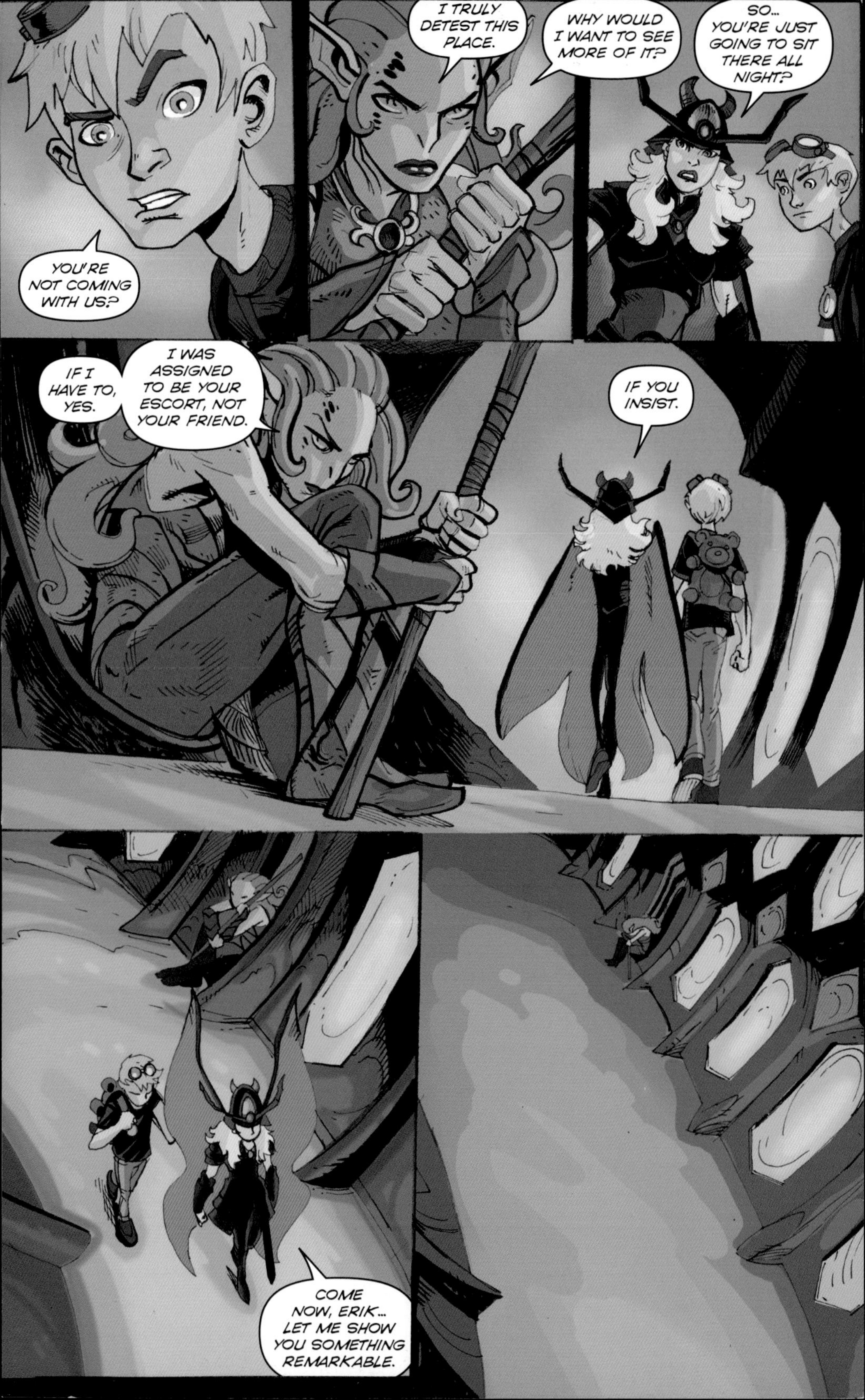
YOU'RE NOT COMING WITH US?
I TRULY DETEST THIS PLACE.
WHY WOULD I WANT TO SEE MORE OF IT?
SO... YOU'RE JUST GOING TO SIT THERE ALL NIGHT?
IF I HAVE TO, YES.
I WAS ASSIGNED TO BE YOUR ESCORT, NOT YOUR FRIEND.
IF YOU INSIST.
COME NOW, ERIK... LET ME SHOW YOU SOMETHING REMARKABLE.

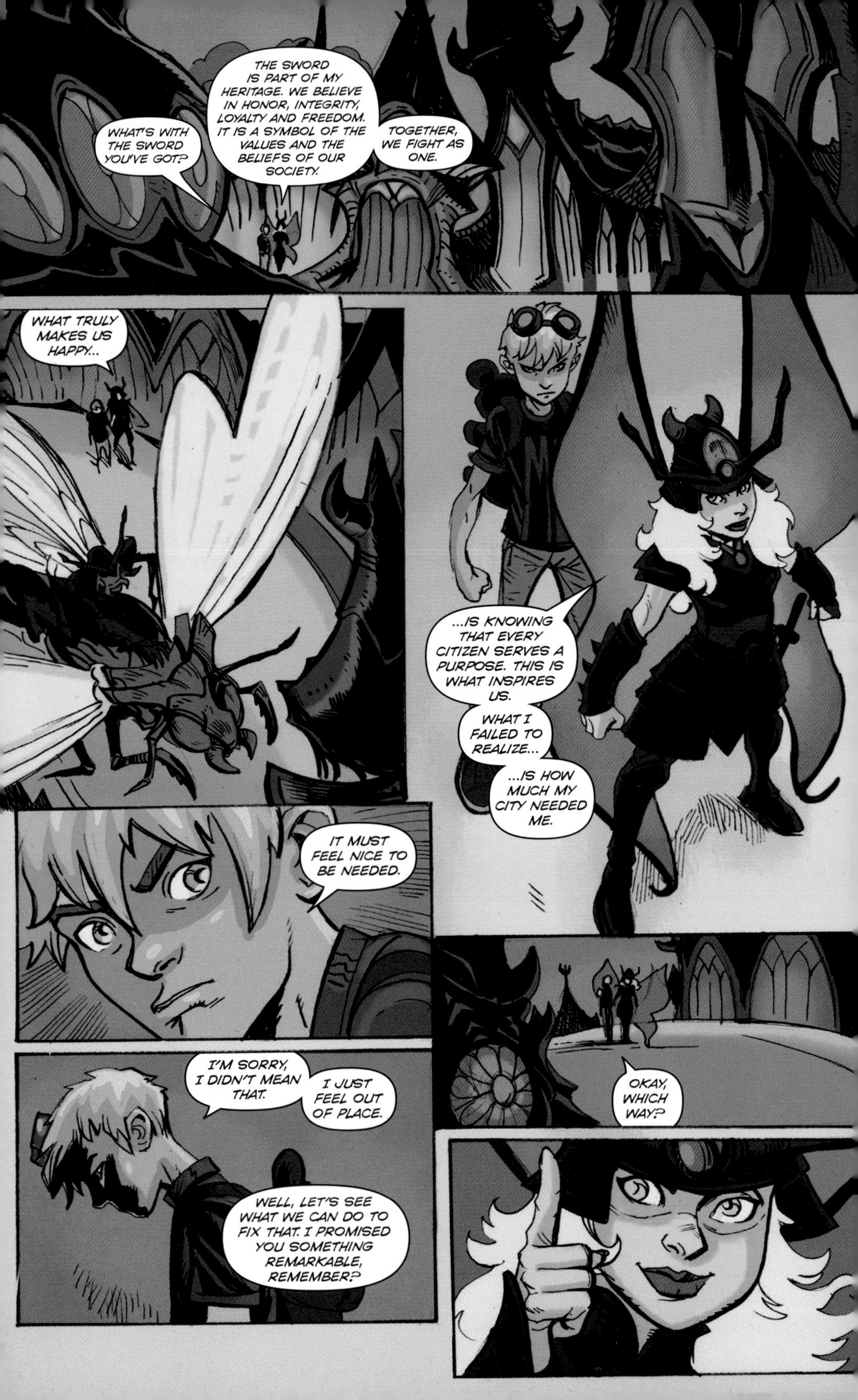
WHAT'S WITH THE SWORD YOU'VE GOT?
THE SWORD IS PART OF MY HERITAGE. WE BELIEVE IN HONOR, INTEGRITY, LOYALTY AND FREEDOM. IT IS A SYMBOL OF THE VALUES AND THE BELIEFS OF OUR SOCIETY.
TOGETHER, WE FIGHT AS ONE.
WHAT TRULY MAKES US HAPPY...
...IS KNOWING THAT EVERY CITIZEN SERVES A PURPOSE. THIS IS WHAT INSPIRES US.
WHAT I FAILED TO REALIZE...
...IS HOW MUCH MY CITY NEEDED ME.
IT MUST FEEL NICE TO BE NEEDED.
I'M SORRY, I DIDN'T MEAN THAT.
I JUST FEEL OUT OF PLACE.
WELL, LET'S SEE WHAT WE CAN DO TO FIX THAT. I PROMISED YOU SOMETHING REMARKABLE, REMEMBER?
OKAY, WHICH WAY?

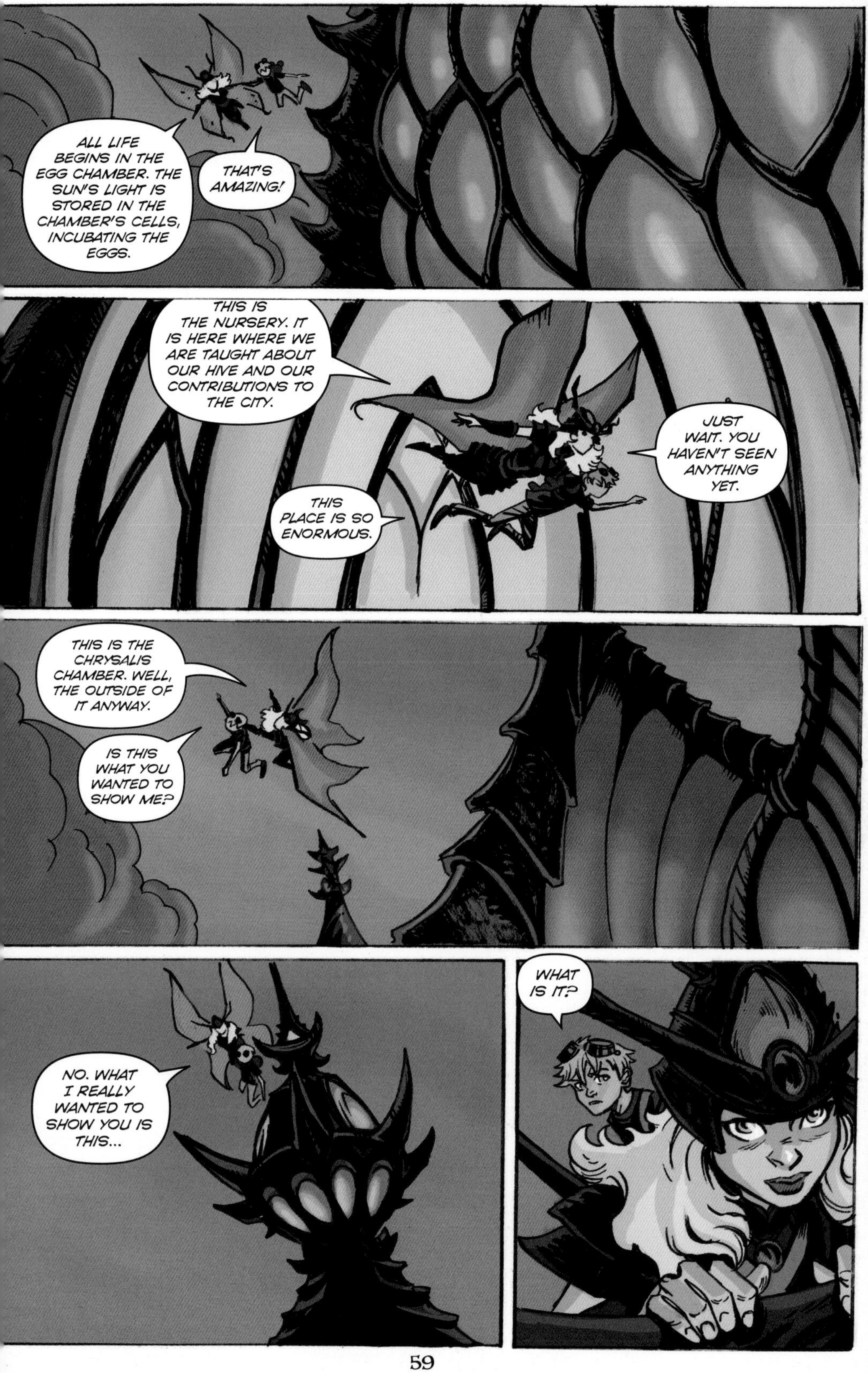
ALL LIFE BEGINS IN THE EGG CHAMBER. THE SUN'S LIGHT IS STORED IN THE CHAMBER'S CELLS, INCUBATING THE EGGS.
THAT'S AMAZING!
THIS IS THE NURSERY. IT IS HERE WHERE WE ARE TAUGHT ABOUT OUR HIVE AND OUR CONTRIBUTIONS TO THE CITY.
JUST WAIT. YOU HAVEN'T SEEN ANYTHING YET.
THIS PLACE IS SO ENORMOUS.
THIS IS THE CHRYSALIS CHAMBER. WELL, THE OUTSIDE OF IT ANYWAY.
IS THIS WHAT YOU WANTED TO SHOW ME?
NO. WHAT I REALLY WANTED TO SHOW YOU IS THIS...
WHAT IS IT?

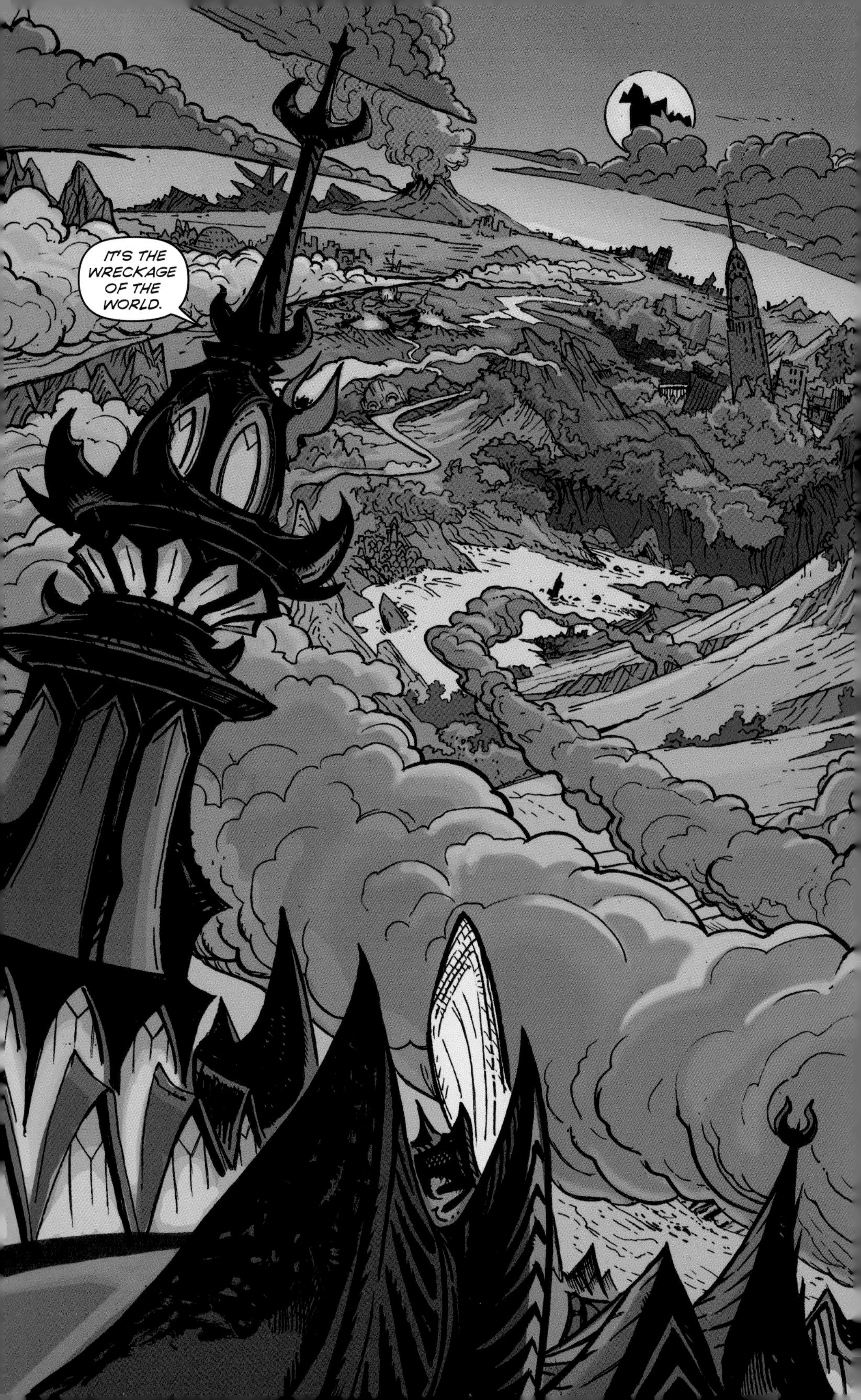
IT'S THE WRECKAGE OF THE WORLD.

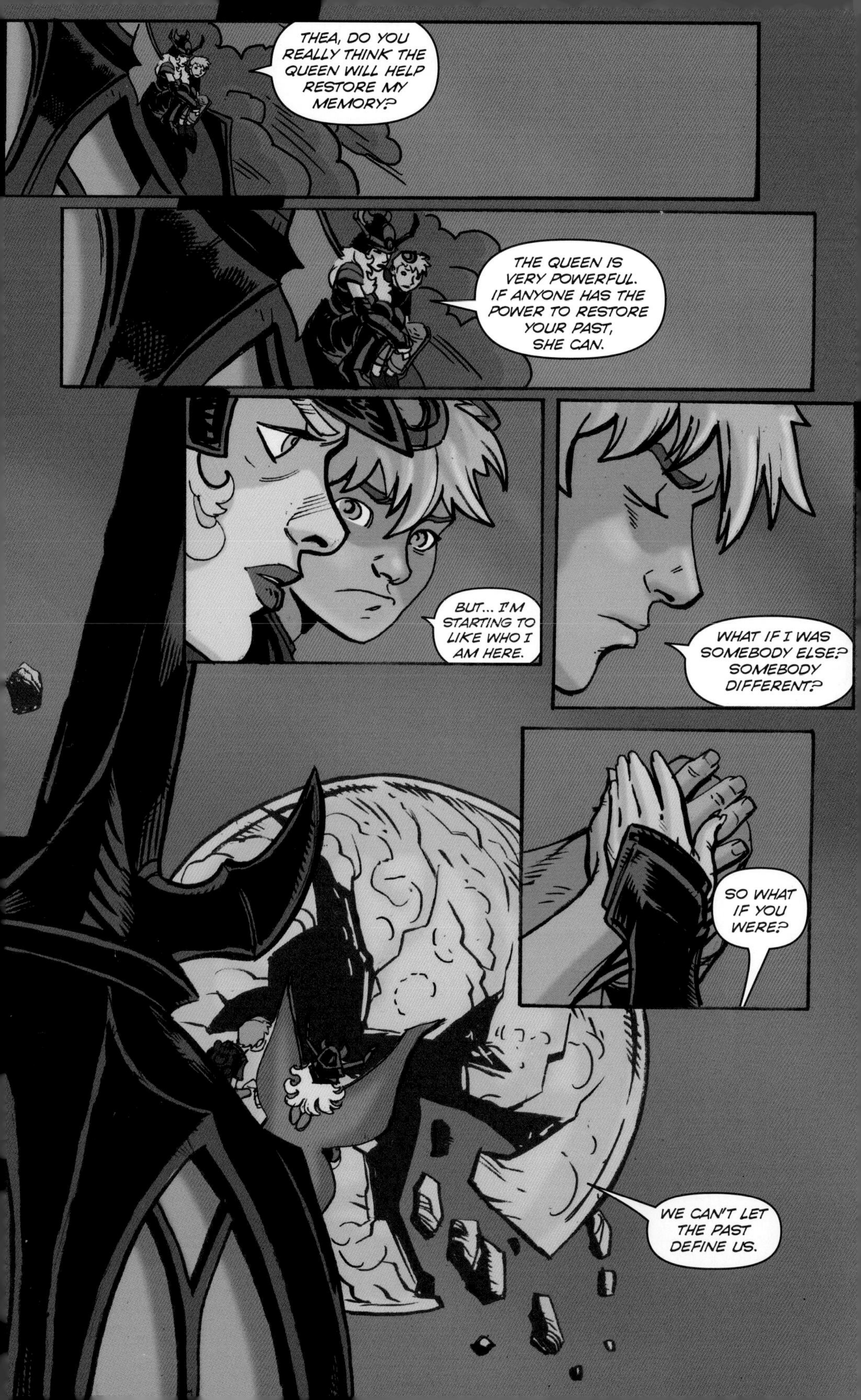
THEA, DO YOU REALLY THINK THE QUEEN WILL HELP RESTORE MY MEMORY?
THE QUEEN IS VERY POWERFUL. IF ANYONE HAS THE POWER TO RESTORE YOUR PAST, SHE CAN.
BUT... I'M STARTING TO LIKE WHO I AM HERE.
WHAT IF I WAS SOMEBODY ELSE? SOMEBODY DIFFERENT?
SO WHAT IF YOU WERE?
WE CAN'T LET THE PAST DEFINE US.

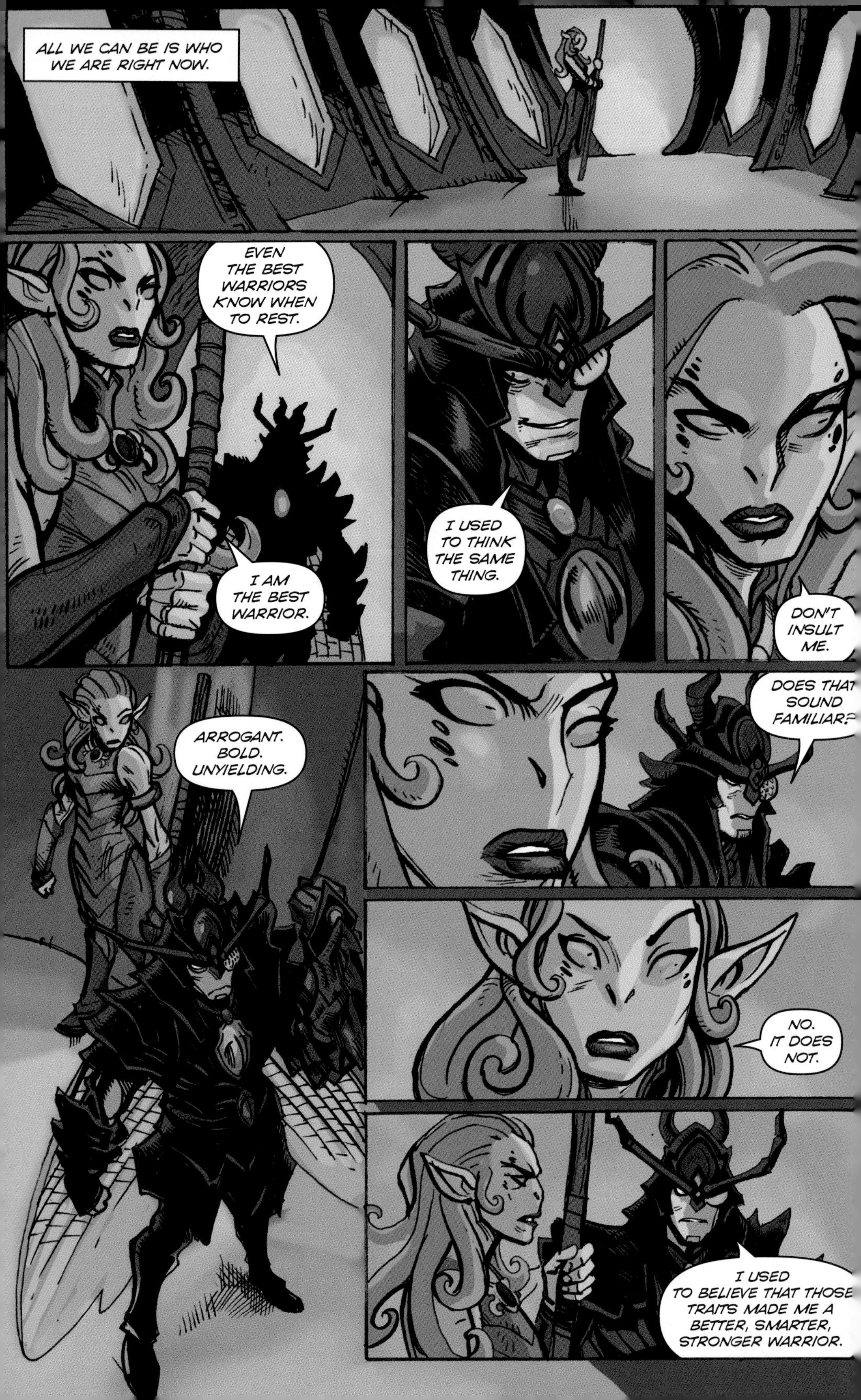
ALL WE CAN BE IS WHO WE ARE RIGHT NOW.
EVEN THE BEST WARRIORS KNOW WHEN TO REST.
I AM THE BEST WARRIOR.
I USED TO THINK THE SAME THING.
DON'T INSULT ME.
ARROGANT. BOLD. UNYIELDING.
DOES THAT SOUND FAMILIAR?
NO. IT DOES NOT.
I USED TO BELIEVE THAT THOSE TRAITS MADE ME A BETTER, SMARTER, STRONGER WARRIOR.

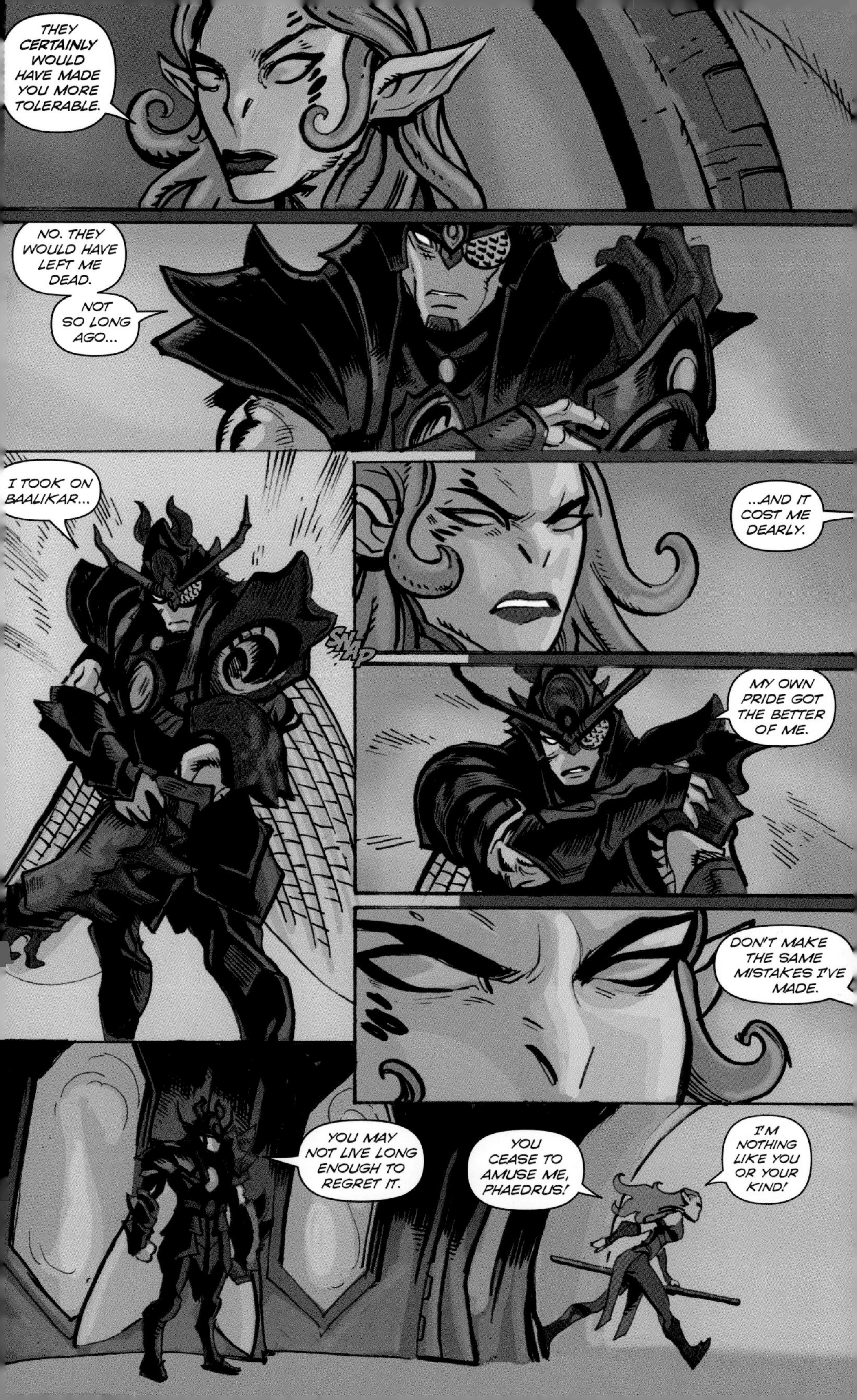
THEY CERTAINLY WOULD HAVE MADE YOU MORE TOLERABLE.
NO. THEY WOULD HAVE LEFT ME DEAD.
NOT SO LONG AGO...
I TOOK ON BAALIKAR...
...AND IT COST ME DEARLY.
SNAP
MY OWN PRIDE GOT THE BETTER OF ME.
DON'T MAKE THE SAME MISTAKES I'VE MADE.
YOU MAY NOT LIVE LONG ENOUGH TO REGRET IT.
YOU CEASE TO AMUSE ME, PHAEDRUS!
I'M NOTHING LIKE YOU OR YOUR KIND!

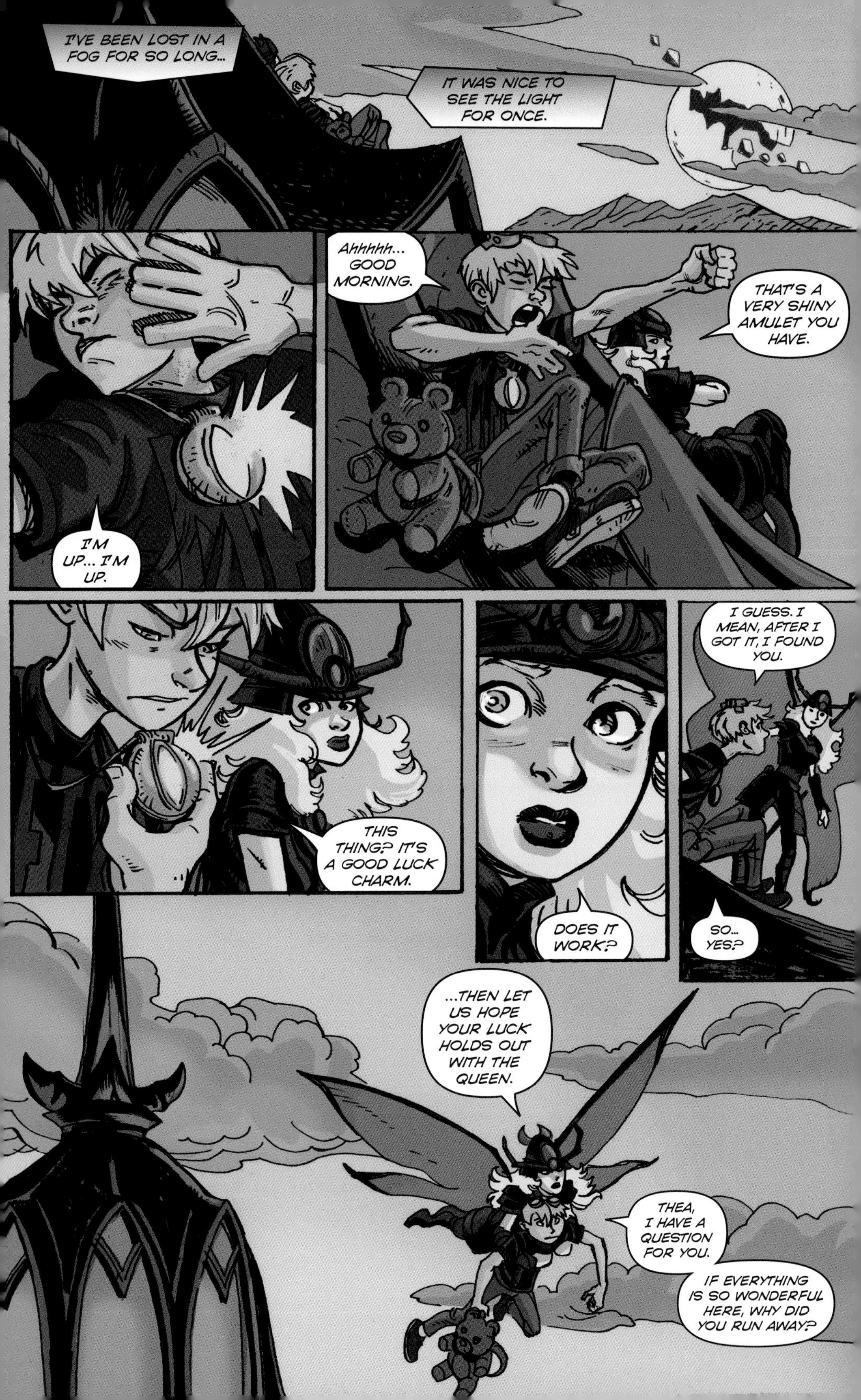
I'VE BEEN LOST IN A FOG FOR SO LONG...
IT WAS NICE TO SEE THE LIGHT FOR ONCE.
I'M UP... I'M UP.
Ahhhhh... GOOD MORNING.
THAT'S A VERY SHINY AMULET YOU HAVE.
THIS THING? IT'S A GOOD LUCK CHARM.
DOES IT WORK?
I GUESS. I MEAN, AFTER I GOT IT, I FOUND YOU.
SO... YES?
...THEN LET US HOPE YOUR LUCK HOLDS OUT WITH THE QUEEN.
THEA, I HAVE A QUESTION FOR YOU.
IF EVERYTHING IS SO WONDERFUL HERE, WHY DID YOU RUN AWAY?

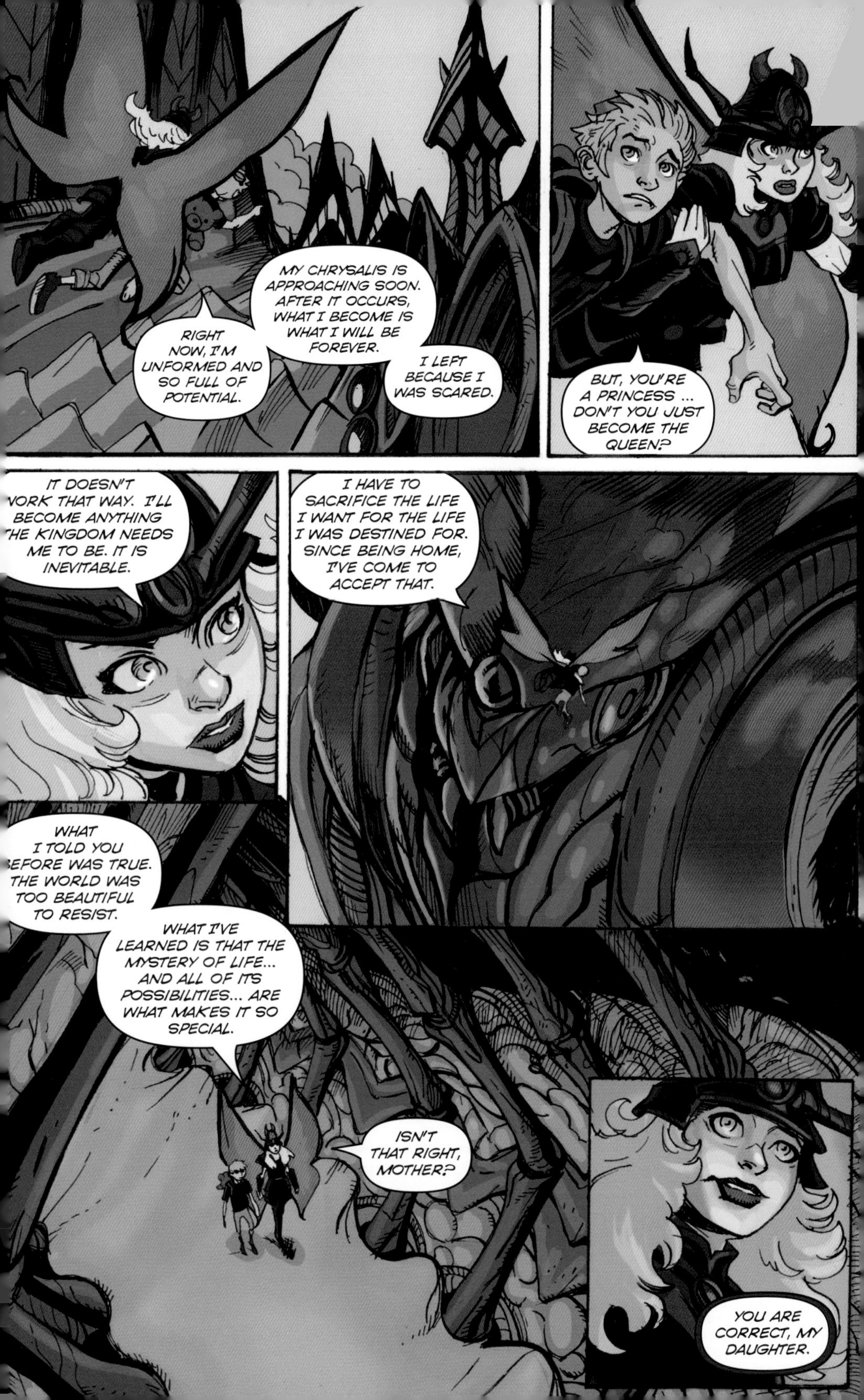
MY CHRYSALIS IS APPROACHING SOON. AFTER IT OCCURS, WHAT I BECOME IS WHAT I WILL BE FOREVER.
RIGHT NOW, I'M UNFORMED AND SO FULL OF POTENTIAL.
I LEFT BECAUSE I WAS SCARED.
BUT, YOU'RE A PRINCESS ... DON'T YOU JUST BECOME THE QUEEN?
IT DOESN'T VORK THAT WAY. I'LL BECOME ANYTHING HE KINGDOM NEEDS ME TO BE. IT IS INEVITABLE.
I HAVE TO SACRIFICE THE LIFE I WANT FOR THE LIFE I WAS DESTINED FOR. SINCE BEING HOME, I'VE COME TO ACCEPT THAT.
WHAT I TOLD YOU EFORE WAS TRUE. THE WORLD WAS TOO BEAUTIFUL TO RESIST.
WHAT I'VE LEARNED IS THAT THE MYSTERY OF LIFE... AND ALL OF ITS POSSIBILITIES... ARE WHAT MAKES IT SO SPECIAL.
ISN'T THAT RIGHT, MOTHER?
YOU ARE CORRECT, MY DAUGHTER.

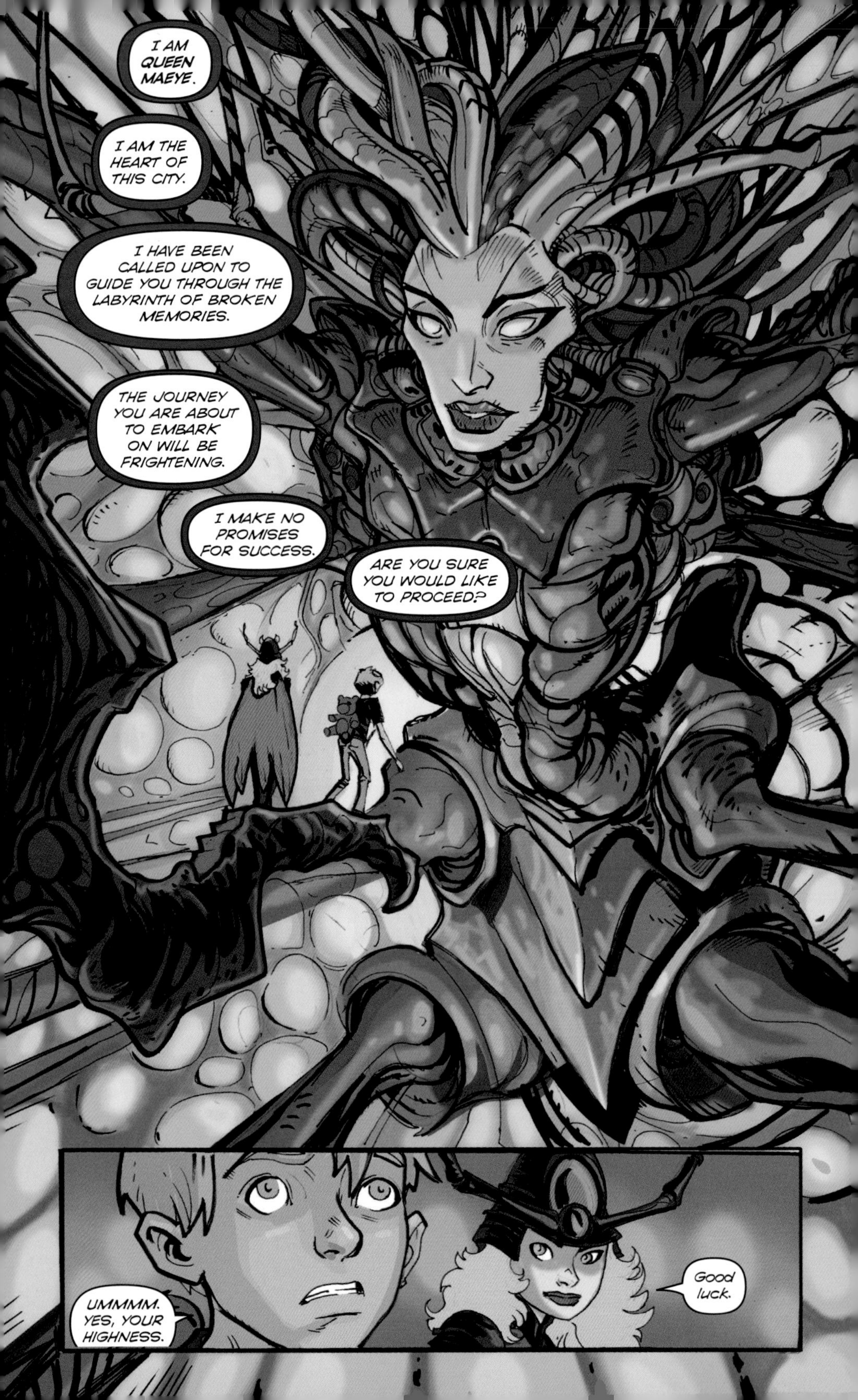
I AM QUEEN MAEYE.
I AM THE HEART OF THIS CITY.
I HAVE BEEN CALLED UPON TO GUIDE YOU THROUGH THE LABYRINTH OF BROKEN MEMORIES.
THE JOURNEY YOU ARE ABOUT TO EMBARK ON WILL BE FRIGHTENING.
I MAKE NO PROMISES FOR SUCCESS.
ARE YOU SURE YOU WOULD LIKE TO PROCEED?
UMMMM. YES, YOUR HIGHNESS.
Good luck.

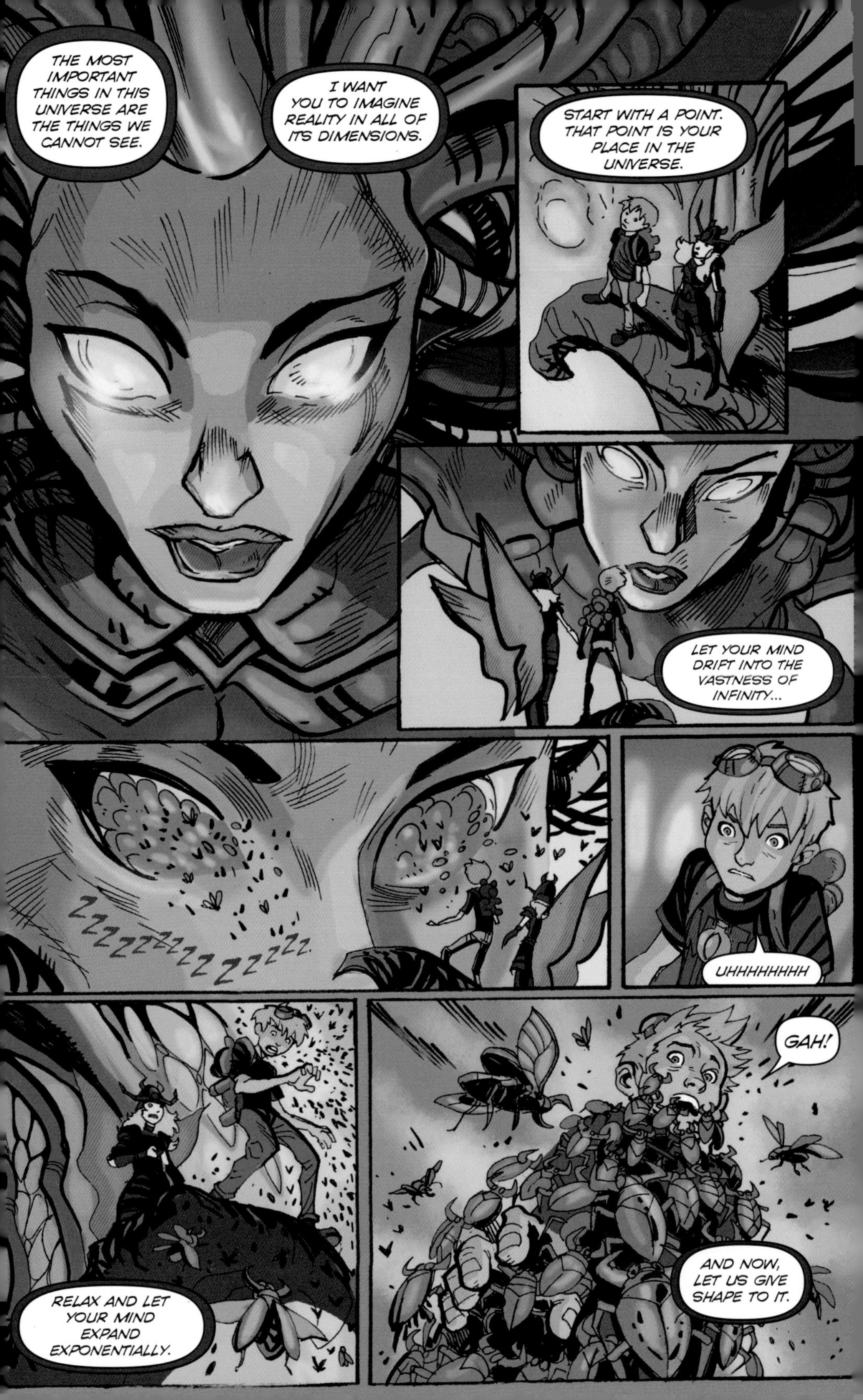
THE MOST IMPORTANT THINGS IN THIS UNIVERSE ARE THE THINGS WE CANNOT SEE.
I WANT YOU TO IMAGINE REALITY IN ALL OF ITS DIMENSIONS.
START WITH A POINT. THAT POINT IS YOUR PLACE IN THE UNIVERSE.
LET YOUR MIND DRIFT INTO THE VASTNESS OF INFINITY...
ZZZZZZZZZZZZZZZZZ
UHHHHHHHH
RELAX AND LET YOUR MIND EXPAND EXPONENTIALLY.
GAH!
AND NOW, LET US GIVE SHAPE TO IT.

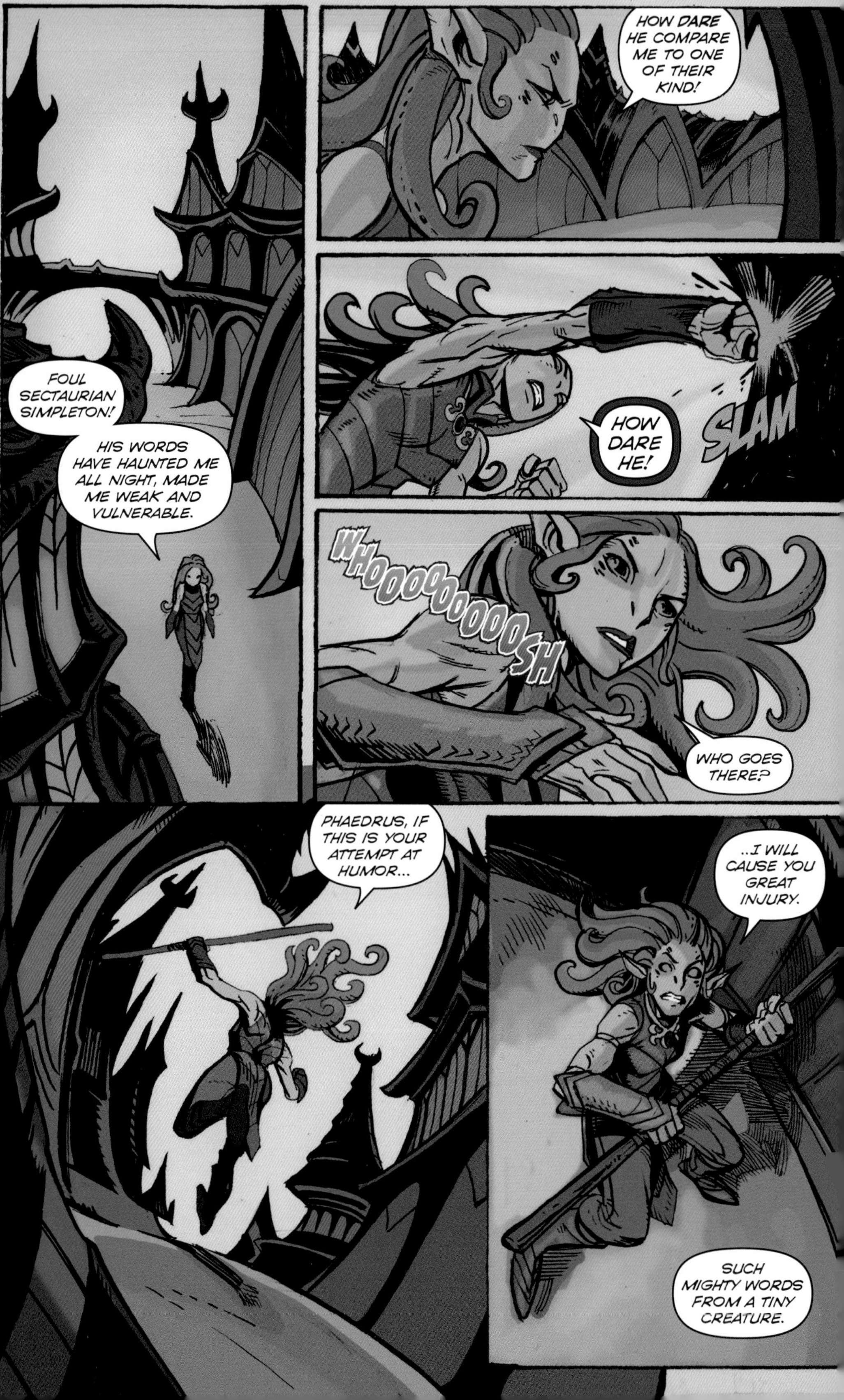
HOW DARE HE COMPARE ME TO ONE OF THEIR KIND!
FOUL SECTAURIAN SIMPLETON!
HIS WORDS HAVE HAUNTED ME ALL NIGHT, MADE ME WEAK AND VULNERABLE.
SLAM
HOW DARE HE!
WHOOOOOOOOOOSH
WHO GOES THERE?
PHAEDRUS, IF THIS IS YOUR ATTEMPT AT HUMOR...
..I WILL CAUSE YOU GREAT INJURY.
SUCH MIGHTY WORDS FROM A TINY CREATURE.

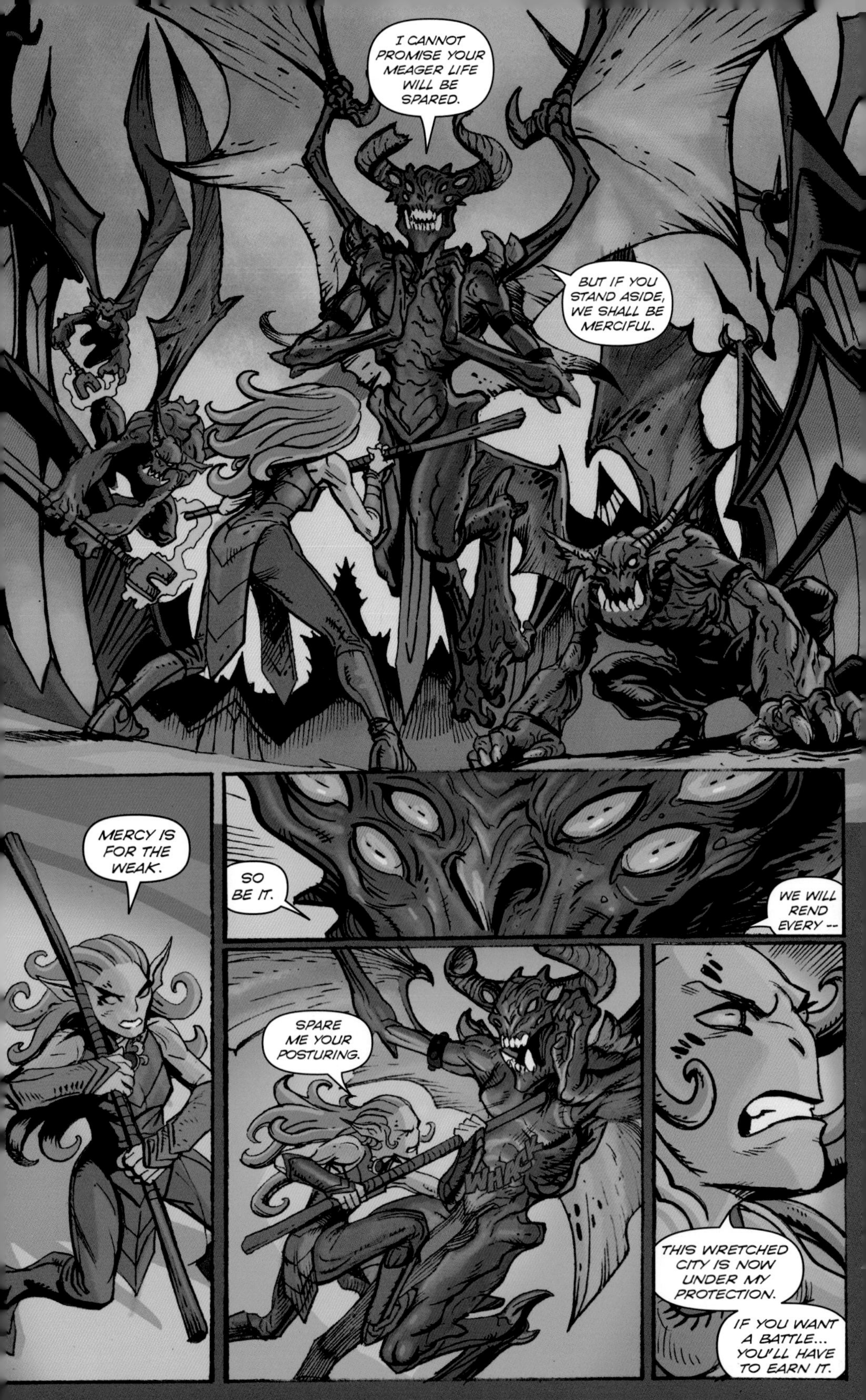
I CANNOT PROMISE YOUR MEAGER LIFE WILL BE SPARED.
BUT IF YOU STAND ASIDE, WE SHALL BE MERCIFUL.
MERCY IS FOR THE WEAK.
SO BE IT.
WE WILL REND EVERY --
SPARE ME YOUR POSTURING.
THIS WRETCHED CITY IS NOW UNDER MY PROTECTION.
IF YOU WANT A BATTLE... YOU'LL HAVE TO EARN IT.

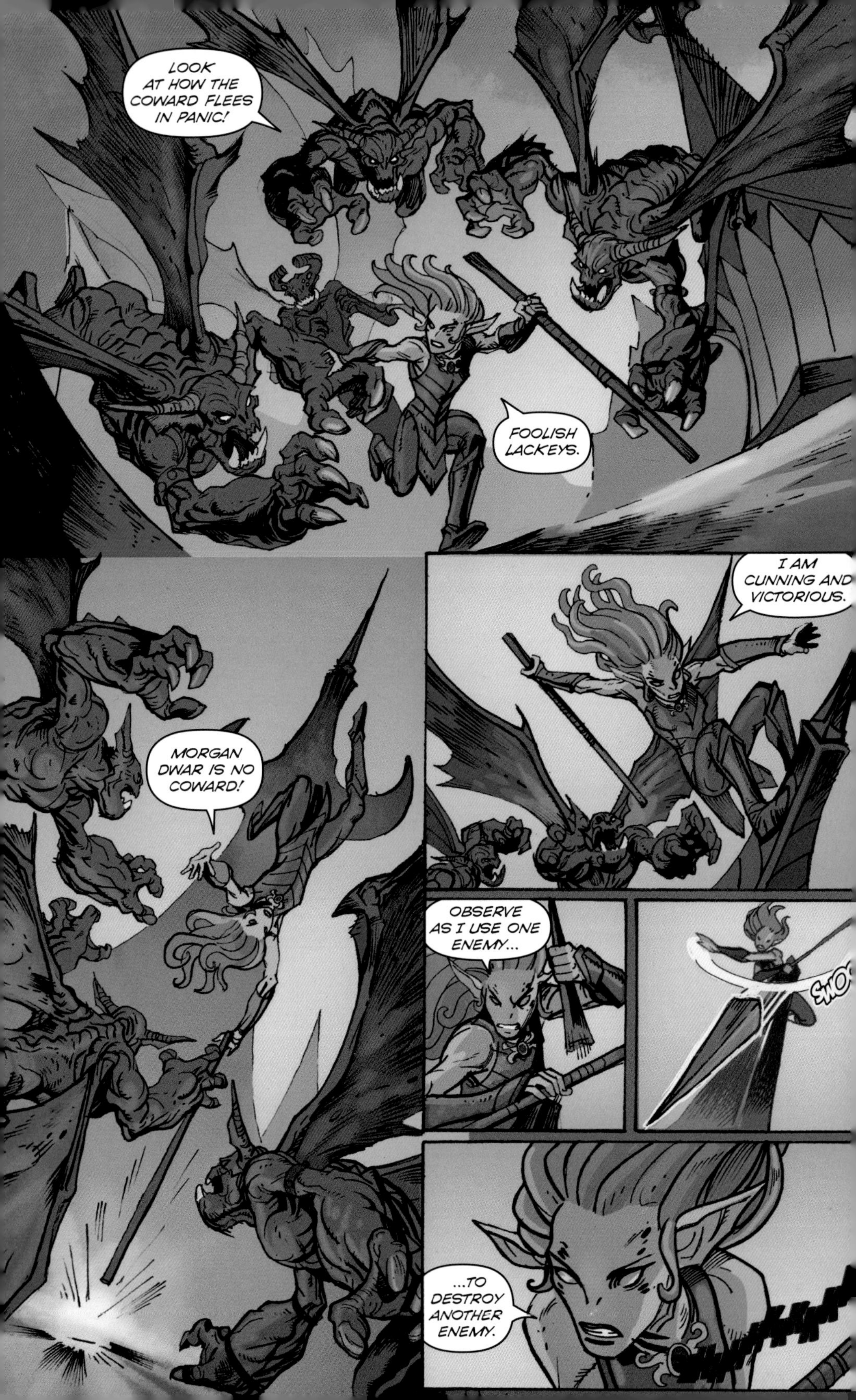
LOOK AT HOW THE COWARD FLEES IN PANIC!
FOOLISH LACKEYS.
MORGAN DWAR IS NO COWARD!
I AM CUNNING AND VICTORIOUS.
OBSERVE AS I USE ONE ENEMY...
...TO DESTROY ANOTHER ENEMY.

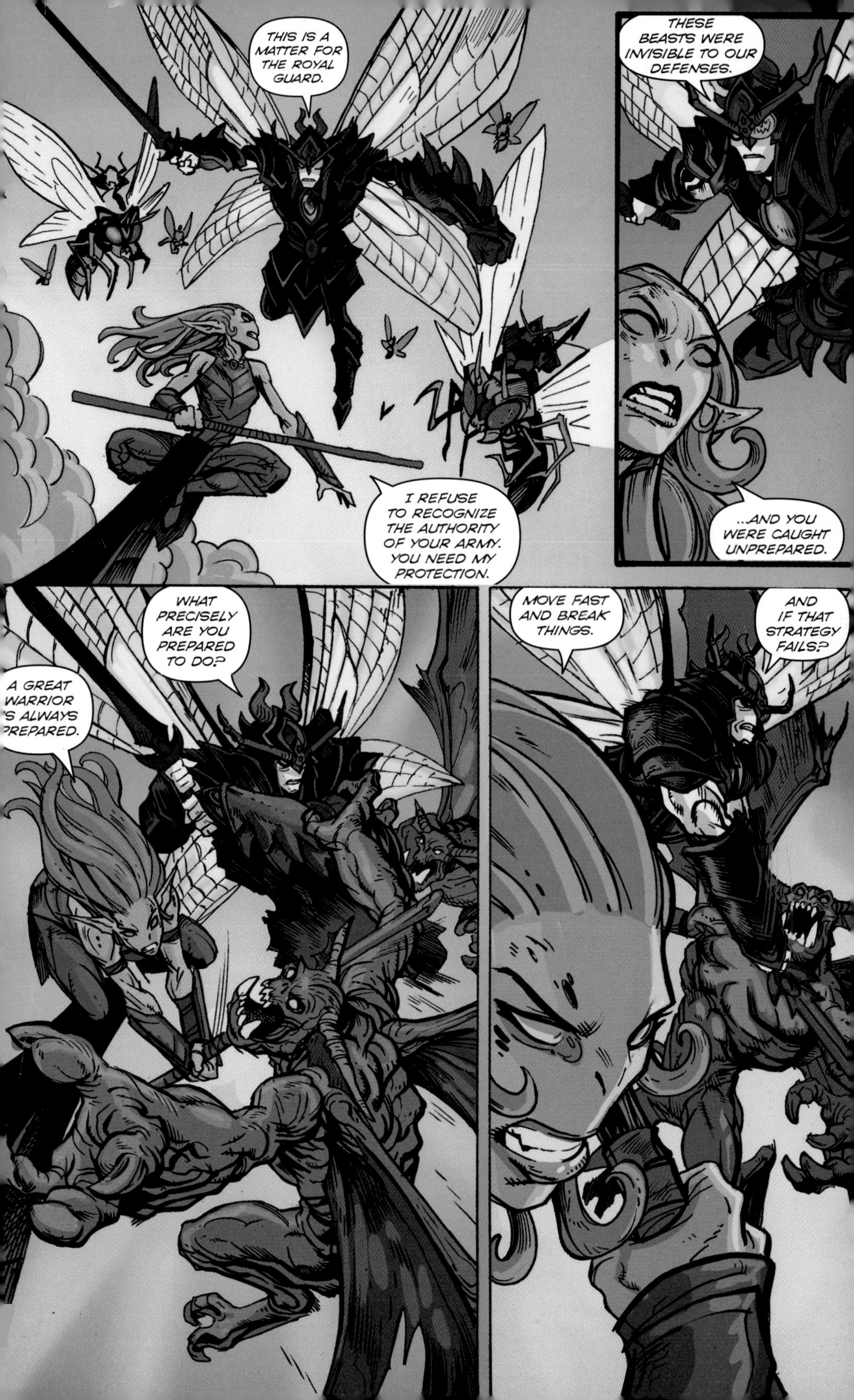
THIS IS A MATTER FOR THE ROYAL GUARD.
I REFUSE TO RECOGNIZE THE AUTHORITY OF YOUR ARMY. YOU NEED MY PROTECTION.
THESE BEASTS WERE INVISIBLE TO OUR DEFENSES.
...AND YOU WERE CAUGHT UNPREPARED.
WHAT PRECISELY ARE YOU PREPARED TO DO?
A GREAT WARRIOR 'S ALWAYS PREPARED.
MOVE FAST AND BREAK THINGS.
AND IF THAT STRATEGY FAILS?

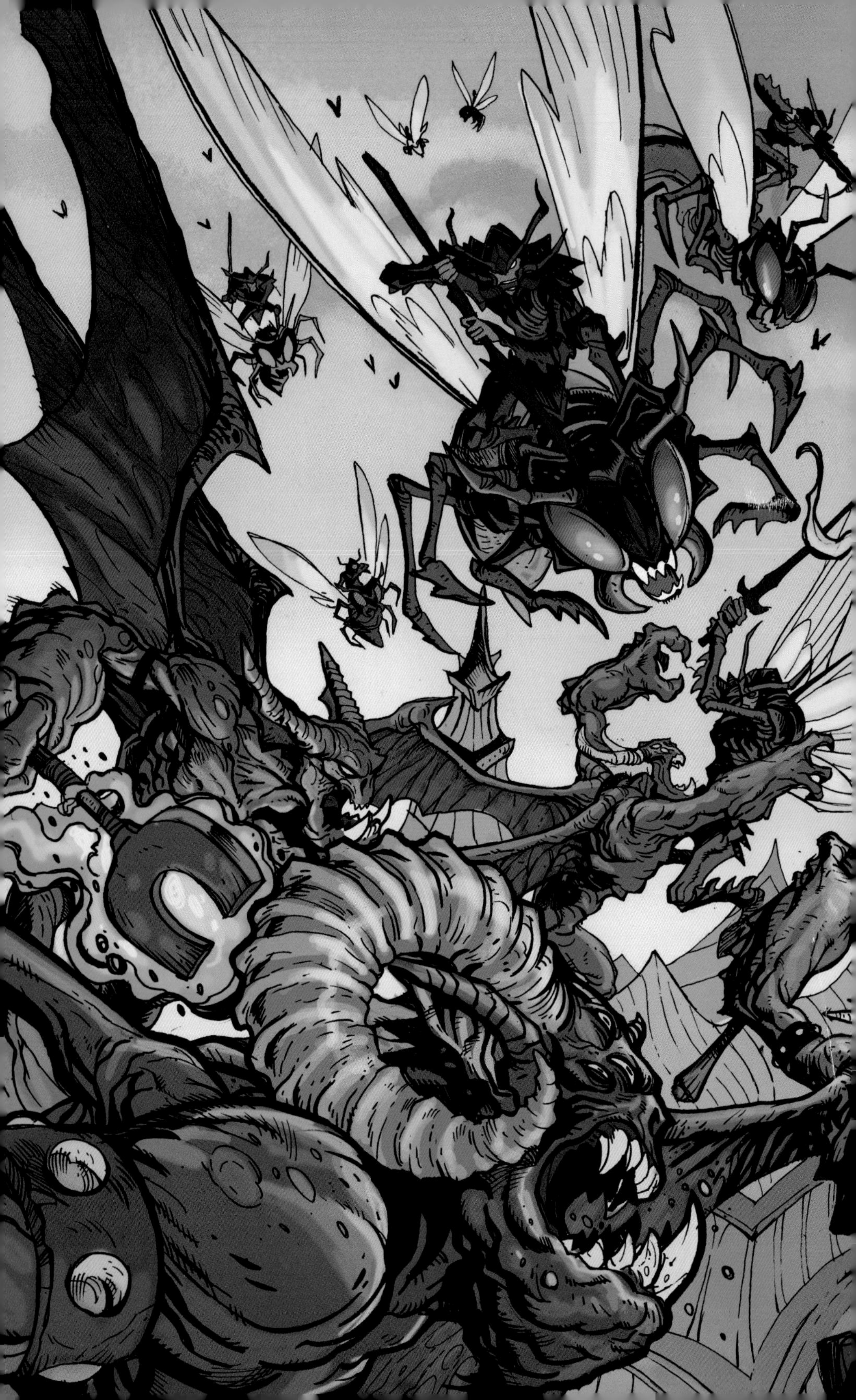

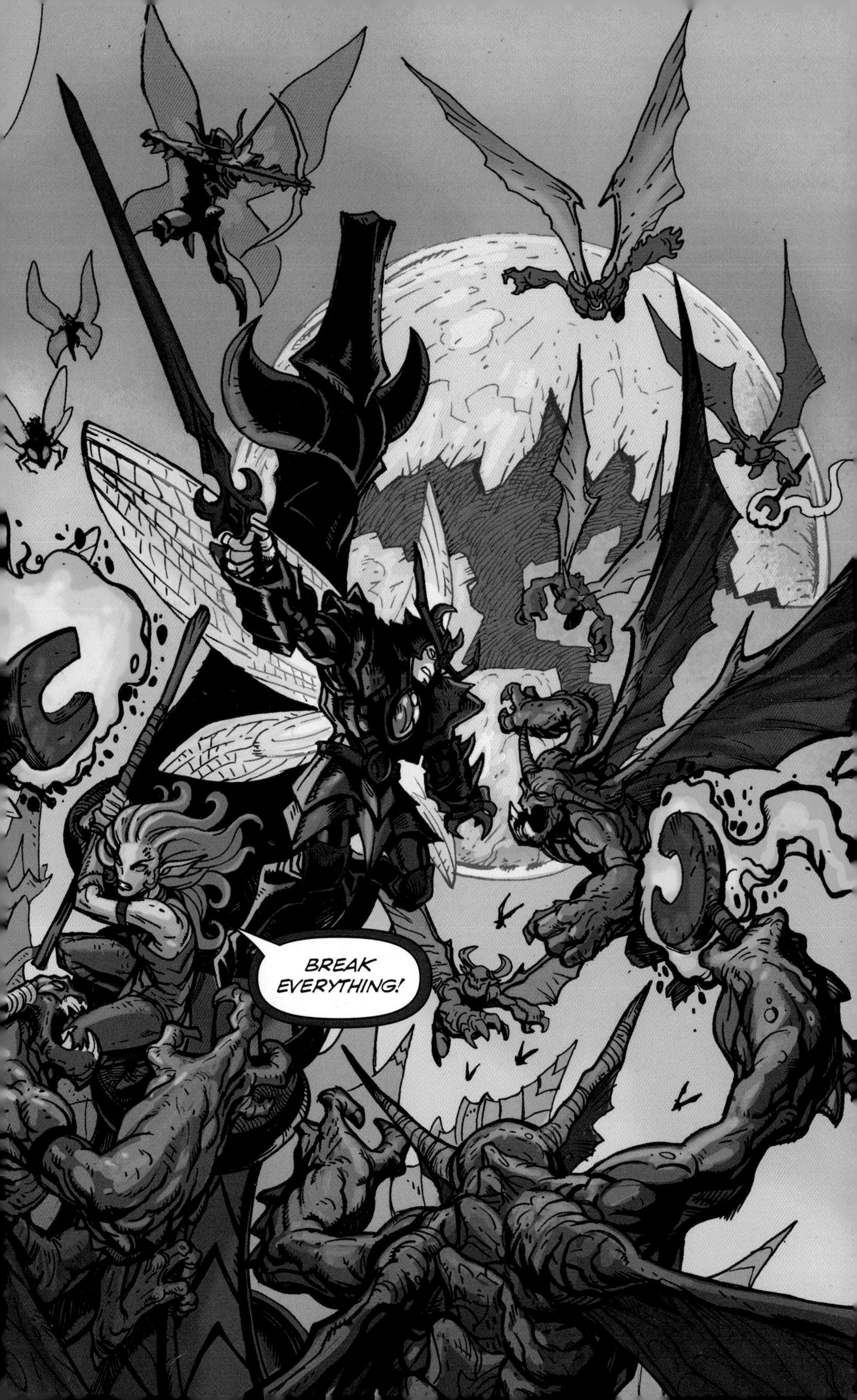
BREAK EVERYTHING!

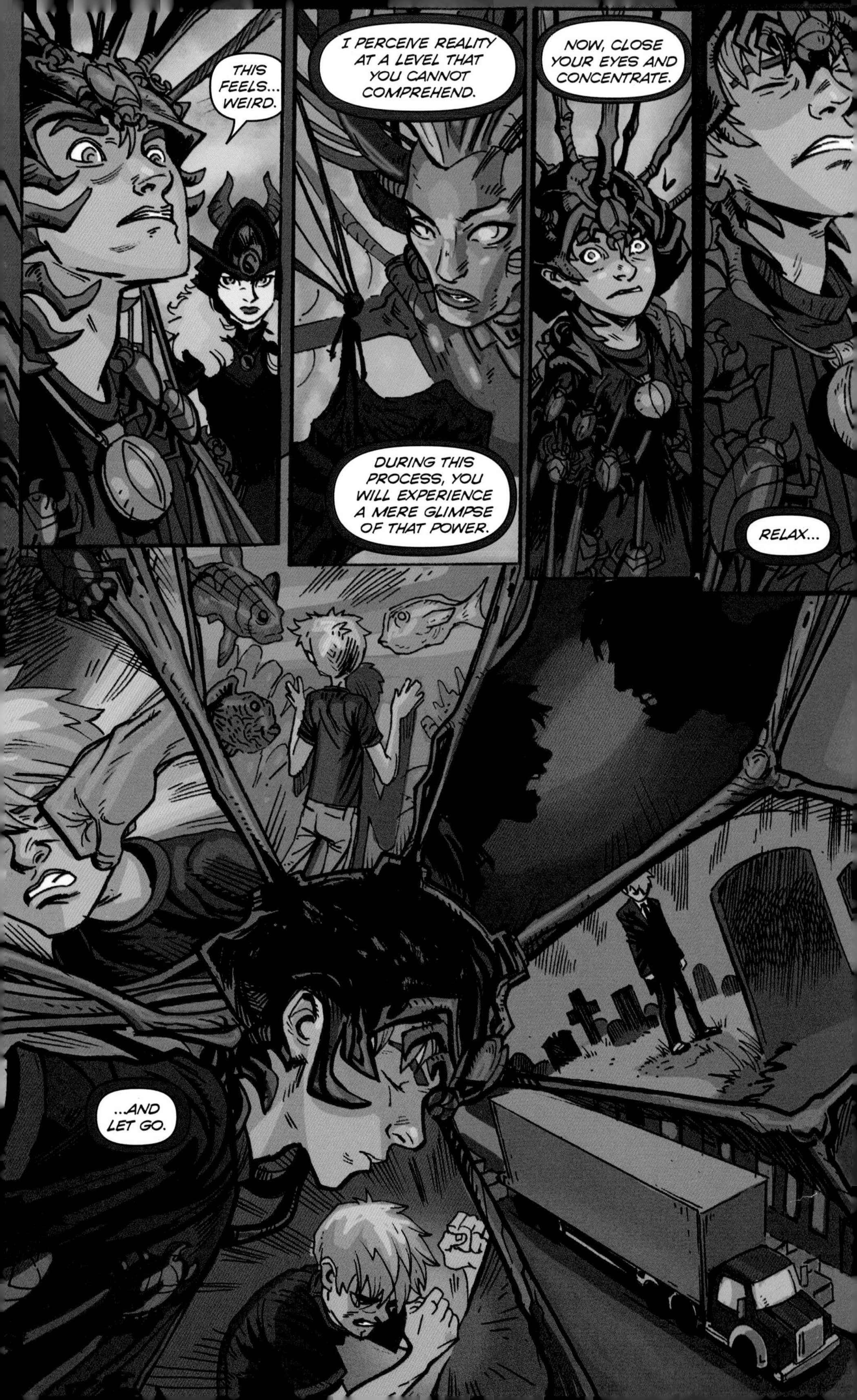
THIS FEELS... WEIRD.
I PERCEIVE REALITY AT A LEVEL THAT YOU CANNOT COMPREHEND.
DURING THIS PROCESS, YOU WILL EXPERIENCE A MERE GLIMPSE OF THAT POWER.
NOW, CLOSE YOUR EYES AND CONCENTRATE.
RELAX...
...AND LET GO.

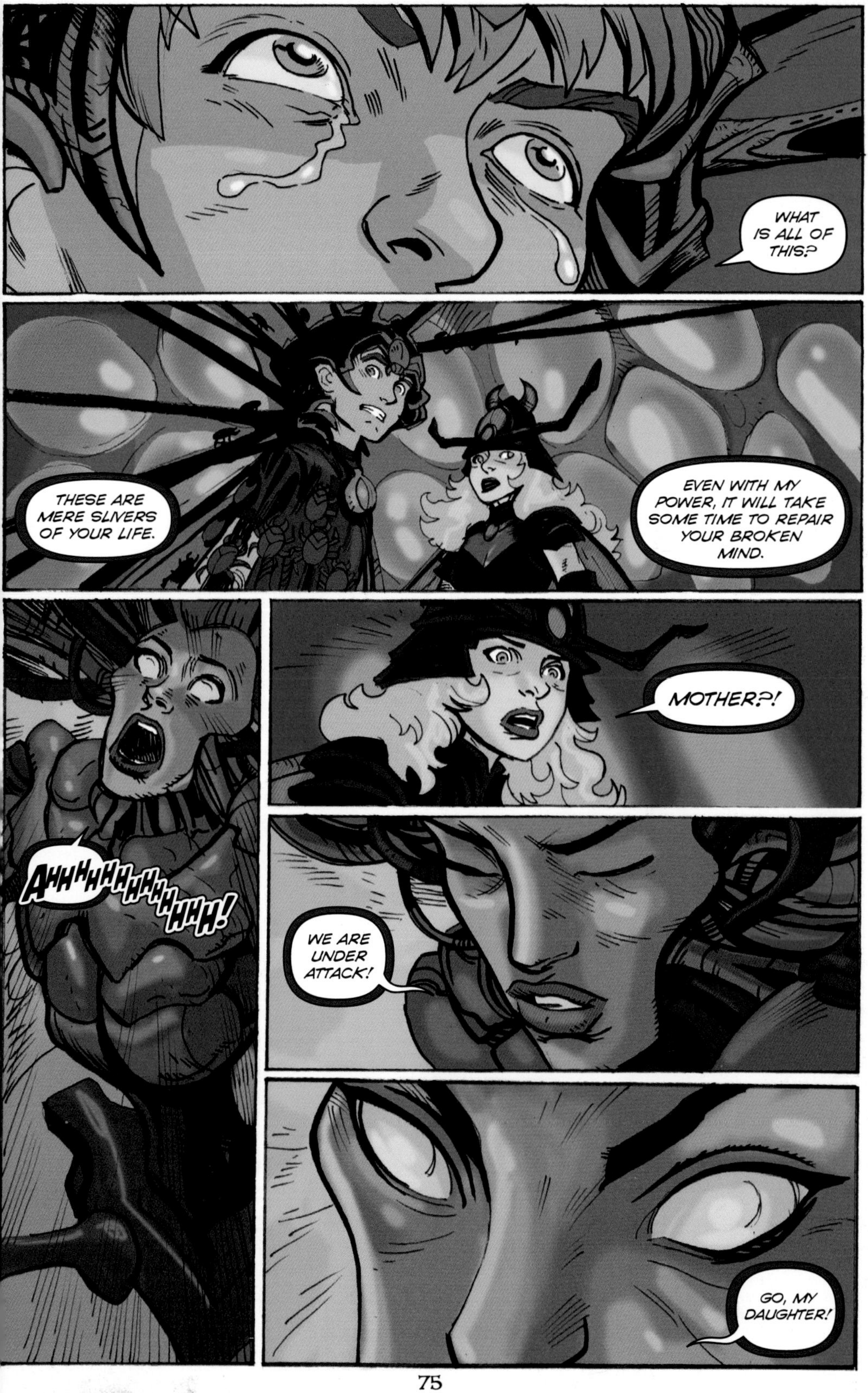
WHAT IS ALL OF THIS?
THESE ARE MERE SLIVERS OF YOUR LIFE.
EVEN WITH MY POWER, IT WILL TAKE SOME TIME TO REPAIR YOUR BROKEN MIND.
AHHHHHHHHHHHHHH!
MOTHER?!
WE ARE UNDER ATTACK!
GO, MY DAUGHTER!

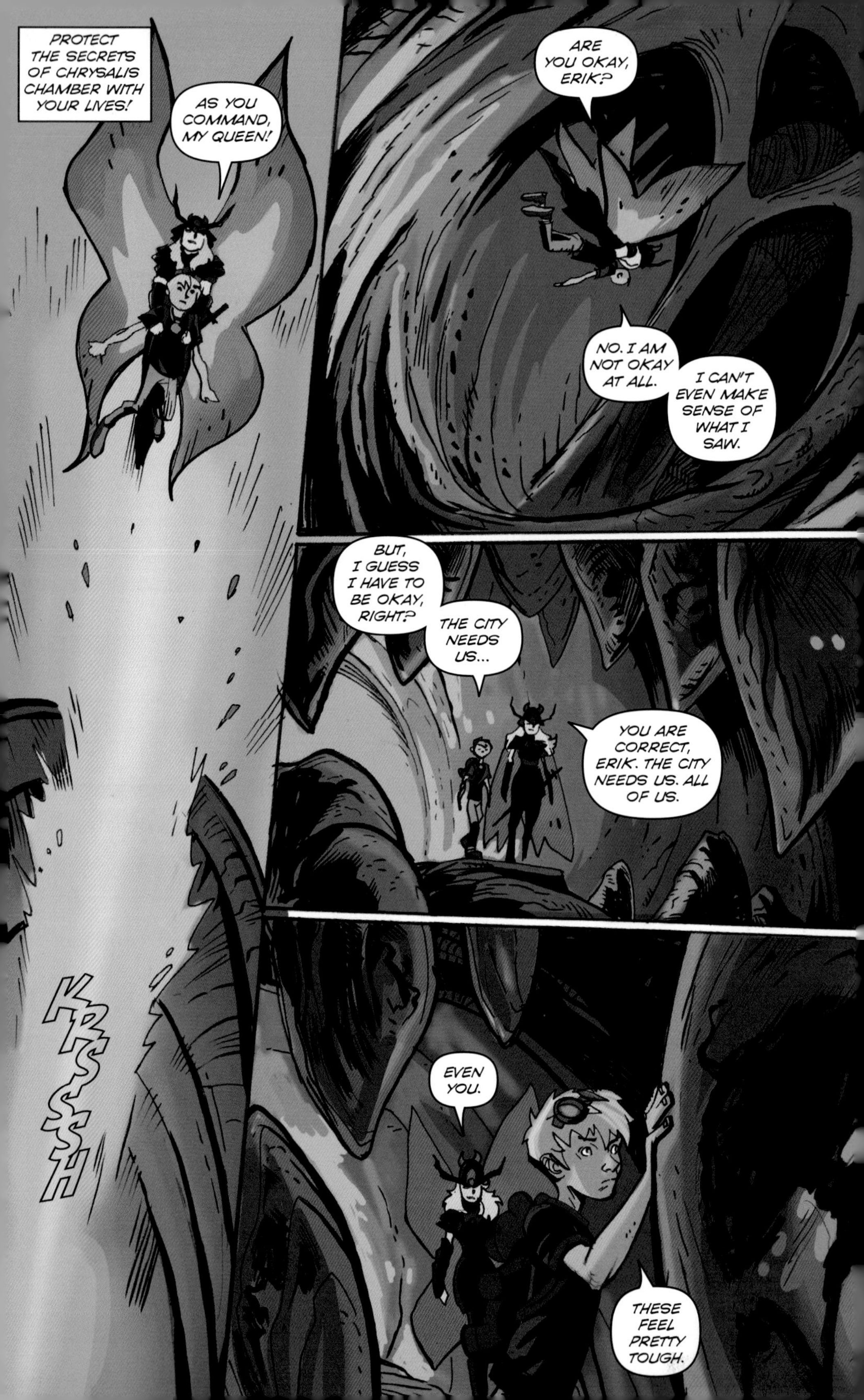
PROTECT THE SECRETS OF CHRYSALIS CHAMBER WITH YOUR LIVES!
AS YOU COMMAND, MY QUEEN!
ARE YOU OKAY, ERIK?
NO. I AM NOT OKAY AT ALL.
I CAN'T EVEN MAKE SENSE OF WHAT I SAW.
BUT, I GUESS I HAVE TO BE OKAY, RIGHT?
THE CITY NEEDS US...
YOU ARE CORRECT, ERIK. THE CITY NEEDS US. ALL OF US.
KRSSSH
EVEN YOU.
THESE FEEL PRETTY TOUGH.

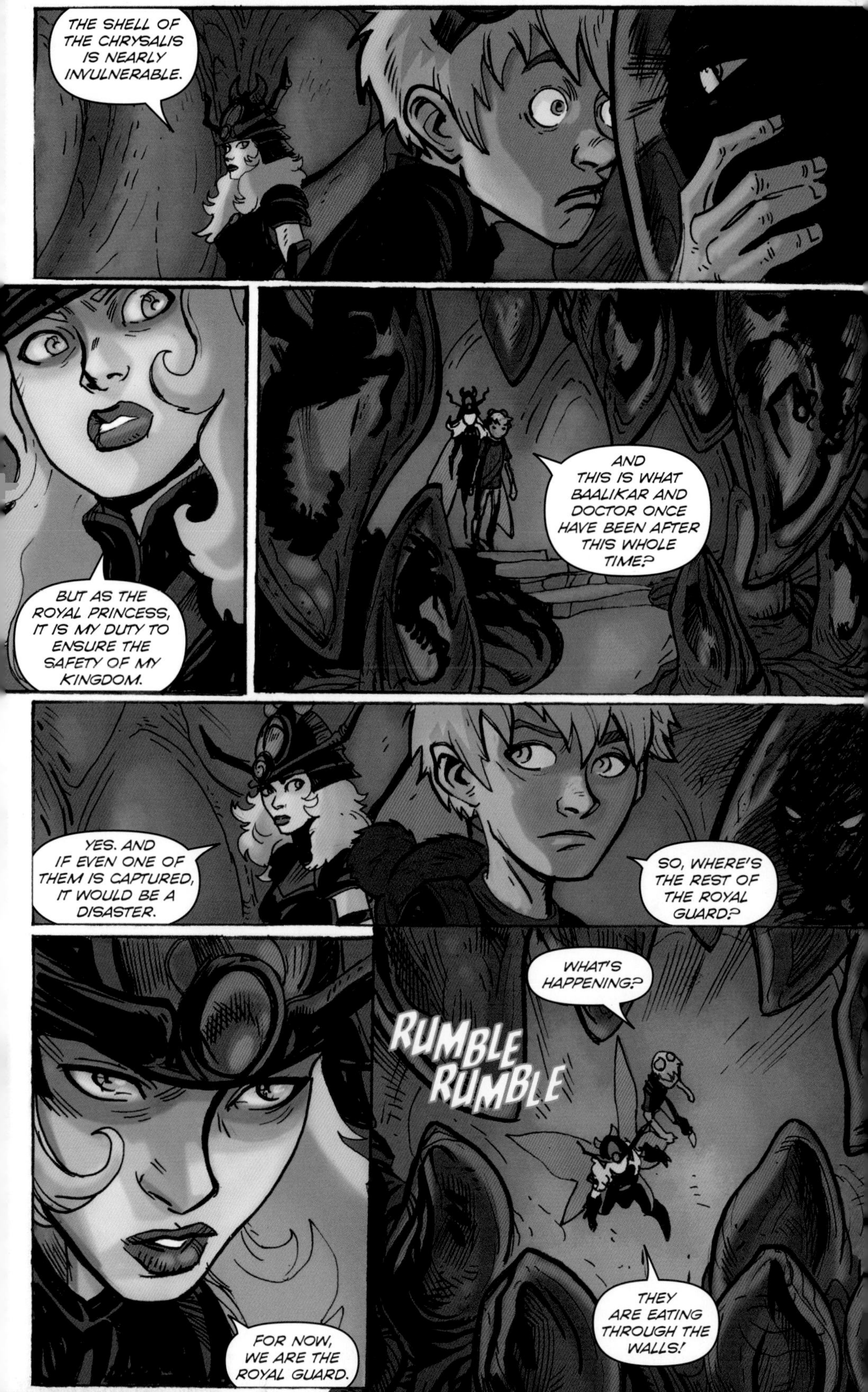
THE SHELL OF THE CHRYSALIS IS NEARLY INVULNERABLE.
BUT AS THE ROYAL PRINCESS, IT IS MY DUTY TO ENSURE THE SAFETY OF MY KINGDOM.
AND THIS IS WHAT BAALIKAR AND DOCTOR ONCE HAVE BEEN AFTER THIS WHOLE TIME?
YES. AND IF EVEN ONE OF THEM IS CAPTURED, IT WOULD BE A DISASTER.
SO, WHERE'S THE REST OF THE ROYAL GUARD?
FOR NOW, WE ARE THE ROYAL GUARD.
WHAT'S HAPPENING?
RUMBLE RUMBLE
THEY ARE EATING THROUGH THE WALLS!

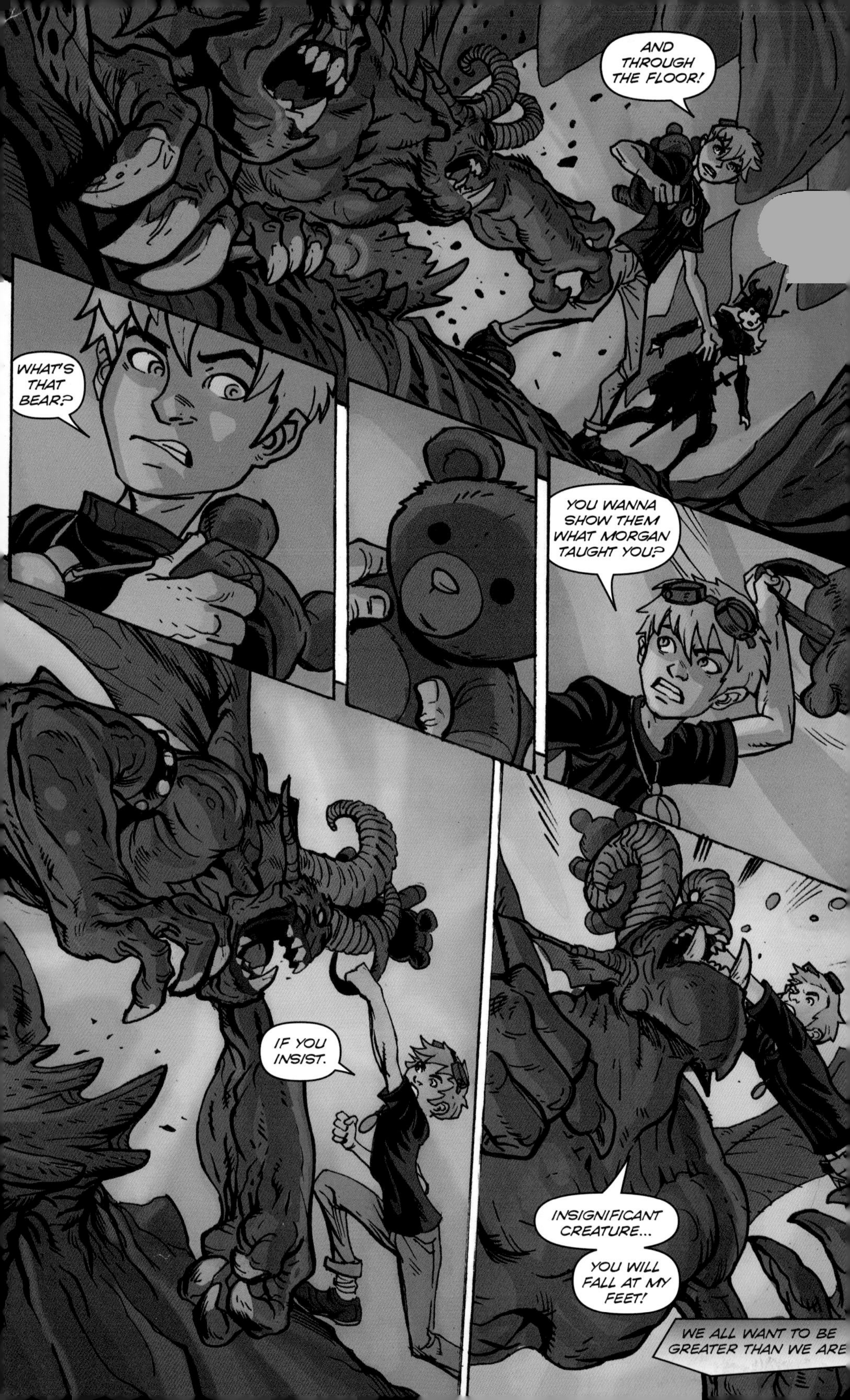
AND THROUGH THE FLOOR!
WHAT'S THAT BEAR?
YOU WANNA SHOW THEM WHAT MORGAN TAUGHT YOU?
IF YOU INSIST.
INSIGNIFICANT CREATURE...
YOU WILL FALL AT MY FEET!
WE ALL WANT TO BE GREATER THAN WE ARE

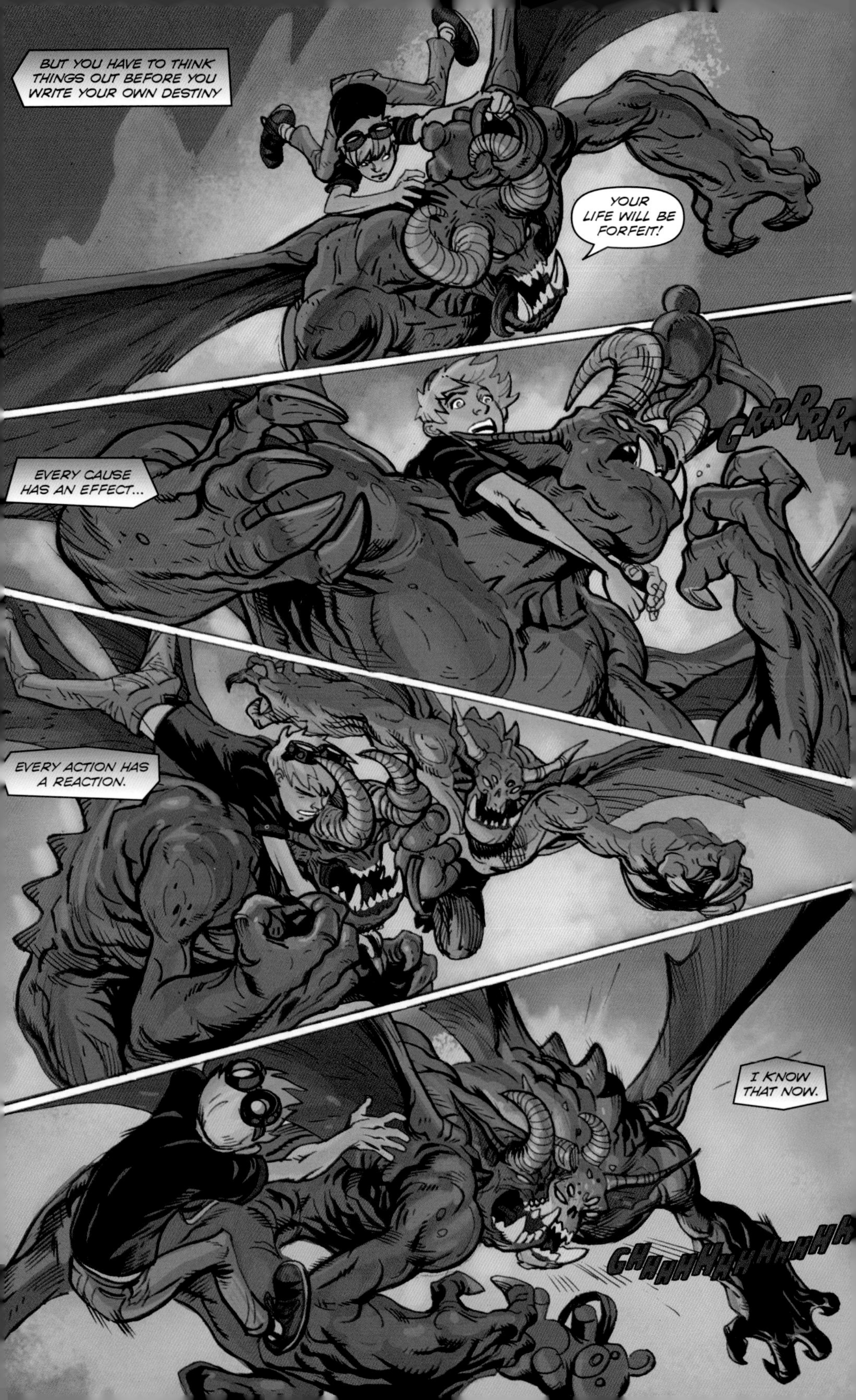
BUT YOU HAVE TO THINK THINGS OUT BEFORE YOU WRITE YOUR OWN DESTINY
YOUR LIFE WILL BE FORFEIT!
GRRRRRR
EVERY CAUSE HAS AN EFFECT...
EVERY ACTION HAS A REACTION.
I KNOW THAT NOW.
GHHHHHHHHHHHH

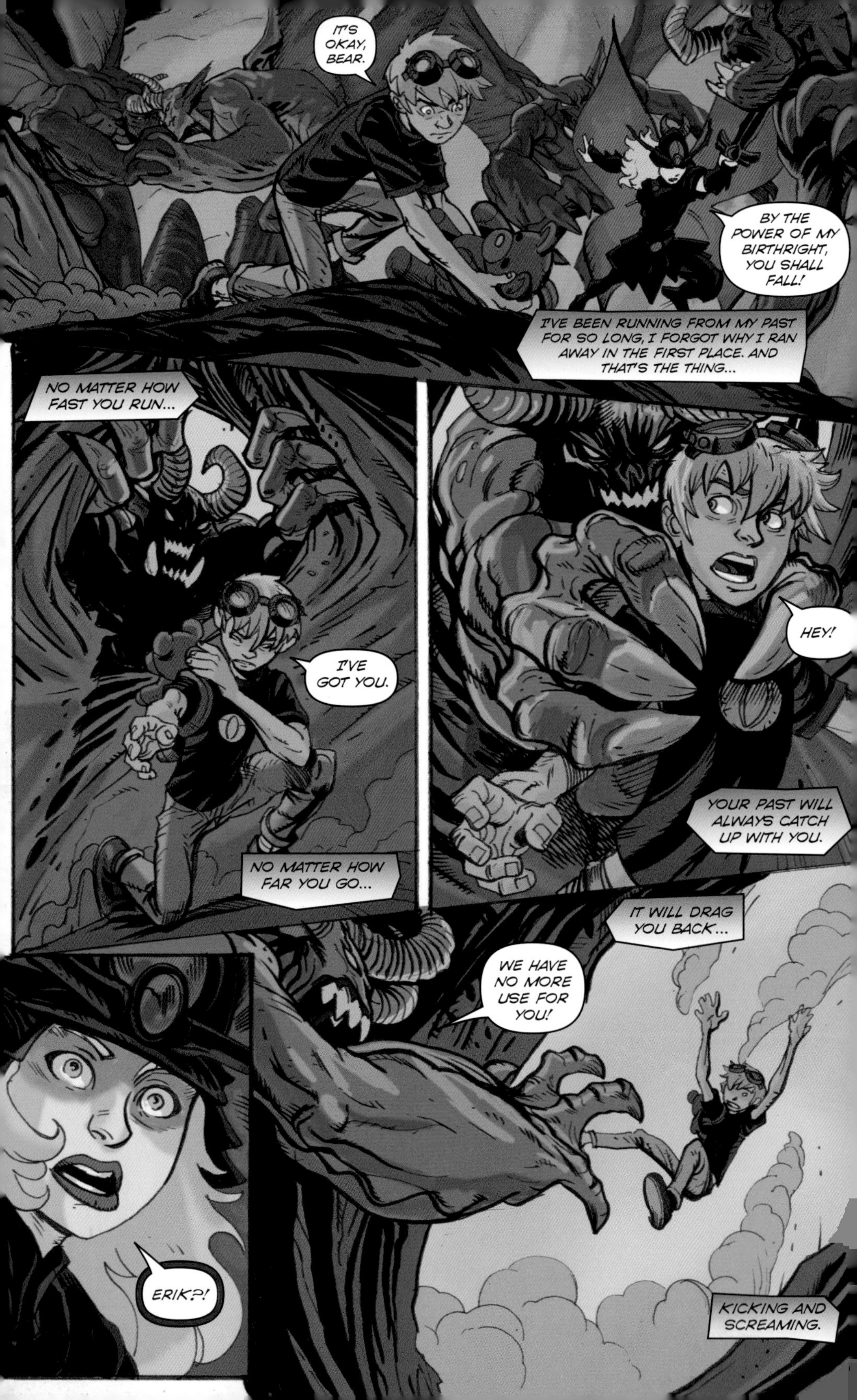
IT'S OKAY, BEAR.
BY THE POWER OF MY BIRTHRIGHT, YOU SHALL FALL!
I'VE BEEN RUNNING FROM MY PAST FOR SO LONG, I FORGOT WHY I RAN AWAY IN THE FIRST PLACE. AND THAT'S THE THING...
NO MATTER HOW FAST YOU RUN...
I'VE GOT YOU.
NO MATTER HOW FAR YOU GO...
HEY!
YOUR PAST WILL ALWAYS CATCH UP WITH YOU.
IT WILL DRAG YOU BACK...
WE HAVE NO MORE USE FOR YOU!
ERIK?!
KICKING AND SCREAMING.

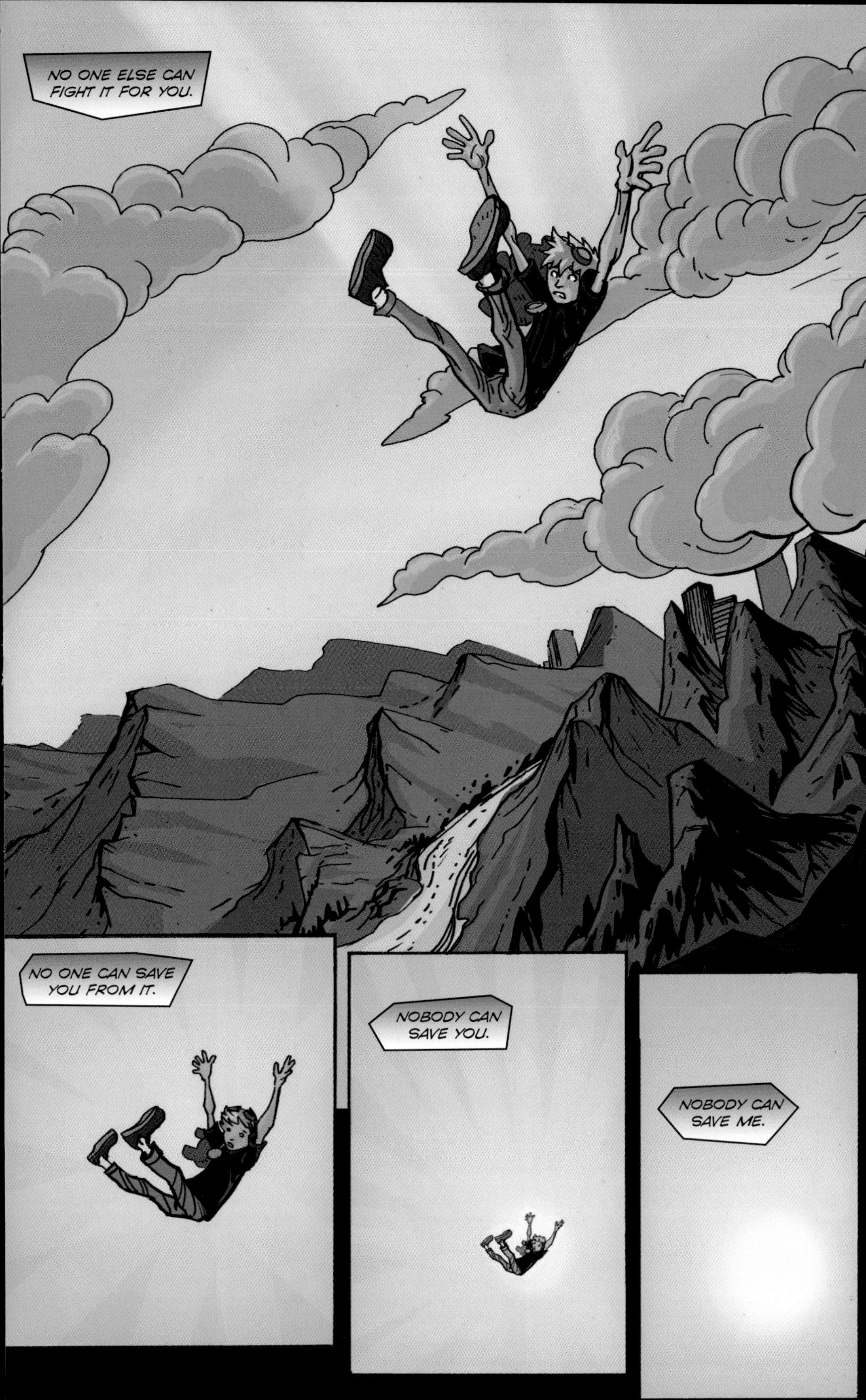
NO ONE ELSE CAN FIGHT IT FOR YOU.
NO ONE CAN SAVE YOU FROM IT.
NOBODY CAN SAVE YOU.
NOBODY CAN SAVE ME.

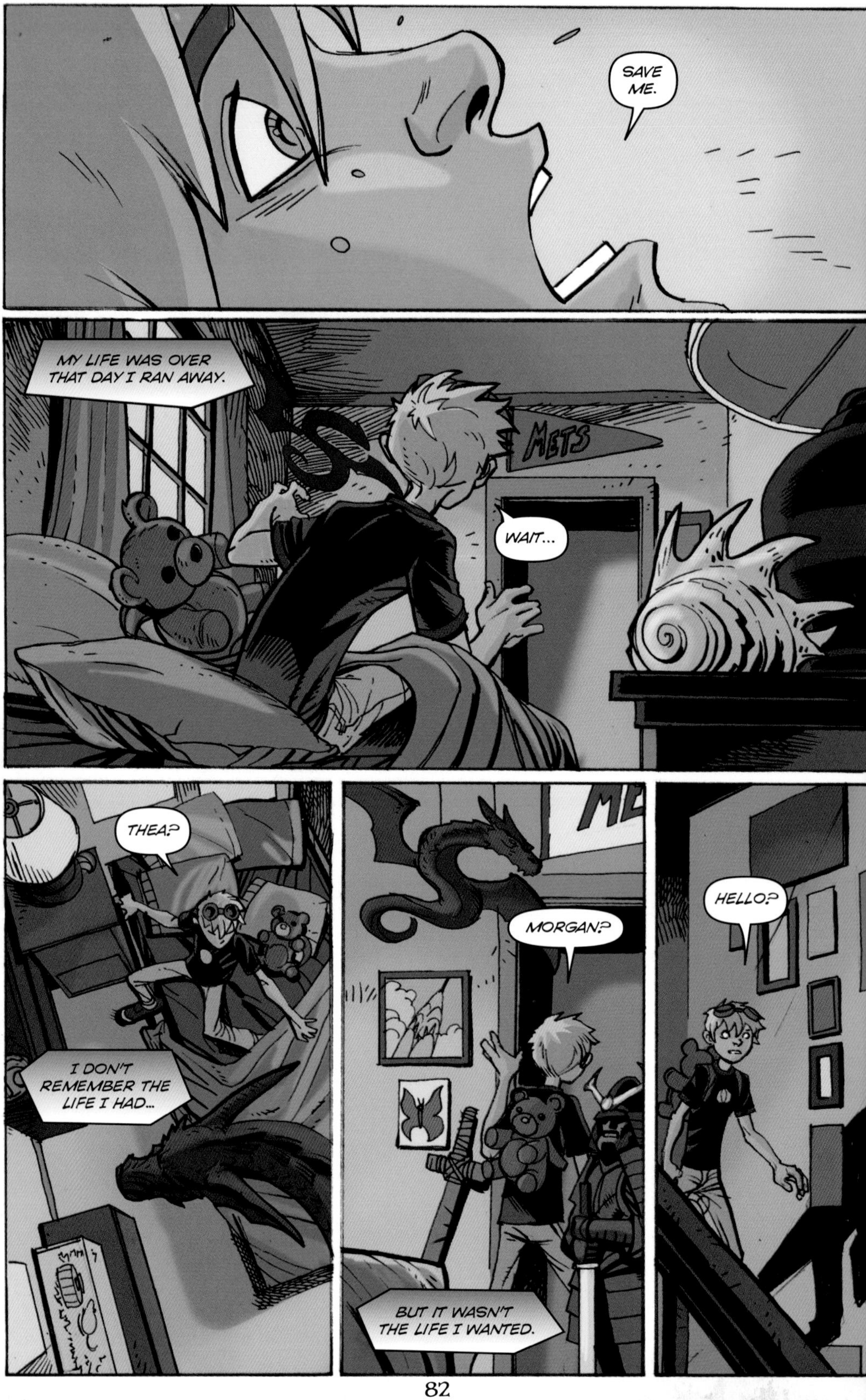
SAVE ME.
MY LIFE WAS OVER THAT DAY I RAN AWAY.
METS
WAIT...
THEA?
I DON'T REMEMBER THE LIFE I HAD...
MORGAN?
BUT IT WASN'T THE LIFE I WANTED.
HELLO?

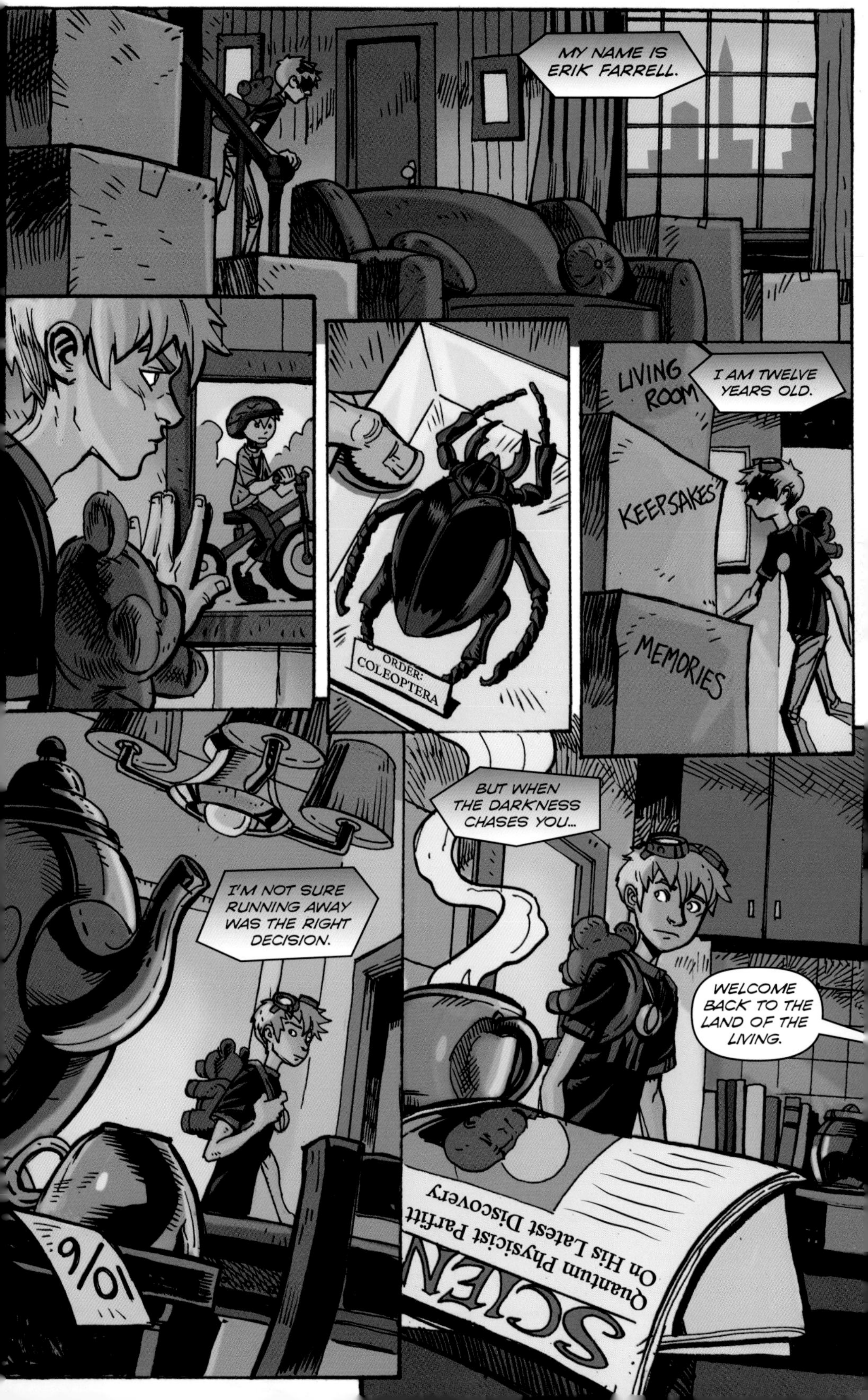
MY NAME IS ERIK FARRELL.
ORDER: COLEOPTERA
LIVING ROOM
I AM TWELVE YEARS OLD.
KEEPSAKES
MEMORIES
I'M NOT SURE RUNNING AWAY WAS THE RIGHT DECISION.
10/6
BUT WHEN THE DARKNESS CHASES YOU...
WELCOME BACK TO THE LAND OF THE LIVING.
Quantum Physicist Parfitt
On His Latest Discovery

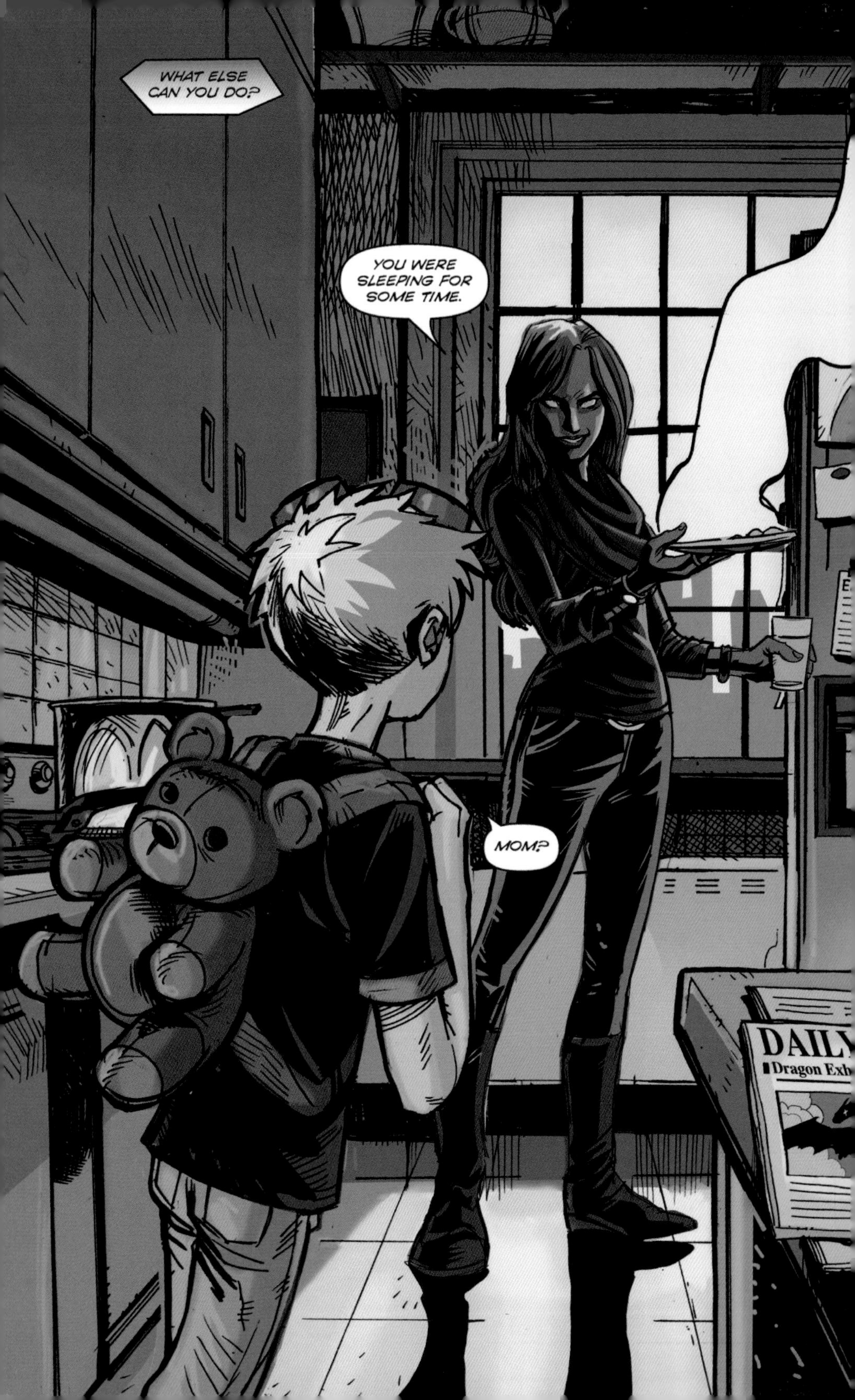
WHAT ELSE CAN YOU DO?
YOU WERE SLEEPING FOR SOME TIME.
MOM?
DAILY
Dragon Exh

WATCH OUT FOR PAPERCUTZ™

Welcome to the scary, science-fictional, second THE ONLY LIVING BOY graphic novel, by David Gallaher and Steve Ellis, from Papercutz–those hard-working, nit-picking editorial-types dedicated to publishing great graphic novels for all ages. I'm Jim Salicrup, Editor-in-Chief and former patient of Doctor Once, here to provide further behind-the-scenes info on Papercutz and THE ONLY LIVING BOY.

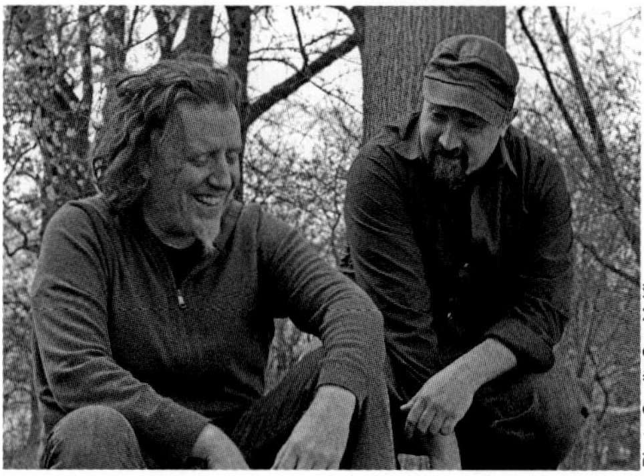
Photo Credit: Caz McKinnon

Artist Steve Ellis and writer David Gallaher getting inspiration for THE ONLY LIVING BOY.

In THE ONLY LIVING BOY #1, I told you a little bit about how Papercutz was founded by publisher Terry Nantier and myself over ten years ago, to create comics and graphic novels for all ages. So, it was simply a matter of time before we worked out a deal to publish THE ONLY LIVING BOY-- a series that was nominated for Best Original Graphic Publication for Younger Readers and for two other Harvey Awards. For those of you just joining us, you may wonder how that's even possible if it's just being published now. The answer is simple. THE ONLY LIVING BOY began as a web comic, serialized at www.the-only-living-boy.com. Papercutz is now proudly publishing the graphic novel edition, available at booksellers everywhere.

I have great admiration for THE ONLY LIVING BOY creators–not just for their creative skills in creating an enjoyable graphic novel series for all ages, but for how they continue to stand behind their work. They spend a lot of time and energy getting out there–to comic conventions and bookstores and comicbook stores–to meet their ever-growing audience, and that's very meaningful. They're aware of how many others–mostly giant, super-successful media companies–are competing for your attention, and they are doing something about it. And I believe it's going to work. I can see Erik Farrell becoming more widely known, to the point where I can see movies, action figures, TV shows, etc., about THE ONLY LIVING BOY.

But as much as I would love to see that all happen -- and for David Gallaher and Steve Ellis to reap the rewards of that kind of success–it's not the most important thing to me. What is important is getting their work to you. Yes, Terry Nantier and I started Papercutz to create a publishing company that we hope will be incredibly successful–but that's because we both want to be able to publish material as great as the comics we grew up with. I have many memories from my youth of getting really excited by great comics. That's why I wanted more than anything else to be a part of the comics world–and that's where I've been since I was 15 years-old.

So, not only do we get to publish THE ONLY LIVING BOY, but we're publishing comics for everyone. Check out the variety of characters that we currently publish on papercutz.com. You'll find well-known characters such as THE SMURFS, GARFIELD, TINKER BELL, and even MICKEY MOUSE, to the latest Nickelodeon stars such as SANJAY AND CRAIG, BREADWINNERS, HARVEY BEAKS, and PIG GOAT BANANA CRICKET to all-new characters such as THE LUNCH WITCH, SCARLETT, FUZZY BASEBALL, and ANNE OF GREEN BAGELS. And there are many more!

I guess what I'm trying to say is that we all love comics, and we hope that you not only enjoy THE ONLY LIVING BOY, but check out some of the other titles published by Papercutz as well. Hey, if nothing else, you might find a great new series to enjoy while you're waiting for THE ONLY LIVING BOY #3 "Once Upon a Time." And, as a really special bonus–turn the page and learn how to draw Erik and Bear! Send us your drawings, and we may publish yours in a future volume of THE ONLY LIVING BOY!*

Thanks,

Jim

STAY IN TOUCH!

EMAIL:	salicrup@papercutz.com
WEB:	papercutz.com
TWITTER:	@papercutzgn
FACEBOOK:	PAPERCUTZGRAPHICNOVELS
FAN MAIL:	Papercutz, 160 Broadway, Suite 700, East Wing, New York, NY 10038

*Submissions to THE ONLY LIVING BOY indicate permission to publish and use submitter's first name, last initial, city, state or province of residence. There is no compensation for submissions and they cannot be returned. Pictures are selected at random.

How to draw THE ONLY LIVING BOY

Ever wanted to learn to draw your favorite comicbook characters?
This step-by-step tutorial will show you how THE ONLY LIVING BOY artist Steve Ellis draws Erik!

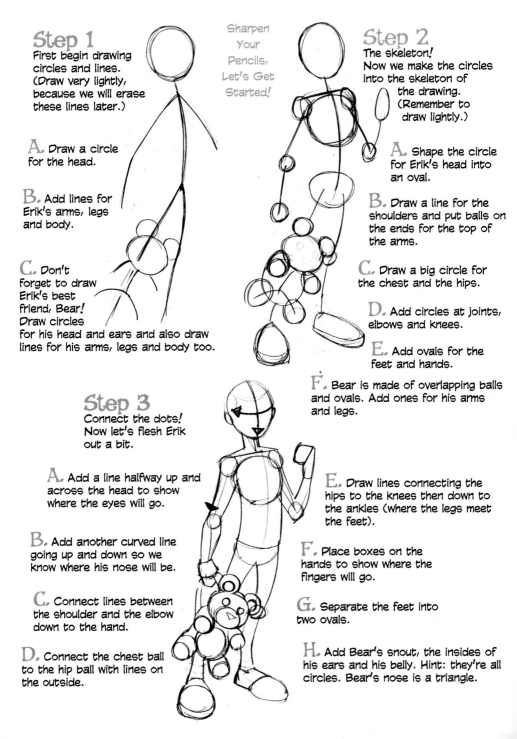

Sharpen Your Pencils, Let's Get Started!

Step 1
First begin drawing circles and lines. (Draw very lightly, because we will erase these lines later.)

A. Draw a circle for the head.

B. Add lines for Erik's arms, legs and body.

C. Don't forget to draw Erik's best friend, Bear! Draw circles for his head and ears and also draw lines for his arms, legs and body too.

Step 2
The skeleton! Now we make the circles into the skeleton of the drawing. (Remember to draw lightly.)

A. Shape the circle for Erik's head into an oval.

B. Draw a line for the shoulders and put balls on the ends for the top of the arms.

C. Draw a big circle for the chest and the hips.

D. Add circles at joints, elbows and knees.

E. Add ovals for the feet and hands.

F. Bear is made of overlapping balls and ovals. Add ones for his arms and legs.

Step 3
Connect the dots! Now let's flesh Erik out a bit.

A. Add a line halfway up and across the head to show where the eyes will go.

B. Add another curved line going up and down so we know where his nose will be.

C. Connect lines between the shoulder and the elbow down to the hand.

D. Connect the chest ball to the hip ball with lines on the outside.

E. Draw lines connecting the hips to the knees then down to the ankles (where the legs meet the feet).

F. Place boxes on the hands to show where the fingers will go.

G. Separate the feet into two ovals.

H. Add Bear's snout, the insides of his ears and his belly. Hint: they're all circles. Bear's nose is a triangle.

Step 4
Starting the details!

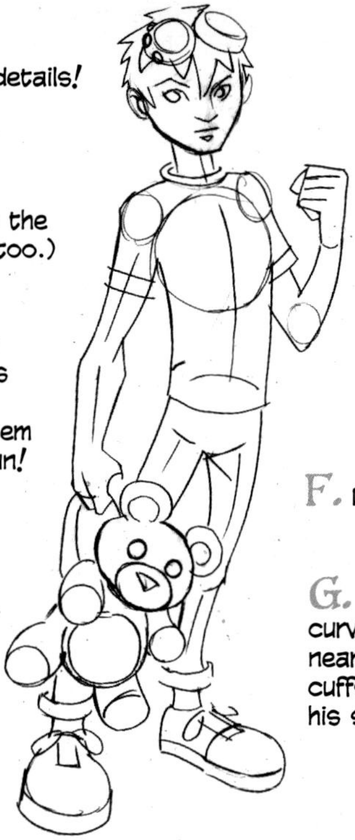

A. The goggles are small ovals. (The buttons on the sides are ovals too.)

B. The hair is just a bunch of triangles going in different directions. Keep them a little curvy and fun!

C. Add the eyebrows above the line for the eyes and make Erik's eyes using open, pointed oval shapes.

D. Put a triangle for the bottom of the nose and draw in the mouth. Adding a small triangle under the mouth looks like a lower lip.

E. Draw in two oval lines for the collars around his neck and on the arms for the edge of his sleeves.

F. Draw in lines for fingers.

G. Add straps to bear using curved lines. Also add half ovals near Erik's ankles to show the cuffs of his jeans and ovals on his shoes for laces.

Step 5
Finishing!

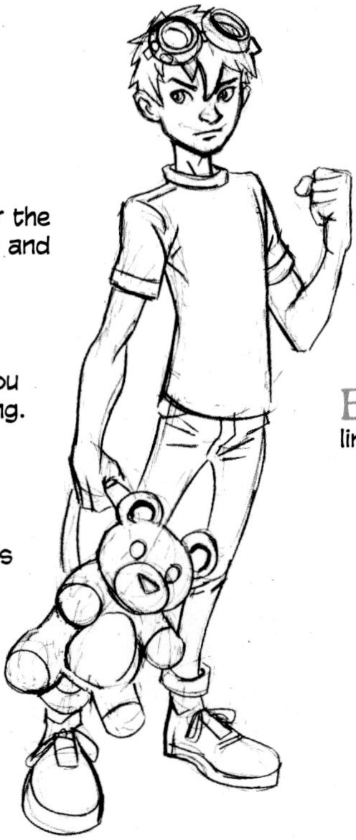

A. Start drawing over the lines you want to keep and erase the extras.

B. Connect the lines you want to finish the drawing.

C. Add creases and folds to arms and legs.

D. Draw circles in Erik's eyes and make him look serious.

E. Erase all the extra lines and you're done!

COMING SOON!

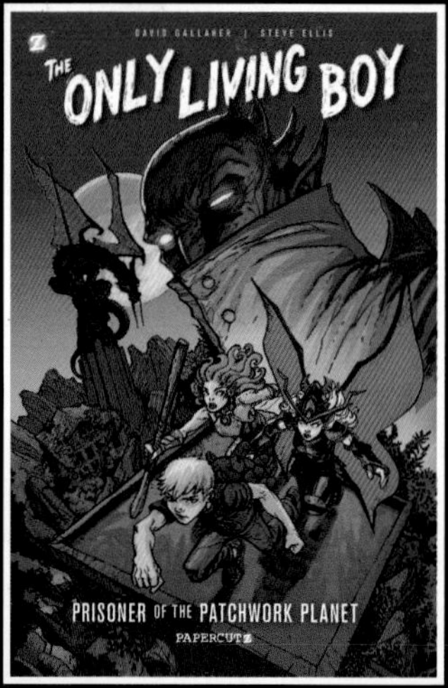
DAVID GALLAHER | STEVE ELLIS
THE ONLY LIVING BOY
PRISONER OF THE PATCHWORK PLANET
PAPERCUTZ

THE ONLY LIVING BOY #1

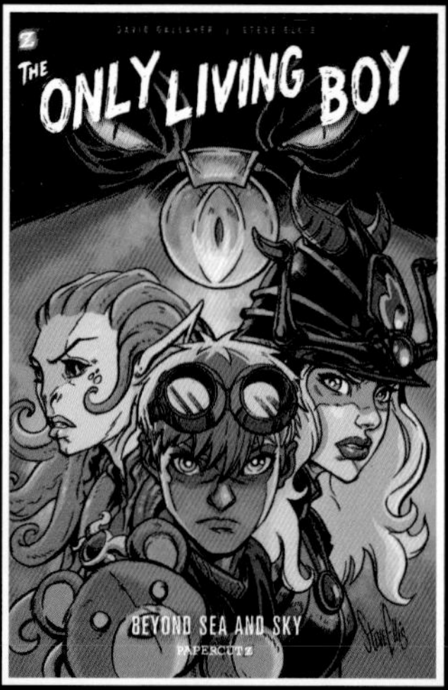
THE ONLY LIVING BOY
BEYOND SEA AND SKY
PAPERCUTZ

THE ONLY LIVING BOY #2

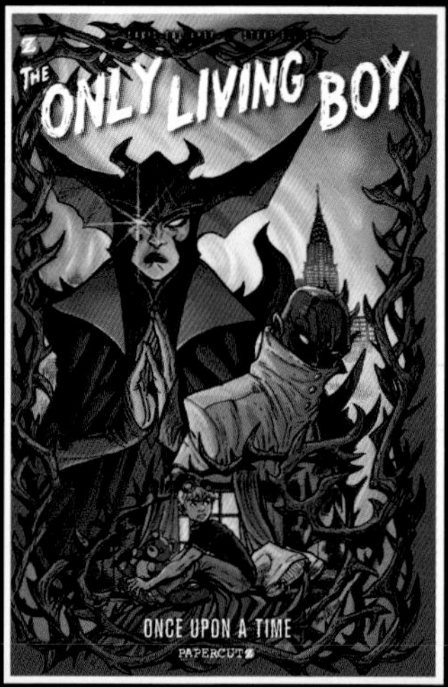
THE ONLY LIVING BOY
ONCE UPON A TIME
PAPERCUTZ

THE ONLY LIVING BOY #3

THE ONLY LIVING BOY

"An all-ages adventure book inspired by pulp serials, Saturday morning cartoons, Jack Kirby, and even the music of Paul Simon."
– MENTAL FLOSS

"A hero with memory loss, scaly monsters, alien heroines, giant evil dragons, underground cities, secrets, this is adventuresome, fast-paced alternate reality action with engaging, layered characters and great, great drawing. Everything you could possibly want in a comic."
– Nick Abadzis, Writer of LAIKA

"Boy meets (alien) world in the excellent sci-fi adventure comic THE ONLY LIVING BOY."–io9

THE ONLY LIVING BOY graphic novels are available for $8.99 in paperback, and $13.99 in hardcover. Available from booksellers everywhere. You can also order online from www.papercutz.com. Or call 1-800-886-1223, Monday through Friday, 9–5 EST. MC, Visa, and AmEx accepted. To order by mail, please add $4.00 for postage and handling for first book ordered, $1.00 for each additional book and make check payable to NBM Publishing. Send to: Papercutz, 160 Broadway, Suite 700, East Wing, New York, NY 10038.

THE ONLY LIVING BOY graphic novels are also available wherever e-books are sold.

PAPERCUTZ™
Papercutz.com